DON'T TOUCH MY TOUCH MY COCKTAIL!

DON'T TOUCH MY COCKTAIL!

A JANE ROBERTS MYSTERY

CAROL CHEN

Copyright © 2023 by Carol Chen.
All rights reserved.
ISBN 979-8-9864396-2-4

The font used on the front cover of this book is "Unfinished Scream," kind courtesy of Christopher King and Wingsart Studio, https://wingsart.studio.

Published by Carol Chen
41 Meadow Drive
Camden, Maine 04843

In memory of Nick and Colin

ACKNOWLEDGMENTS

Thank you, thank you!...to my sounding boards and my readers—Cheryl Ayer, June Bower, Cookie B. Breton, Tom Campbell, Patt Chen, Lisa Cummings, Terry Gerritsen, Barbara Higgins, Barb Karl, Dorie Klein, Rick Kot, Cindy Lang, Charlene Scholtes Margo, Peter Michelena, Nancy Ninnis, Deborah Oliver, Richard Olson, Cheryl Rogers, Marc Rogers, Roz Schweber, Mathew Thomson, Tim Whelan.

A Very Special Thank You to my book cover designer, Taylor Curry, for all his patience and that lovely, deadly olive....

DON'T TOUCH MY COCKTAIL!
Cast of Characters

Jane Roberts, Public Safety Officer
Storm Nosmot, homicide detective and Jane's mentor
Israel Tenner, PSO assistant
Helen Orbeton, PSO receptionist
Harriet Buxton, Director of Human Resources, Maine State Police
Joseph Adderley, Jane's superior at Maine Crimes Unit-Central
Finn Gallinen, police officer

Troy Overlock, employee at Calderwood Boatyard
Frank Overlock, Troy's father
Lorraine Overlock, Troy's mother
Jerome Williams, manager at Calderwood Boatyard
Troy's co-workers: Randy, Todd, Spencer
Joe Miller, Troy's co-worker

Trudy Moody, former Town Clerk
Wilbur Moody, Trudy's husband
Noreen Pushaw, Wilbur and Trudy's daughter
Bernie Pushaw, Noreen's husband
Jason Coombs, Bernie's co-worker

Egor and Yaroslav, Russian ship managers
Spartak, Russian sailor
Dimitri, Russian sailor

Konstantin Balankoff, Jane's beau
Torrance Balankoff, Konstantin's sister
Samantha Lloyd, caterer
Nathan Herinton, Samantha's beau
Maggie Banner, owner of Grand Harbor Inn
Ryan Young, Maggie's boyfriend
India Barton, assistant at Grand Harbor Inn

Grace Cleveland, owner of Apple π
Cora Gould, waitress at the Pub
Hamidi Louca, organic farmer and self-defense instructor
Sonny Mannix, State ferry captain
Rajiv Basrak, former crime lab investigator, now owner of
   Indian restaurant, Curry in a Hurry
Salem Pratt, semiconductor multimillionaire
Chanson Pratt, Salem's wife
Geneva Pratt, Salem and Chanson's daughter

Zen-Ti (ZT) Smith, Black-Asian entrepreneur
ZK (Zen-Kan) and ZM (Zen-Mo), relatives of Zen-Ti

Gluella Trott, creator of LOBSTER BRIDES!
Gaspard Pariballou, Gluella's attorney

Hitch McGill, U. S. Senator from Texas
Shelby McGill, Hitch's wife
Alex Champus, FBI

Wilton Savoy, Marketing Chairman of J. T. Karl's Wild
   Open
Diane Savoy, Wilton's wife

Ray Bun, Black-Cambodian entrepreneur

Jay Bun, Van Bun, Man Bun, and Tiny Bun, relatives of
  Ray
Winnifred Billings
Kenmore Billings, Winnifred's husband
Kendall Billings (deceased)
Zara Billings, Kendall's widow

PART ONE

1
The Swiss Alps
Early December 2019

In the distance, the two dark shapes move together through an open alpine field knee-high in snow, trailing behind them boot-punched strands of deep, black impressions lasting only seconds as swirling, snowy gusts whip away all trace of their presence. The steady rhythm of the two, side by side, breaks occasionally when they strain their thighs through dense drifts and gullies. A heavy, complicated blizzard began slamming the Swiss countryside in the morning, and now earth, sky, and forest are layered together in one towering winter trifle.

Snow devil and minx, she leans down as he turns to glance towards the woods. One swift scoop of the heavy snow, and her mischievous yelps are ricocheting towards his head with the snowy bomb. He whoops a startled cry as the snowball bursts across his neck. He grabs a broad chestful of snow, racing after her down a steep incline until he has her front and center. WHOOOOOOOSH! Her sable *(faux!)* hat and long, brown hair are drenched in white. The frenzy of the storm unleashes them into its wild gyrations. She is shrieking; he is hollering; he dives towards her and downs his fleeing prey. Chokes of giddiness, snow stuffing up noses, stinging snow sifting towards hot skin beneath coats...two bodies tumbling into winter's vast confusion.

They trek back to the chalet, their laughter jostling with the panting and gasping inside their lungs. Faster than they realize, daylight is sliding off the white world into chilling valleys of darkness. "Let's start a fire in the small sitting room," he says to her. "We can warm up in there, and I'll get us some chocolate and cognac from the pantry."

....

"Do you have a small knife we could use?" she asks.

He kneels down beside her before the fireplace, gives her the knife, and watches as she places a chocolate square on the blade.

She holds the steel near the fire, using one mitten as protection from the growing heat. Slowly the deep dark square begins to lose its form, spreading into softness, at which point she captures the smooth, sliding sweetness on her finger and offers it to him. She touches her finger to his lips, and he licks down the treat.

She repeats the warming with another chocolate square and sweeps the melting ounce into her own mouth. They savor the sweetness and clink their glasses of cognac before downing the warm liquor, hoping to quench their chill. He adds more logs to the fire, and the small room becomes warm enough for them to remove their damp outer clothing. Warmth grows from the fire, and warmth returns to their skin and to their insides with each eager glass of cognac.

They are laughing and recounting silly, funny things that happened in childhood. Her eyes glance downward and then up again to his face. She wants to look at him forever...to drink in this perfection. His field of raven hair sweeps off his forehead in elegant folds...the black-Irish who strayed into the Russian herd. How could a man be so beautiful?

The silence between their eyes is total, absolute. There are no words. She stays still as she undoes her top button. He is looking at her...his what? His kooky, brash, American-would-be-Mongolian princess? He is about to speak, but says nothing.

She reaches for his hand and unbuttons two more buttons with his hand guiding her fingers. The orange-honey flames of the fire move towards them, though going nowhere, when she dips her finger into softened chocolate and moves deeper inside her blouse. She circles her finger round and round, round and round, until he lowers his head towards her, and when his lips join the sweetness of the chocolate and where her finger rests, they are far beyond talking and laughing. They are barely breathing...there is no breathing.

....

They stumble and tumble into the bedroom, and she unfurls from their laughter—but not from him—to catch her breath over the hand-carved beauty of the wood cupboards, the soft Persian carpets burying her toes, the huge bed with its intricate tapestries—beets and artichokes?—it has to be a Kaffe Fassett design! Floating before her is a vast, white cloud of feather topper, flannel sheets thick as pancakes, billowy marshmallow fluff quilts. It's all too much! She's having a major interior design seizure.

Her heart puffs wildly, expanding like the gorgeous, puffy bedding before her, but being who she is, she obliterates the wondrous spell. "Oh My God! How are we ever going to sleep on this gigantic whoopie pie?!" None other than Konstantin Balankoff scoops up none other than Public Safety Officer Jane Roberts and nuzzles into her ear as he piles the two of them on top. "Who said anything about sleep?"

2
St. Frewin's Island, Maine
Monday, December 9

Tonight St. Frewin Island's local entrepreneur and "eco-spreader" Bernie Pushaw (aka call sign "Godzilla") was about to encounter the phenomenon known as "walkie talkie cross pollination." Bernie was the kind of island rascal who quit drinking four times a year, and he smelled like it—always smearing tooth paste over his teeth after he'd guzzled his quota, and exuding that minty fresh breath when he sauntered by you, his slanted eyebrows arched in mischief. But to his credit, Bernie stuck to the grimy grind and managed to pay the bills, which deprived his wife, Noreen, of Divorce Reason #1.

Right now Bernie was coordinating with his colleague to pick up the usual barrels of septic waste from the St. Frewin's Island Public Works lot. That was where the septage was randomly tested for toxic chemicals and elements. If a given barrel tested at acceptable levels, Bernie et al. trucked the containers out to the "Environmental Fields" on the north side of the island, where the State Department of Environmental Protection permitted St. Frewin's to recycle septic tank contents from local residences and boats at anchor. While this program was coming under scrutiny for its hazardous impacts, Bernie and his crew were still deemed "legal" when they incorporated the waste into the 200 acres making up the "Environmental Fields." Time, earthworms, fungi, and bacteria pitched in and reworked the septage into respectable fertilizer, though with the rise in toxic wastes, people were starting to wake up to all the shit in their shit, so to speak. It was becoming an issue, as Bernie would tell folks.

He flipped on his walkie talkie to the usual channel and tried to make contact with his work buddy, Jason Coombs, aka call sign "Dracula." Seemed like there was a hell of a lot of static bouncing around in the air waves tonight.

URNK!!!...TSCHSHSH!!!...ZIiiii...URNK!...SCHWEEee!!

"Come in, Dracula. Come in. This is Godzilla. Over."
CHSHSH!!!...ZIiiiiiii...URNK!

"Dracula, COME IN...damn it all. COME IN!" *Where the fuck was all this fuckin' static comin' from*?!? Bernie/Godzilla wondered.

"So'd you get that flat tire fixed yet, Godzilla? Over."

"Shore thing, Dracula...while you been sittin' there pickin' on your ass, Boy. Over."

"Yah, well my sorry ass still works, if anybody wants to know. Like you all care, Godzilla. Over."
TSCHSH!!!...ZIiiii...URNK!!!...URNK!...SCHWEEEeee!!

"PIZ-DETS!!!" [Russian for "Damn it!"] "Who iz deez? PIZ-DETS!!" The Russian thug was momentarily confused. He was not Dracula, and he was not whom Bernie had intended to reach by walkie talkie, nor had the thug intended to speak to Bernie.

But Bernie knew when someone was pulling his leg. He woofed into his mike. "Whut you sayin', Dracula? Piz Diet? Somethin' about a pizza diet? A Pizza Diet?! Don' tell me that's all yer eatin' now, is it? What's that all about? Any pepperoni slices in theyah for me? Heh, heh...Over."

"Nyet pizza diet. Nyet! ...Black gold! Vee gut da black gold, OK? Now you peek up!" The Russian thug tried to clarify his goal. Who else could it be at this time of night trying to reach him but his American contact?

"Well, hol' on there, Dracula. Your accent's pretty cute, Boy. Where are you? We're not picking up at the usual place?" asked Bernie, who had no idea he was now talking to the walkie talkie of a Russian thug.

TSCHSH!!!...ZIiiiii...URNK!!!...URNK!...SCHWEEeee!!

"PIZ-DETS! Vat you say? Nunsenz! You peek up at da boatyard...right on da dock. Da beeg boatyard, da? Right ah-way!" commanded the Russian thug.

"Yo, Dracula! Hold on to your hosses, man! I'll swing by in a minute...at the boat yahd you say? Hang on to your hat. I'm comin'," Bernie assured his listener. "And don' forget me on that pizza. Black GOLD you sayin'? Don' know what that might be. Maybe hamburg with pineapple on top? Kind of a funky combo, but that'll be fine by me. Over."

ZIiiiii...URNK!!!...URNK!...SCHWEEeee!!...TSCHSH!!!...

Bernie was thinking to himself he might as well go get those boatyard barrels first thing. His bud, Jason Coombs, sure sounded pretty hot under the collar about those barrels, pizza or no pizza.

3
Earlier in the Year
November

Ferry passengers walking by the petite woman sitting at one of the computers in the State Ferry Terminal internet cafe on the mainland might have thought she was a sweet, young thing engrossed in a research project on the screen. Gluella Trott's small, delicate shoulders and hands and pale blue, innocent eyes could be misleading...*Mary had a little lamb,* and a soft mouth and gentle voice as well.

Her graphic designers and webmasters had submitted the final version of her newest website, and she needed to be sure every last pixel was in place, that the overall branding would pull in the right candidates. She was all business at the moment, scrutinizing the colorful graphics and promotional text on the computer and trying to read everything as if she were a hypothetical wealthy man...a rich man hungry for someone.

In truth, Gluella Trott was a piece of hard-bitten sinew among purveyors of romance. She could care less about chocolate kisses, heart-shaped candies, and roses—they had no place in her business plan. For Gluella, it was vital to perfect the "hook" when your clientele were people looking for love. Conveniently, her biggest partner in this enterprise was the public itself. And, more pointedly, the primal voids in their distraught psyches.

Her business thrived on those severe, black pits of loneliness that could engulf people's rooms day and night, no matter how much great TV, music, and books they had at hand. It thrived on human beings' inner emptiness and their sexual cravings gnawing on their bodies and minds, which couldn't be chased away with a good hamburger and fries. It thrived on people's hearts in despair over the lack of at least one special person in their lives to whom they were special, too, where both parties wanted the same special at the same time: Intimacy...if only.

Gluella was confident she had the expertise to give her clients the means to meet fellow dots who might be ripe for connection. Whether the dots did connect and then stayed connected was up to the individuals. What happened after that was not her job.

Gluella was long gone from the picture at that point. She wasn't there to play therapist or miracle worker. And really, who had ever truly been able to dissect love, or cultivate love, or make it obey?

Today was the launch of Gluella's latest effort in pulling heart strings: LOBSTER BRIDES! Her goal was to offer a personal tool for the lovelorn women of Maine's coastal and island communities. She was pitching global romance between wealthy, foreign gentlemen and shorefront ladies who knew how to put on a New England lobster bake and take everything off when the steam got hot. Gluella envisioned Euros and foreign currencies piling up before her eyes. And she loved her logo featuring gorgeous, smiling "female" lobsters whose ruby red claws were sporting sparkling diamond engagement rings in place of the usual stubby rubber bands binding the claws. If that didn't say it all, time would tell.

After two hours spent scrolling down through the organizational details, the enticements, and the personal data and photographs, Gluella phoned her webmasters to give them the green light, and LOBSTER BRIDES! went live. Before she exited from her site at the end of the afternoon, her venture had over twelve hundred hits from around the world. Twenty-four of them from one port city alone on the Caspian Sea. What a global world it was. And everyone starved for love.

4
Monday, December 9

At the sound of the Public Safety Office door flying open with the blustery cold, receptionist Helen Orbeton gripped her wool shawl around her middle. In walked Trudy Moody, rolling along like a Macy's Thanksgiving Day balloon in her fire-red parka and day-glo yellow gloves.

"Whew! Way too cold out there, Helen. How've you been?" Trudy asked while waving off the raw December air and yanking her parka zipper down along her bulging flannel layers.

"I'm doing all right, Trudy."

"What about Josiah, Helen? Is he doin' OK up to Warren?"

"He's all right, I guess. Prison is what it is. There's not much to say, is there?" Helen looked somewhat blank. But she was pragmatic and sturdy, and her son behind bars was simply part of her life. Now a widow in her late 50s, Helen had the love and support of Dr. John Leckman, St. Frewin's GP and vet. He was her family, too.

"Well, did you hear the latest news?" Trudy chattered on. "Ted Hatch went and rammed his car right into his wife yesterday afternoon! Happened on the mainland. Can you imagine?!"

"Must not be getting along too well," Helen remarked.

"Nettie Hatch is going to survive, but that's no way to treat your wife, especially when she's nearly a saint!" Trudy stamped her feet and shook herself all over. *Just like a dog,* Helen thought as she watched Trudy let go of the cold.

11

Carol Chen

During her decades-long career as the Clerk of St. Frewin's Island, Trudy Moody had managed the Town's books on births and deaths, marriages and rabies shots, dog tags, ocean fishing licenses and brush burning permits. Some days she was thankful to be retired, but she still made it a point to keep everyone on their toes with her astringent life force—including her husband, Wilbur; her daughter, Noreen; Bernie Pushaw, Noreen's deadbeat spouse; and most of the municipal staff on the island.

Helen was glad to see Trudy drop in. She hadn't seen her in a while, and it was awfully quiet without Public Safety Officer Jane Roberts around to keep things lively. The Abenaki County Sheriff's Deputy did call in to Helen every other day to check on the peace out on the island. For the past week, however, Helen had generally been alone at her desk while Jane was away on break.

"Do you fancy some eggnog, Trudy?"

"Eggnog? At this time of day, Helen? Don't tell me you're startin' to tipple now. Are you?" Trudy leaned towards her with narrowed eyes.

"That's absurd," Helen laughed.

Trudy looked around the office. "You know, Helen, I can understand that you haven't put up your Christmas cheer yet. You probably aren't gonna feel very festive this year, what with your only child in the slammer and all that. But that's OK. Because that's exactly why I'm here."

"Aren't you the dynamo, Trudy!" Helen said with trepidation.

"I'm gonna help you deck the halls, so you and Jane and the public can have a real nice holiday spirit in here. I've got a bunch of decorations in my car...I'll get started right away," Trudy announced, heading back towards the door.

DON'T TOUCH MY COCKTAIL!

"That's so kind of you, Trudy. But you know what I'm thinking, now that I've gotten to know Jane over the past year? She's liable to want to take charge of the decorations herself. She can be a stickler for detail on the office visuals, if you know what I mean." Helen was trying to keep it all diplomatic, but she could almost hear the tinsel bomb ticking inside Trudy's brain.

"Don't be silly, Helen. Jane won't have time to hang up all the right stuff. She'll be buckin' in her saddle the minute she gets off that ferry. God knows we have more than enough drunks and rowdy people now that the snow and the holidays are here. Jane will be up to her neck in OUIs and cars slidin' off the road. She won't be thinking to put Baby Jesus in the manger, I can tell you that much."

"I'm not so sure we're going the stable route this year with the donkey, the three kings, and, well, shepherds, Trudy," Helen said ever so slowly. She was trying to avoid lighting the fuse that would touch off the Holly Jolly explosion.

"I never heard such rubbish, Helen! What's gotten into you anyway? You've got yourself a shiny new Public Safety Officer and that qualifies you to go forgettin' the Immaculate Conception and 'Lo, A Child Is Born'? And what about bunting?! Huh?! Have you given up on bunting? And wreaths, and bells and stuffed stockings?!!"

"Trudy...easy now. Yes, you're a little bit right." Helen was trying her best. "Things are different with Jane here now, but there's always room for compromise, don't you think? Especially at Christmas time?"

"Don't give me that doe-eyed look of yours, Helen Orbeton. I am not gonna waste my breath lecturing you. You are old enough to know the St. Frewin's Island public offices have always put their best foot forward at Christmas, and I'm gonna make sure we do it up good, and we do it right. So don't tread on me, Helen. Don't even think of it! The holidays are for goodwill towards our fellow men...'Let nothing you dismay'...remember? 'Tidings of comfort and joy'...have you forgotten that?!" Trudy stormed out the door and began hauling her boxes in from her car.

....

Two hours later, Trudy's molten holiday lava had sufficiently pooled and cooled off, and she turned a complete circle to take in her magic. Twelve little figurines and barnyard animals making up the crowded scene of the nativity were now ensconced in a stable on a small table in front of the office white board. Trudy especially liked the large fold-out picture of the rolling hills of Bethlehem she had plucked from an old issue of *National Geographic,* which she taped to the white board as a scenic backdrop for the crèche. Elsewhere around the Public Safety Office, tired-looking red and green plastic swag and lights and Styrofoam wreaths decked the walls helter skelter, from window to window.

"This looks a whole lot better, Helen, than when I first walked in here. You have to admit," Trudy insisted.

"Trudy, what about this area among the bushes and shrubs on your big picture of Bethlehem? I see a bunch of soldiers holding submachine guns, all ready to shoot at people."

"Oh, don't mind that, Helen. Here, I'll just slap some of these Santa Claus stickies to cover up those troops and their gear." Trudy said.

DON'T TOUCH MY COCKTAIL!

Helen was peering closely into the stable. "The one thing I hope you'll hold back on," Helen suggested, "is placing the newborn babe in the manger so early in the month. After all, he wasn't a preemie, was he? Let's give it another week and a half or so...then we can pop the little guy into his hay bed. What do you think of that?"

"Really, Helen, it's like you've become an atheist overnight! Do you no longer ask the question, What child is this?" Trudy was heating up again.

"You know, could you excuse me, Trudy, just a minute, while I run to the rest room?" Helen asked. She needed salvation now.

When she returned, Trudy had packed up her loose ends and left for the day. Joy to the World! rang in Helen's ears.

....

A short while later Samantha Lloyd stuck her head in the PSO office and was happy to see Helen holding down the fort. "Hi Helen! Are you enjoying the sanity while Jane's away?"

"I'll be glad when she's back next week, Sam. It's been bleak without her," Helen admitted.

"I just wanted to check quick on the parking permits for the big New Year's Eve party Salem and Chanson Pratt are holding this year," Sam said. As the island's favorite caterer, Samantha Lloyd commanded a holiday work load guaranteed to knock the ordinary human being flat on the ground. But not Sam, who could plan, orchestrate, cook, dictate, placate, and please everyone from the likes of Rasputin to Camilla Parker Bowles.

15

"Are we sure we've got all our t's crossed for snow plowing the roads down to their house on Young's Point? You've alerted the road crew and they're all set, right?"

"Yes, everything's in order, Sam," Helen confirmed as she looked over the public works schedule. After they ran through a few other details, Sam headed for the door. "Good luck with all the cooking you've got ahead of you!" Helen called out as Sam took off.

Helen finished her mug of eggnog before closing the office for the night. But she jumped back a little as she downed the last of it. At the bottom of her cup sat the strangest object. When she pushed her eyeglasses to the top of her head and took a closer look, who did she see but the little porcelain Baby Jesus! Staring up at her as a reminder that he had to be born at some point. THAT TRUDY! Dumping the Child of God into Helen's cup when she had left the room earlier. It wasn't in Helen Orbeton's psyche to think such thoughts, but "What a Bitch!" did cross her mind.

5
Monday, December 9

"Well, Sugar Plum," Zen-Ti cooed into the phone, "you've got to make some kind of choice here, or we're wasting my breath and your money." Zen-Ti took a swig of his Tsingtao beer and shook out his arm holding the phone. He gazed around his office in Lowell and started counting the number of bullet holes in the opposite wall. High time to get that Swiss cheese covered up. The whole place could use some paint. His Bay State-street rank was on the up and up. His office should look like it belonged to top dog of the nation, even if he wasn't that dog...yet.

Zen-Ti was still waiting for Chanson Pratt to respond. She did not. He had no idea how Chanson, the wife of one Salem Pratt, a Texas semiconductor multimillionaire, had tracked Zen-Ti down for this special job. And he wasn't going to pry.

"OK. Look. I'll go over the list with you one more time. Like I say, we offer a shmuggysbord: You want mariticide, we'll just send him to the farm. Or we can give him a Picasso—on the face, maybe on his chest or back? Maybe Three Knee Deep? Or we can just dump your better half in the trunk of our car, drive him down to Massachusetts, and bring him back to you in a few days with not too many dents, but maybe he'll be a wiser guy. You know what I mean?"

"Zen-Ti, I am so sorry, but I couldn't understand that list of yours. Could you please translate all of that for me? I don't see how we're going to do business if you keep talking gang slang." Chanson asked nicely. She was facing

17

away from a big mirror in her Texas home, while looking behind her with a small mirror in her hand to see how her latest haircut shaped up in the back. And she was silently asking herself how she ever got to this point. But she was determined to see things through.

"Look, Sweetie, in this line of biz, you don't want to go barking all this shit over the phone. What if some nosey ear's listening to me and you? That's why we use gang slang. It doesn't take any brains, Honey! Keeps trouble off our backs, you get it? But for you, Buttercup, I'll make an exception. I said kill him, cut him up somewhere on his bod, stab him a little, or just take him for a spin down south and back without any man handling. Lady's choice."

"Oh God...no murder, Zen-Ti! No blood at all!" Chanson was aghast. "I just want to scare Salem nearly to death so he'll wake up and clean up his act."

"Sure thing, Chiquita. We can do just what you want. What's your gripe anyway? Is your hubby a Mamma Man or a Gump?"

"What?"

"You know, like, gay?"

"Not at all!"

"Well, is he on bug juice or brake fluid?"

"No! Heaven's no!" Chanson gasped, on the hunch that either of those liquids had to be something toxic.

"Then why are you going to all this trouble, Lollipop?"

"Oh dear. This is getting too complicated. I don't know what to do, Zen-Ti." Chanson began pacing the marble floor and looking out her huge glass windows to the vast skies of Texas. "It's been years since Salem has had any real feeling for me...for us. Our marriage has become a worn-out shoe. And he's so caught up in his work, his corporate returns, and now I think he's mortgaged everything but our dog to foreign financiers. We could go broke for all I know! I just want it to all go back to who we once were. Do you know what I mean? What do you think? Will Salem wake up and smell ME again?—never mind the roses! Can you help us?"

"Whoa there, Pop Tart! Sorry I asked. Sounds like you got the same problems like everyone...short on Fucks and Bucks. But I'm no marriage knot counselor, and I'm sure as hell no ATM. No can do. You just have to pick something off the schmuggysbord."

"OK. I have to pull myself together here. Let's just make it a simple kidnapping. OK, Zen-Ti? No violence. No harm. Just whisk Salem away for two days and then deliver him back to me all in one piece. You can shake him up enough so he'll be really thankful to get back home, to our life together. All I want again is his love, and his attention. But I don't want you to hurt him," Chanson said.

"Got it, uh huh," Zen-Ti was shaking his head to himself. "No biscuits; no hand candy. No dum dum."

"There you go again, Zen-Ti! Translation please?"

"Yes, Babe. I'm saying zero on the guns, no knives, we won't be packing weapons. Sound good to you?"

"I guess so," Chanson sighed, trying to avoid her innate ambivalence. "As for payment, this middle man you set me up with, this Tony Abanditono, will hand over my down payment to you on December 23. You're all squared away, right? Then you bring Salem back to me in Maine, safe and sound after our party, and Tony will pay the rest of my money. Is that how it works?"

"Money talks, Cupcake. Every time. Now, tell me. With all these old fogies at your gig on New Year's Eve, what's Cigarette Man going to be wearing so we can tell who he is?"

"Let me think...let's plan on Salem wearing his silver and gold striped tuxedo jacket. It's so loud, you won't miss it."

"And how about you, Cookie? What kind of feathers are you going to be flying for New Year's Eve?" Zen-Ti asked dreamily, half to himself.

"I don't know yet, Zen-Ti. That's not the point," Chanson grumbled.

"Take it easy, Gum Drop! Take it easy. I'm just shooting the breeze with you. I'll quit."

"OK. I'm hanging up now, Zen-Ti. Please just stick to the plan...our New Year's Eve party at our summer home. That's 18 Young's Point on St. Frewin's Island off the coast of Maine...and you better wait until near midnight when everyone's had enough food and alcohol. That way they'll be too full or too busy with the countdown to notice you snatching Salem away."

"Yes, Ma'am. 10-4." Zen-Ti hung up and continued scrolling through the society shots of Chanson Pratt on the web. *She's one fancy Frosted Flake on the outside,* he thought...but up came his STOP sign. Clients were Clients; Biz was Biz. Still, as far as the birds and bees, he was betting this Frosted Flake was sweet as a honey-glazed chocolate dip donut. *Sweet as can be...yeah, Baby.*

6
Monday, December 9
Night

Bernie Pushaw slowly looked around him as he stood in the near darkness of the main dock at the Calderwood Boatyard. It was fucking cold out tonight, and way too creepy quiet. His truck dashboard read 14 degrees Fahrenheit on his way over, so he figured that must be why he was shivering. He hugged himself and jammed his gloves under the bulky armpits of his ancient parka. He didn't think of himself as a wimp, but he was feeling damned spooked and lonely. No moon, no clouds, and just one wobbly security light way off to the corner made it all the worse. Big black shadows of towering yachts completely shrouded in plastic wrap swallowed up the near and the far, leaving Bernie with the willies and not much depth perception.

That's when he turned on his flashlight and swept it around until he finally saw the two drums of waste that Dracula had left for him on the dock, just like he said over the walkie talkie. But these drums were little guys compared to what Bernie hoisted daily. Must be some crap from somethin' the size of a dinghy, though come to think of it, that didn't make much sense. No sane captain was out on the ocean around here in early December. But maybe the boatyard had drained the crap out of some small tub they were working on right now. Didn't matter. It wasn't Bernie's lookout. He was just the eco-spreader.

He got into his truck and drove it right up to the barrels. Then he maneuvered the heavy drum lifter at the back to raise the containers, one at a time, onto the truck bed. He climbed up into the truck and secured the barrels. When he turned on his flashlight again to make sure the load was secure, Bernie noticed the funny words on the two barrels. Some kind of gibberish on the ten-gallon drum: Премьера белужья икра. And those Chinese stick figures on the other: 中国大陆金块. Weird was all his frozen brain could think in the cold of the black night. St. Frewin's Island was getting weirder and weirder.

....

Two nights later on the beach near the public ferry landing, the Russian thugs, who had erroneously handed off their ten-gallon barrels of Premier Beluga Caviar and Chinese gold to Bernie Pushaw, were sweet-talking to Troy Overlock, their American contact from the Calderwood Boatyard. The first thug spat at Troy, "Ty che, blyad?" [Russian: What the fuck?] The second growled in a tense, low pitch, "Schas po ebalu poluchish, suka, blyad!" [Now I'll fucking kill you bitch, motherfucker!]

The Russian thugs had called each other Egor and Yaroslav, and that's about all Troy knew. He was trying to make some big dough on the side. How hard could it be to drive two small barrels down to some D. C. townhouse for some total strangers?

But Troy never made walkie talkie contact with the Russian thugs the night of the fiasco. He had no idea what time he was supposed to pick up, and he didn't have a clue where the goods were now. His attempted explanations were lost in the thugs' supreme certainty that Troy was a total liar, which inspired them to give their fists some fresh air. Troy's face quickly lost its good looks with every direct punch to his head.

Egor tried to explain to Troy how he and Yaroslav now owed—impossibly!—nearly fifty million dollars for disappeared product—a fucking five million for caviar and another forty-three million plus for gold...all owed to "BEEEEG Boss" back home in the port city of Makhachkala on the Caspian Sea. All thanks to Troy screwing up their delivery.

But Troy never caught the dollar figures or the numbers didn't register, because he went in and out of consciousness, and he had never been much good with math anyway. At some point, he was praying for death, but the thugs did not grant him his wish. They hauled his slumped body behind a shed on the beach and left him to his fate. Egor and Yaroslav then hurried back to the dock, jumped into their Donzi speedboat, and tore off into the frozen, black night. No one but the moonlight caught sight of the two small, black devices that were flung into the air as the boat receded. No one saw the two small, black objects disappear beneath the skin of the sea.

7
Tuesday, December 10

"Oh, man! Are you serious, Helen? The Channel 9 TV crew is showing up in two days instead of late next week? And you're saying they insist on the scheduling change? What a total disaster!"

Konstantin Balankoff leaned his mouth close to the back of Jane Roberts' neck and blew on it while she was on the phone with her Public Safety Office in America. She tried to shush him as he started licking her ear.

Sensual Jane would have given anything to remain playing Naked Heidi in the Alps for five more days—Naked Heidi, who was shriveling fast into Responsible Jane, who was being called home to her job in Maine as the Public Safety Officer on St. Frewin's Island. Naked Heidi wanted to gut Responsible Jane and toss her down a Swiss crevasse forever.

Seriously though, could Jane explain how in the world she and Konstantin Balankoff had turned into an item? Their bonding seemed to happen overnight. Not that anyone bothered with courtship anymore. Jane was amazed she didn't have to plot or scheme this time around. She didn't pray, or beg, or fabricate ways to get together. She hadn't had time to buy sexy new underwear. She never even panted. Konstantin came to take her on a picnic one day—simply a summer picnic on St. Frewin's Island—and Jane was a goner. All his. And he seemed to feel the same towards her.

DON'T TOUCH MY COCKTAIL!

"All right, all right. Tell them I'm on my way back. But I swear to God, Channel 9 is on my hit list!" *And they've reduced my paltry love life by about sixteen orgasms, the pigs!*

8
Wednesday, December 11

What would Mainers do without the occasional winter thaw? That little window of opportunity now and then when the frost and the snow backed off for a day, giving everyone a chance to race around madly and put to rest some final outside chores. Being that kind of a day, it was a good day for Bernie to haul the two oddball drums out of the storage area and add their contents to a bunch of septage and spread the whole caboodle over the thawing fields.

After he plowed the furrows where he would deposit the barrel contents, Bernie got his equipment in place to maneuver the first barrel so he could dump its contents into the spreader truck. He shook his head and gagged as the cap of the first barrel came free. He had so many years of the scent of human crap under his belt and up his nose, the stench of that waste just rolled off him now. But the contents in this barrel??? Jayzoo Cristo!! Fuckin' BEEZAR as far as Bernie could tell. And the smell?! God Almighty! Awfully fishy? Or salty smelling? Whatever party-goers shit in this barrel must have stuffed themselves to death on Morton's Salt. Every man, woman, and child swallowing a whole goddamn round navy-blue container, girl and umbrella and all! Bernie had never smelled such fucking brine. And how could this stuff look so oozy black? Maybe too much spinach on their plates? Bernie couldn't imagine eating that much spinach if you paid him....

DON'T TOUCH MY COCKTAIL!

Once that mess was done and over with, Bernie tackled the Chinese barrel of crud next. What the hell?! As the drum was tilting and emptying out, Bernie heard the continuous chortle of solid chunks cascading into the spreader. Sure didn't sound like septage. Since when did septage sound like pebbles? How could his job be turning into such a goofball day? He hadn't had a drink in twenty-four hours. It was like the day itself was shit-faced...not Bernie. All he usually did was spread the same old crap. What was with this new shit? Should he give a shit?!

Intelligent gent that he was, he decided to stop at the end of the second furrow to jump out of his machine and commune with the trench before him. He bent down and with his working gloves on, picked out of the frosty ditch a few of the black chunks of the second barrel now coated with the disgusting briny glue of the first barrel. He pressed the chunks in his gloved hands; he smelled the chunks. There was no way before God and man that anyone was gonna tell him this shit was simply shit. It didn't feel like it. It didn't smell like it. It weren't just shit, Dumbo! What the fuck? What was this?

9
Thursday, December 12
Noon

Lieutenant Joseph Adderley and Homicide Detective Storm Nosmot were sitting together at Baxter's Bar and Grill in Hallowell and exchanging thoughts on two of their ongoing cases. They both sipped on coffees and waited for their "All Aboard Burgers" to arrive—everything under the sun piled on top of an organic beef patty.

The Channel 9 midday show *News of You!* was just coming on, and the camera began zooming into what Adderley and Storm both realized was the State Ferry Terminal on St. Frewin's Island. They could see the ferry docked at the landing, its stark spire jutting forth in the winter sky. Storm felt a sudden uneasy vibe that the huge, glossy black shaft was beckoning everyone like a vacant cross, hungry for a body with outstretched arms to adorn its empty horizontal crosspiece.

"Well, well, well," Joseph Adderley sat back and stared. Who should the Channel 9 broadcast host be speaking with, but their own Jane Roberts. The two officers looked at one another with question marks in their eyes.

"Wasn't this interview supposed to occur next week?" Storm asked. "I thought the theme was going to be 'Merry Christmas from St. Frewin's.'" He shifted on his bar stool.

"This could be a recipe for disaster, Storm. We didn't brief Jane yet on how to handle the interview. Now she's about to go rogue and adlib her way through the whole damn thing!" Adderley shook his head. "We better buckle our seat belts. Especially if Harriet Buxton gets wind of this...." He sat back with a frown taking over his face.

A drone camera panned over the harbor towards Jane on the pier. She was hopping from one foot to the other in her hot orange down jacket and faux fur-lined trapper hat. The drone moved past bundled-up, curious onlookers and then circled round towards the enormous, black Styrofoam fenders lining the V-shaped ferry crib. The thirty-foot high stanchions were faceless monoliths guarding the island from invasion...but an invasion of what? By whom? Maybe Jane would reveal all to the TV audience.

Adderley and Storm held their breath as Jane commenced with her spontaneous thoughts about her job as the island's Public Safety Officer. They both agreed they should each order a Manhattan, on the theory they would each need one before the interview was through, even though this was their lunch break.

The lively banter between the TV host and PSO Roberts simmered along at a congenial pace. "I'm glad she's focusing on positive aspects," Adderley said to Storm, who raised his Manhattan in relief.

The topic turned to the daily running of the office. Jane described what a typical week entailed and what tasks were involved, including her current efforts to plan their budget for the new year. "Now, I want you to know that the Public Safety Offices on all our island communities could use as much State support as you can convince your legislators and the Governor to give us," Jane pumped it up. "If the voting public is watching this broadcast...Ha ha!!...you better believe I'm making the ole pitch for more funding!" Adderley gritted his teeth.

Jane continued on her spin. "I mean, we certainly don't want the hearty, hardworking Mainers who inhabit some of these most scenic square miles of our State to feel like they're not getting their fair share of the taxpayer dollar, right?" Adderley took a generous swig of his drink to distract himself from whatever Jane would spill out next.

"Did you know that tiny little St. Frewin's Island with a year-round population of some 300 people accounts for about 10% of the gross annual statewide income that flows to tradesmen? This is thanks to the building boom we have out here, and the constant renovations long-time summer residents enjoy making on their summer estates. And don't forget our WiFi-free tourism. This island economy is cooking! And it keeps on cooking right through the winter."

"Well, she's made some good points there," Storm remarked. He took a loving look at his burger, followed by a loving bite.

"You should also know the fishing and boat building industries on St. Frewin's each account for 15% of the gross annual statewide income that flows to fishermen and boatbuilders. So what sense does it make for the State to stick to a tight-fisted fiscal program for the island communities?!" Jane exclaimed.

THAT DID IT. "Pour me a Glenfiddich," Adderley growled to the bar tender. "And don't be stingy."

"St. Frewin's deserves more social spending," Jane hammered on. "Because, let's face it, life out here is not always a dream come true. We have our share of problems like any community. I can't honestly stand here and pretend we don't have issues surrounding alcoholism and opioid addiction, domestic violence and abuse, dogs running loose, night deer hunting, undersized clam harvests. You name it...we've got it."

"Jesus Christ, Storm. Our office should have been informed about this rescheduling so we could preview and coach Jane about spilling her guts." Adderley stared at the three drops of liquid sitting at the bottom of his glass.

Jane began teetering as a sharp wind picked up. "Why did we think she would stick to the sunny aspects of her job?" Adderley asked Storm.

A TV crew person ran to Jane's side to provide a human buffer from the windy gusts, to allow Jane's mike to continue broadcasting clearly. It was becoming apparent the weather might be more than the TV crew could handle with their equipment. Hats and straps and papers were now blowing out of view. As Jane continued to wax on about the state of St. Frewin's, the drone camera focused in on the ferry terminal's now infamous hygienic sign:

Tickets that have been held in people's mouths will not be accepted.

"So tell us, Jane," the interviewer asked. "You had a real shock this past summer with the death of Ruth Farrow. What impact did that event have on your role as Public Safety Officer?"

"Uh oh," Storm said. "There's the Grim Reaper question."

"Ah...Ruth Farrow, my first murder case. May she rest in peace," Jane said, hands together, and looking straight into the camera. "What I want you and all your viewers to know is that murder is not a daily special on our island menu. In fact, despite the points I made earlier, we live in an absolute Paradise here on St. Frewin's," Jane said to the audience. "It doesn't get any better...."

Gasps punctured the broadcast, and one of the TV assistants closest to Jane began shouting, "Oh no! Look! Look at him!" Jane turned towards the shore. The cameras followed her spin. The cameras kept rolling and zoomed in for the "*News of You!*" experience. Storm and Adderley followed the action with their mouths wide open.

Something resembling a man stumbled from behind a shed on the beach and began wobbling towards the ferry dock where Jane and the TV crew stood. His bludgeoned mask reminded Jane of the plum dumplings her grandmother used to make...plum dumplings now slashed open to crimson flesh where there should have been face. He cried out miserable sounds and keeled over into the sand.

Jane realized what was happening and started calling out to the TV techs, even as they swung their lenses towards the shore and continued to stream it all live to the midday audience. "Cut! Cut! CUT THE CAMERAS!" Jane yelled, while pushing and shoving the TV personnel away from their view of the victim.

"Look, Lady." One of the techs who had moved too close to the water caught himself in time. "I don't give a damn if you're the Public Safety Officer out here. We've got a job to do."

"So do I, Sir. And I'm telling you to back off."

"Maybe you don't get it. This monster mash is gonna give our viewers a whole lot more entertainment than you and all your hot air."

DON'T TOUCH MY COCKTAIL!

"Entertainment?" Jane said. "You can't show a little respect for this guy's family? What if his mother's turning the TV on right now?"

"So what? It'll make your job easier when she calls in to say that's her son. Right? Hey, you'll be thanking us before we're through."

"Why don't I take down your name, in case we need to follow up," Jane said.

"No name. You can call the network. They'll handle it." The camera man turned to continue recording the fallen man.

Jane could not contain herself. "You know, they could not have sent a bigger asshole to do your job today. You are one shabby so-called professional. I may get you for tampering with a crime scene."

"Too late to apologize, Lady. Don't even try."

Lieutenant Adderley sputtered a muffled curse into his scotch. This is how the fall of the Roman Empire must have unfolded...one little incident in one little, remote colony at a time, eroding into disruption and frenzy...the frail march of a fringe civilization taking its first rickety detour down the tubes.

"Attention, Everyone! ATTENTION! This is now a crime scene! You have to leave this area NOW!" Jane continued hollering, waving her arms in the wind. "You've got to get your people out of here IMMEDIATELY!" Jane roared into the faces of the receding camera crew, who alternated between filming her rage and filming the downed body. "SHOW SOME RESPECT FOR THE WOUNDED!" Jane yelled, jumping up and down and now whacking some of the TV crew to emphasize her demands. "Didn't you hear me? You can't be here any longer! GET THE HELL OUT! SHUT THIS DOWN!"

Adderley dropped his head to the bar counter and wept. Storm patted him on the back. Storm couldn't cry for laughing, and then his laughter became funny tears. Why should any of this be a surprise to them? How could it have turned out any other way with Jane on the job?

Storm felt a secret ping inside his chest. Looked like he'd be heading out to St. Frewin's very soon to solve the case of this pulverized man.

10
Thursday, December 12
Afternoon

The size 13 cowboy boot heels propped up on the mahogany battleship desk in the Washington, D.C. inner sanctum belonged to Senator Hitch McGill of Texas. So did the mounted head of a blackbuck antelope and all the framed memorabilia. Nearly everything else befitting of a longtime legislator's office—heavy drapes, dense carpets, brocade settees, stately chairs, antique cabinets, classic lamps—was the property of the Architect of the Capitol. So much political clout on his CV, Hitch mused, yet he and all his fellow legislators were not permitted, as a rule, to outfit their own offices. So much for diversity! He had never managed to swallow this aspect of his job.

Hitch McGill extended his lanky frame along his Herman Miller chair (kept hidden in a closet during official meetings!) and stretched his lower back to release his roiling stress. He was furious over whether he was about to have a heart attack or if he should make damn sure his Russian flunkeys each had one instead. If these reformed Bolsheviks wanted the Congressional votes to go their way, they had to make it worth Hitch McGill's time and effort to swing things in their favor.

Over the past fifteen years, Hitch had become accustomed to Moscow's modest gifts...elegant dinners, surprise cases of vodka, and those occasional lovely kuklas whose long hair swung in rhythm with their long legs. But as Hitch's influence in the United States government grew, Russia's stagnating economy and its bid for global prominence were being further undermined by more and more wild cards zinging in from all over the globe.

Whatever the subject of the Senate bills—nuclear disarmament, European energy security, oil tariffs, scrambled NATO and bacon—these Ruskies needed Hitch now more than ever. So they had better be ready to Pay Big. And Pay Big they said they would...to Hitch's surprise.

"Pay Big" meant caviar and gold...not just those pathetic one-ounce jars of cheap salty ball bearings and the occasional golden cuff or wristwatch. No. "Pay Big" now meant barrels of the stuff, all under the radar. One ten-gallon barrel of each this year....one barrel of Premier Beluga Caviar and one barrel of gold, preferably gold nuggets spray-painted black to hide their gleam in transit.

So where the fuck were Hitch's barrels? And what about this spazz, Troy Overlock, who was supposed to have pulled into Hitch McGill's townhouse driveway on Wednesday night to deliver the goods? What kind of game did the Bolsheviks think they were playing? Were they considering shorting Hitch? The barrels were tracked by GPS, so Kremlin's finest had no excuses. Just check their damn tracker log and find out where the hell the Senator's prizes were hiding.

Hitch's pragmatic tit for tat that was shuttling between his patience and his hunger for results had gone on long enough. It slammed to a halt. He lowered his boots and legs to the floor and took up his phone to badger Egor and Yaroslav for a plausible explanation. Otherwise, he would feed them whole to their boss in Makhachkala on the Caspian Sea.

DON'T TOUCH MY COCKTAIL!

················

"So you're trying to tell me in your shitty, broken English that you mixed up the GPS tracking of my barrels with your GPS tracking of an entirely separate delivery? ...of what? What's that? Knock-off Bottega Veneta handbags going to a dark web outlet in Kittery, Maine?! You're saying you confused MY caviar and MY gold with fucking arm candy? You idiots! How do you expect me to vote in favor of Mother Russia when you're leaving me high and dry with nothing for my blinis or my family's blinis or my buddies' blinis this New Year's Day? Why would I ever answer your calls about Chechen terrorism again if there's no barrel of gold sitting at my doorstep by tomorrow night? You know who's going to get fucked here, Egor? You are, My Big Fat Pelmeni!"

················

"OK. Now you're talking. You're saying you sent out a drone to track my barrels once you realized the wrong person picked them up. And that drone has footage of the fate of my barrels? So what are we waiting for?! Send me the fucking footage so I at least have an inkling of what you're talking about! You're making no sense...say that again? Someone buried my barrel contents in a shit field? What the hell does that mean? Right, yes, OK. Send me those tapes right away. I need to get a handle on your fuck-up NOW!"

Hitch McGill took a moment to catch his breath and then he opened the door to his legislative assistant's office and handed her his laptop. "Geneva, please set up my computer to play some incoming videos from the outfit called 'Slavic Imports.' Don't start the videos; just set

37

them up. And then please look up 'Environmental Fields' on St. Frewin's Island in Maine, OK? Let me know right away whatever you find. And then I want you in here to look at those videos with me to tell me if you can make any sense of them. Mind you, this little exercise of ours is Strictly Confidential!"

....

"OK. So let's focus on those two barrels. Right there. Got it," Senator McGill said with the image of his two barrels filling the laptop screen.

"Oh dear, Senator McGill. This is so weird!" exclaimed Geneva Pratt after their first few minutes of watching the screen.

Silence from the Senator...and grimacing.

"It looks like some man is pouring one of your barrels into a spreading machine. And he's driving towards some ditches dug into the ground. That's what Environmental Fields is all about, by the way, per the web. It's a site where the St. Frewin's Public Works is legally permitted to recycle septage waste from homes and boats."

"Septage waste?! Good God," said the Senator.

"Oh, oh...now I can see some kind of thick black goop trickling out of the spreader hose into the furrow. Look at that disgusting stuff!" Geneva exclaimed. "Ewwww!...it's awfully black and sticky looking, don't you think? Like black mayonnaise maybe?"

My god damn CAVIAR!!!! ...IN A SHIT FIELD!!! was what the Senator was thinking.

"Now the worker is putting the contents of the second barrel into the spreader and he's driving along with everything spilling out on top of the black goop and then into another trench. The stuff coming out looks awfully chunky...I have no idea if that's human waste or not. Do you think it looks like excrement and all? Oh, sorry! Pardon my language. I guess it looks like, well, like cute little black nuggets, don't you think?" Geneva asked.

My god damn Chinese gold!!! The Senator was perspiring and moaning in woe.

"Uh oh. Now the spreader is applying something that actually does look like real human waste. Oh no! Smack on top of where he spread your two barrels! Yuck! OK, OK. He's stopped the machine and he's stepping down to take a closer look. Ugh! Oh! Disgusting! He's actually picking the stuff up. He looks confused and amazed. Oh My God! ...Ha ha!! Ha ha!! I can't believe it! Now he's taking a leak right on top of everything in the ditch! Ha ha!! Gross me out!"

"THAT TOTAL ASS KEBAB! WHOEVER HE IS, I'M GOING TO KILL HIM!!"

"Hang on, Sir. Here's another shot of our focus area— must be a day or two later...sort of looks like they got awfully bad weather, which has frozen everything into a solid lake of crap with huge crusty chunks on top. Gosh, what a mess! I am so sorry, Senator! It's a toxic dump, isn't it? So gross! I mean, this is so pathetic...whatever...you had in your barrels. I hope it wasn't that important."

The Senator locked his bulging eyes on Geneva Pratt and struck a pose...vigorously. His corrugator muscles burrowed into his brow. His nostrils flared their outer wings and stayed there. He brought his six-foot frame up high and began pacing the room with clipped military steps. He was about to diffuse his behemoth frustration, but first he wanted it to well up and bite off some vital part of Geneva Pratt's head.

"You know, Geneva, when one hears a man say 'I'M GOING TO KILL HIM!!,' that should provide one with sufficient insight into how that man feels about the situation. And if that man has prefaced the entire incident with 'Strictly Confidential!' that is a further indication of the gravity of the matter.

"Nonetheless, in a cloud of obliviousness, you ignored the wails of despair emitted by that man. You blurted out the simpering and the hackneyed—'ewwww' and 'gross' and 'yuck'—and all topped with roars of laughter!! Does it not occur to you that such mindless utterances demonstrate an acute lack of empathy? And might all of this seriously suggest a dire need to improve your sense and sensibilities and suppress your emotive outbursts during work hours, in order to even begin to understand the real world, let alone the world of politics? DO YOU FOLLOW ME?!"

"That's very perspicacious of you, Senator. I'll keep in mind everything you've pointed out," Geneva said as she gave Hitch McGill a long and thoughtful look. His face reminded her of her own father, and she felt a fleeting twinge of misplaced allegiance. "Since I overheard everything you were yelling into the phone to your 'Egor' earlier, I am fully apprised of the pile of shit in which you've landed. No, wait...in which your assets have landed. I'll be happy to telephone Egor right away to arrange for his thugs to get over to the Environmental Fields to retrieve your Chinese gold." Geneva walked towards the door and looked back at Hitch McGill. "I think you will agree with me, Sir, that you've kissed your caviar goodbye, yes?" Geneva gave a polite nod and walked out the door, back to her desk.

DON'T TOUCH MY COCKTAIL!

Hitch drew in a long breath and held it until the door was closed. "By golly, that girl just may have some of her mother, Chanson, in her after all," Hitch said to himself. He stared up at the curved horns of his blackbuck antelope and thought back to when his pal Salem Pratt had first told him about St. Frewin's Island and the amazing, whimsical ban on the internet. Imagine that.

Hitch had no idea St. Frewin's had unplugged from the world-wide web after a horrific car collision wiped out an entire family years before. Official cause of said vehicular homicides? Distracted driver on cellphone. Not whimsical at all.

But to Hitch, it had been a miracle. No local, federal or global digital surveillance capability in that neck of the ocean. Imagine that...he now thought, with bitter, bitter resignation.

11
Thursday, December 12
Afternoon

Jane bounded up the steps of the PSO, her long, crazy hair flying in the air. She would have loved to fling open the front door but for the fact that without prior notice to or permission from Jane, the door had been transformed into a dump picker's garish concept of Garbage Noel. *How the hell do we have this shiny coral-orange CELLOPHANE covering the whole God damn door and a wreath MADE OUT OF GREEN GINGERALE BOTTLES AND RED COKE CANS?!?*

Jane buried her disgust. She had to get into the office right away to call Lieutenant Adderley and Storm about the battered man she and several ferry attendants had moved from the beach to higher ground. Before the county ambulance took charge, Jane had pulled the victim's wallet from his pocket. According to the driver's license, Troy Overlock was their man. And more than one islander confirmed that Troy Overlock worked at Calderwood Boatyard.

Helen looked like she was holding her breath when Jane entered. Jane stared at the walls in disbelief, taking in Trudy Moody's festive Christmas handiwork. Without saying a word, Jane walked into her office and dialed Major Crimes Unit-Central. This new victim was more important than Jane's confusion over how some idiots had managed to infest the PSO office with all this holiday rubbish...and that dog-eared Bethlehem scene?! She was certain it could not have been Helen.

"Lieutenant Adderley?"

"We know Jane. We know. We saw all of it on *News of You!* Storm will be on the first boat tomorrow morning."

"Lieutenant Adderley, I'm really sorry about the paparazzi out here today. It wasn't at all how I meant things to turn out...what with that poor Troy Overlock appearing out of nowhere, half-beaten to death, and all the chaos."

"I wouldn't call the TV news camera people 'paparazzi,' Jane, but what's done is done. Not to worry for now. Just make sure your victim is in safe hands."

"Will do, Lieutenant Adderley. Thanks for your support on this one. We alerted Abenaki County General Hospital about Troy Overlock. He's unconscious, but Dr. Leckman, our island GP, was available to look him over and clean him up a bit before the ambulance arrived to transport him. I'll call you with a report when I have an update. And I sure hope we won't have to bother you more than this over the holidays. Merry Christmas to you and everyone at Maine Crimes Unit-Central."

"Thanks, Jane. Same to you. Do a good job. Try to avoid trouble," Lieutenant Adderley advised. Wishful thinking...why did he bother?

....

"So, Helen—this Troy Overlock who's been badly hurt. Do you know him?"

"Oh dear. Yes, he's Frank and Lorraine's son. He lives with them. Down on Radar Lane. Sweet boy...well, now a man. What happened?"

43

"All we know is that he showed up on the beach and then, BAM!, he passed out during today's TV interview. Severely beaten."

"That's horrible. Now what?" Helen said.

"I don't know. But I'm going to find out. And I've got to run over to see his parents. And then I'll head back to the ferry to do a site walk of the general area where he fell," Jane said.

Helen spoke again. "Jane—Sorry to switch topics. There's an entrepreneur visiting the island, and she wants to talk to you about her latest venture...something about Lobster Brides! Not sure if you've heard about it?"

"Doesn't sound familiar, Helen," Jane said.

"Well, this Gluella Trott would like to meet with you tomorrow morning—that's Friday, December 13th. Do you think you'll have time? I know you're busy with this new case and you've just returned from your vacation, and Oh! Your new assistant officially starts work tomorrow. Israel Tenner is his name. He stopped by the office earlier today to introduce himself while you were on TV. I think you'll like him, Jane...." Helen's voice petered out.

"Helen, what amazes me is that I was allowed no role in choosing this new assistant. MY new assistant. Does that make any sense? What if I HATE this guy? What if he's another Finn Gallinen? What if he smells like rotten fish?!" Finn Gallinen was Jane's least favorite colleague on the force.

The front door opened before Jane's comments became thin air. In walked a blondish young man who didn't need to be told to work on his posture. "Hey...Hi there. Just thought I would stop in before the day was through to see if my new boss was in. You must be Officer

Jane Roberts. I'm Israel Tenner...the rotten fish...," he said, holding out his hand, a wide grin on his face.

"Ha ha!! Oh boy. Well, I already like you more than I knew!" Jane's laughter rang out. "Don't mind how I talk. You'll get used to it." She walked right over and gave Israel a welcoming handshake.

"No offense taken. And now I'm here to help, Officer Roberts. Put me to work."

"Well, first things first, Israel. I'm Jane. You can call me Jane. Do you have all your gear moved in? Are you settled enough to start work right away...I mean now?"

"All set. Just say the word."

"OK. Let's go see Lorraine and Frank Overlock and break the news to them about their son, Troy. Troy showed up at the ferry beach today and collapsed onto the ground...it looks like someone totally pummeled him. And we need to inspect the ferry scene and see if we can find anything useful concerning our victim."

"Sounds good, Jane. I'm glad I'm here."

"Ditto, Israel." And to Helen, Jane called out, "Are we in luck or what, Helen?! And, sure, book Glue whoever she is for tomorrow. But, seriously, Helen. Did you say Gluella? Who goes through life with that kind of name? Who names their kid Gluella? Anyway, let's make it 11 AM, so I can first pick up Storm tomorrow morning and get him started on our case. Thanks!" Jane motioned for Israel to exit before her.

"Helen!" Jane stuck her head back in and yelled as she was about to close the door in leaving. "Make sure you ditch this cantaloupe-colored wrapping paper and plastic waste that's plastered all over our front door! ASAP Please!!"

And then Jane leaned in further and whispered in glee, "Helen! This Israel looks like a young Robert Redford!"

12
Friday, December 13
Early Morning

Spartak Volkov paid no attention to the nasty weather and the precarious footing in the chunky, uneven rows of tainted snow where he found himself this dawn. The thin, gray light was enough for him to look at his hand-held video player and begin to line up his position in relation to where the missing barrels had been spread on the earth. Egor and Yaroslav had dropped him off on the island at dawn and told him not to contact them until he could return with proof in his hands of his findings. They wanted to see nuggets of blackened gold from the "Environmental Fields," which was where he now stood.

His cronies back in Makhachkala had laughed at him for grabbing this winter assignment. "You dummkopf!" they kept yelling. "Why don't you wait until the summer smuggling trek to Maine? That way you'll have sunny days and lobster rolls." But Spartak had his reasons, and they were keeping him warm and cozy right now while he looked for the landmarks that would place him where the black gold had been buried.

He could see a red barn as he played back the video on his screen showing the gold being spread in the field. He looked around him, saw the red barn nearby on his right, and estimated the location of his trench. He stumbled some hundred feet towards his chosen area and bending down, he aimed his hammer and pick and broke through to the chunky black layer. The little black rocks looked like what he needed, so he grabbed a handful and stuffed it in his pocket. So far, so good.

"Hey, you! Hey! What are you doin'? What's goin' on?" Spartak jerked his head up, astonished to see or hear anyone at this early hour...especially when the person was yelling and running towards him. He froze. Bernie Pushaw did not. He raced towards Spartak over the icy, chunky plain of frozen curds and crud.

"What the hell you think you're doin' diggin' up my shit hole, Boy?! Who are you anyhow?!" Bernie hollered, equally astonished to see anyone at this hour of the day at Environmental Fields.

"I am Spartak! Spartak!" Spartak was unnerved, he was cold, and the tight stocking he was wearing over his head to blur his features was distorting his heavily accented words.

"Star Trek?! Whoa, now, Star Trek! Don't go gettin' funny with me, Boy. It's too fuckin' early in the mornin' for all this. Next thing I know, you're goin' say you're lookin' for Mr. Spock. Right?! Ha ha!! Gottcha there, don't I? Ha ha!! But you tell me, Star Trek...What the hell are you doin' in all this shit?!"

"Peace and Love! Peace and Love from Russia!" That's all that Spartak could think to blubber in his effort to calm things down here. But it all sounded like muffled froth coming out of his smothered mouth, which further confused this already tense encounter. Bernie started to explode. "Russia? Zat what you said? You God damn commie hippie!!!" Spartak assessed his odds and suddenly spun towards the woods and started running, running as fast as his boots could handle the slippery, icy, pocked snow field, which was not fast at all. He fell repeatedly and rose again. He could hear Bernie hollering and a quick look back showed Spartak that Bernie was heading to his nearby truck. Spartak ran and ran.

Bernie grabbed his taser gun and started chasing after Spartak. Spartak's eyes were crimped under the stocking and he could not see clearly where he was going. Bernie on the other hand was wearing boot grippers, and he was able to fly across the snow and bricks of ice scattered across the surface. He closed in on the fleeing Russian, his sure-footed effort quickly wiping out the distance between them. Bernie prepared to blast his taser at Spartak, and taking aim, Bernie let loose his electrified wire guides as he screamed his blood-curdling war cry at his ideal, imaginary target. "TAKE THAT!!!!!!, TRUDY MOODY!!! YOU BLOOD-SUCKIN' BITCH OF A MOTHER-IN-LAW!!! ZAP!!! ZAP!!! GOTCHA, YOU OLD BAG!!!!"

Spartak tripped and fell from the impact of the taser, but his heavy winter coat blocked the full thrust of the taser darts. They momentarily pierced the stiff, woven fabric, but only enough to create a faint electrical circuit. As Spartak fell, the darts quickly slid off him, due to his thick clothing. The electricity barely reached the core of his muscles. His muscles did not lock up on him entirely...they were still his muscles!

He realized in a few seconds that he could stand up. He trotted unsteadily at first, then quickly feeling whole again, he rushed towards the woods and kept running, more freely with every flying footfall because the ground began to slope upward and changed over to a dense layer of pine needles and turf. *Run, Spartak, run—keep running* he told himself, as he raced into the forest, a wolf dissolving into nothingness.

Carol Chen

After his initial lightning sprint, Bernie was bent over sucking in cold air, his chest begging for an oxygen tank. He couldn't go on. His GP had told him all the little Alfie Olays in his lungs were too blasted from like 80,000 cigarettes, give or take a few packs. And his toes were numb from all the drinks he'd tossed back for decades. Serves him right, his wife Noreen would be quick to say.

But Bernie had done his part. He would report all this to Jane Roberts and let the law take over now. That's what she was here for, public safety, right? No use her sittin' on her ass when the government was puttin' a check in her hands twice a month. And God bless her that she had refused to breathalyze Bernie bi-monthly like his wife had begged Jane to do. At least Roberts was packin' some brains upstairs.

One more lightbulb went off in Bernie's pickled brain...it was a pretty bright light bulb for an old fuck like him, he had to admit. He headed back to the equipment shed for something to start digging. He weren't no dummy.

And a little while later, another lightbulb circled back round to Mr. Pushaw. "Peace and Love" was what that turkey had yelled out, but sure as hell it sounded like "Pizza Love" for a moment. Pizza Love...Pizz Diet...Pizza Diet...Bernie was going to stew on all these strange words when he got home tonight. Somethin' odd was startin' to wiggle here. Noreen, his ever-lovin' wife, was good at word puzzles. Maybe she could help figure it out.

13
Friday, December 13

"You are going to love Storm Nosmot," Jane assured her new assistant, Israel Tenner, the next day when they were heading over to the ferry to pick up the homicide detective. "He's really one of the most level-headed people I've met in ages. And he's patient with newcomers, so I think you'll find it's great to work with him."

"Too bad we didn't find any juicy evidence at the ferry beach yesterday," Israel said.

"I know. Figuring out a crime can take a lot of patience. Storm's always telling me that. We're never sure what we'll run into when we search, and much of the time, we don't find it right away."

"Do you think it was kind of the same with Troy's parents?"

"Not much to go on, you mean? Maybe. But remember, they're in shock. We showed up at their door to let them know their son is half dead and struggling for his life in the hospital. It's not the time to hammer them with questions. We'll give it a few days, interview Troy's friends and colleagues, then circle back to his parents. Keep the faith, Israel. We can do this."

....

Helen walked into Jane's office in the late morning to announce the arrival of Gluella Trott...yes, it was still "Gluella," and "Trott" with two Ts at the end. Jane took a deep breath and motioned for Helen to close the door.

"What is this woman all about? Just one sentence is all I need."

"I'd say charming and alarming, Jane," Helen said with scrunched eyebrows.

"I should have guessed," Jane steamed. If someone seemed absurd before you even met the person, that had to give you an inkling, right? Jane really didn't want to hear about Gluey's latest venture when she would rather be tracking down clues to Troy Overlock's attack. She wished she were with Storm and Israel, who had driven over to Calderwood Boatyard to talk to Troy's boss and coworkers. Maybe someone would remember something to explain his assault.

"And about Troy Overlock, Jane," Helen said. "The hospital called to report that he's stable but still unconscious. The doctors want to keep him in a coma for a few days so his brain can recuperate. So no visitors or questions for now."

....

"Thanks for meeting with me, Officer Roberts," Gluella began, not even bothering to hide her quick assessment of Jane's body with a calculating eye. And Jane didn't bother shooing away formalities and familiarizing it to "Jane." Her professional yardstick was staying smack where it belonged. Who knew what this dingbat had up her sleeve.

"I just wanted you to be in the loop about my new venture—LOBSTER BRIDES! I've started a website for coastal Maine women who are looking for successful foreign husbands." Gluella handed Jane a pile of colorful flyers and a stack of cards printed with her basic pitch and information. "Obviously, the flip side of the coin is that I am assisting well-to-do foreign men to find brides along Down East Maine."

Obviously. Jane peered at the flyer depicting flabby maroon crustacean paws handcuffed in cheap looking diamond rings. *Is this what Gluella thinks is alluring?* Tiny mussels and whelk shells stood strangely in place as teeth in the lobsters' shrill smiles. *I have never seen such hideous graphics! Is she serious?* Jane looked up at Gluella Trott. *How the hell did she get that name? Do I dare ask her? And is that a little pack of chin hairs I see grazing along her right jawline? She looks like a Shirley Temple doll gone to seed. Maybe even a shrimpy child bride herself, but I bet that sweet look on her mug is a front for some kind of wily barracuda....*

"I don't mean to ruffle your romantic shore dinner here, Gluella," Jane began, waving a brochure, "but how do you plan to weed out the sharks and bottom-feeders to be sure only well-to-do foreign men dive into your lobster tank?"

"Oh, we've been extremely cautious with our algorithms on that aspect. No riff raff or gangsters allowed," Gluella explained with an automated smile, while stroking the chunky sausage curls on either side of her small head. "Candidates who sign up on our site must go through a rigorous financial vetting process. And the initial entry fee? Phew!" she emphasized, waving her hand under her nose, "is out of reach for all but the truly rich. Not to mention the renewal fee ladder, as you can imagine."

"It all sounds impressive, Gluella. Can you divulge any details about this vetting process?" Jane asked, her skepticism starting to twitch its ears.

"Absolutely." Gluella leaned forward and continued in her intent, soft voice. "Each applicant must provide his financial summary and the contact information for at least two of his major banks so we can verify the applicant's appropriateness. We contact all bank references before the applicant can gain entrance to our stable of Lobster Brides!"

"Your 'stable'? That sounds kind of—I don't know—something or other politically incorrect, doesn't it? But, all right. So...let's say Mr. Singapore gets past your vetting process and falls in love with Ms. North Haven, but it turns out Mr. Singapore is a front for a devious criminal who's out to get Ms. North Haven's money. Or let's say Mr. Singapore has three wives and is looking for a female lobster to round out his harem. How do you monitor those kinds of potential fraud?"

"I'm afraid you're straying into our protected corporate intellectual property, Officer Roberts. I'll have to decline going into details. I hope you can understand." Gluella folded her hands in her lap, and Jane could sense her shutting down at about thirty miles per hour.

"If you say so, Gluella. But you brought all this to my attention on your own initiative. I'm simply trying to look for black holes in your Love Boat here before the victim of some kind of international robbery or immigration bigamy lands sobbing on my desk. By the way, did you beta test your promo graphics along the way? You know, run them by some random members of the public to get feedback?"

"I'm glad you asked, Jane. The Lobster Brides! branding is the product of hundreds of hours of interviewing potential female participants and getting their input on how they would like the male world to perceive them. We're taking the platinum high road in every way," Gluella emphasized, with a tinge of tetchiness beginning to leak out of her baby doll face.

"I guess I should just step back and wish you well with your efforts, Gluella," Jane admitted. "But I'm wondering about this enthusiastic picture on the back of the brochure," she said, tapping on the image with her index finger. "I see a naked Lobster Babe with angel wings and high heels jumping out of a boiling hot steamer pot and yelling, 'I DO!' Are you sure the message you're projecting is accurate? I mean...sometimes there's a fine line between matrimonial intent and sexual relations. Are you seriously promoting marriage possibilities for your female clients...or just good old flesh for your male clients?"

"Aren't they initially or often one and the same?" Gluella asked in syllables that shot out of her mouth like BB pellets. "But not to worry, Jane. Leave it to the operations research professionals to iron out the formulas in this kind of business. I'll let you know how we're doing in a few months. And thanks again for your time and input." Gluella gathered herself together and hurried out of the office before Jane could even think to say goodbye.

"Helen—Did you catch any of that?" Jane asked in wonder.

"Well, bits here and there. But the interesting thing, Jane, is that I've heard lots of gals on the island saying they've signed up to be listed on Gluella's website."

"I'm surprised not one bit, Helen," Jane said in a tired voice. "Maybe it's this place?"

"No," Helen answered. "Just life."

14
Friday, December 13
Late Afternoon

There were probably some thirty people who assembled in the PSO later that afternoon for the community seminar on "Dope and Dogs." With the legalization of marijuana had arrived the sorry side of the coin...dogs inadvertently getting high, which could kill them.

"So, let me recap," said Dr. John Leckman, the island's general practitioner for humans, who also served as the local veterinarian. "Our basic tools in preventing psycho-pharmaceutical episodes, or death, in our furry friends are these:

1. Keep all marijuana products and chewing gum out of reach of your dog and never, never leave any of those items lying around where your dog can find them.

2. Don't discard gum wads or marijuana in your yard, on the ground, on the side of the road, in parking lots, in parks, or anywhere, except in a sealed bag to go in the garbage. And conversely, pick up any gum or roaches you see on the ground and discard them safely.

3. If your dog suddenly begins to throw up, to act shaky or skittish, to shy abruptly from your effort to pet its head, and to show unusual unsteadiness in its legs, call your vet right away and get medical attention for your dog. Marijuana and xylitol sweetener in gum can kill your pets."

Dr. Leckman began to take questions from the audience, and a general discussion followed on dogs' tripping. The meeting was winding down when the office door opened up to Bernie Pushaw, who had that look on his face that suggested he was both sober and on a "Good Citizen" mission. Everyone could tell right away. Those bedroom eyes of his were not glazed, and he wasn't swaying leeward and windward. He delivered his news with his inimitable initiative and gumption. "Jane! You gotta hear about this pinko freak I found out in the fields this AM! There's somethin' very hairy goin' on!"

"Really, Bernie? Now what?" Jane guided him towards her office, while several of the people at the seminar stuck around to make small talk and eavesdrop a little if they could. However, after Jane closed her office door behind her and Bernie, there was little for anyone to hear. Just then an unknown man walked into the office, startling the stragglers who had continued chatting about hallucinating dogs.

Helen looked up and stared when she saw a stranger with a head that looked like a shrink-wrapped Jerusalem artichoke. "Sir, can I help you?" she asked, leaping up from her seat. People were now backing away and starting to whisper among themselves. Was this a masked bandit? Who was this guy with a stocking over his head? Was this a holdup?

"Pleece...I come in peace. Peace and Love. Telephone? You haf telephone? I nid telephone...."

"Oh my God, Stan!" Frieda Helmstadt whispered to her husband. "He must be a terrorist!"

"What makes you think that, Frieda?" Stan whispered back. "You told me there weren't no jihadists except maybe at Hannaford. You told me we didn't need to get that danged terrorist insurance! And now you think you're lookin' at one right here in the Public Safety Office? Come on, Frieda...what's got into you?"

"But he wants the phone and he's got pantyhose all over his head, Stan!" Frieda pulled her husband towards Jane's office as she continued speaking in her lowest voice. "And he can hardly speak English, so he must be a terrorist!"

Helen acted as fast as she could think. "Ah, Sir, why don't you have a seat right here near my desk while I go get my boss. She'll help you make your telephone call? Yes? My boss will help you. Telephone...yes?"

Spartak Volkov thought he understood what Helen was saying, or at least she seemed to speak kindly to him, which he hoped was a good sign. He sat down where she pointed.

Helen walked over to Jane's office and tried to get past Stan and Frieda Helmstadt to alert Jane. "Helen!" Frieda hissed in Helen's ear. "Do you want us to run home and get Stan's rifle?! We can be back in a jiffy!" Helen looked at Frieda in shock. "Frieda!" she whispered back sharply. "Don't you dare do a thing! Don't go taking the law in your own hands. Just stay put!"

Helen knocked on Jane's door and let herself right in, closing the door behind her. "Jane—Bernie. Sorry to interrupt, but Jane, you've got to come out to the main office. There's a man out there and we may have a situation. He seems strange or foreign? I think he wants to use our phone."

"OK, OK. Excuse me a minute, Bernie. Let's go see," Jane said as she opened the door and left her office with Helen, with Bernie leaning out to take a peak.

DON'T TOUCH MY COCKTAIL!

"Jane! Jane!!" Bernie started bellowing. "Son of a bitch!! That's him!" Bernie shoved his way quickly towards Spartak. "That's the pinko commie guy I told you about!!"

Spartak looked to where he could bolt, but the locals still hanging around for all the excitement had already moved to block the front door. Spartak held up his arms and started babbling, "Peace and Love! No harm! Peace and Love!"

"Shit, if this goon isn't the biggest sap!" Bernie growled and then looked at Jane. "You gotta do somethin', Jane. He should be arrested, don't ya think?"

"All right, everybody. Let's just take it easy," Jane said to the wide-eyed people present. "I'll bring our visitor into my office and try to straighten out what's going on, OK?" Jane took Spartak's arm and said "Peace and Love" back to him, since that was one English phrase he seemed to know. And she kept saying it to him as she led him to her office. She looked back at Bernie and winked at him. "Great job, Bernie! Thank you! I'll catch up with you later, OK?"

15
Friday, December 13
Later in the Afternoon

Jane had Spartak take a seat and she closed the door. He tried to speak again, but his voice was such a blur, he began pointing to his mouth and nose in anguish. It was all so idiotic, Jane was flummoxed. But then she got it...it should have been obvious! But how was she supposed to know some bizarre foreigner would show up in her office this afternoon with a nylon stocking suffocating the living daylights out of him?

She opened her desk drawer, took out her scissors, and showed them to Spartak. He tried to smile, but his lips got nowhere. She said "Peace and Love" again and made a clipping motion with the scissors. He shook his head yes. She leaned towards his face and very slowly began cutting the ridiculously tight stocking from underneath his chin and slowly up the side of his cheek and so on until she was able to pull the rest of the taut mask off his head.

"Ohhhhh, Spasibo! Spasibo! Ya lyublu tebya! Ha ha!!"

Oh, great. Just great. This guy is Russian. I should have guessed. BUT! I can call my secret weapon. I can call Konstantin's sister, Torrance Balankoff.

Jane got Helen on the interoffice line and asked her to ring up Torrance and ask if she could come down to the PSO right away, a matter of public safety.

While Jane waited to hear from Helen, she gave Spartak the OK sign with her fingers, hoping this was a universal concept. He was rubbing everything to try and bring it all back to life—his eyes, his ears, his nose, his lips. He was smiling. *OK,* Jane thought. *Détente was working so far.*

Helen beeped Jane's phone. Jane picked up. "Jane...Torrance is on her way. Five minutes max." And eight minutes later, Helen knocked on Jane's door and made way for Torrance to enter.

"Thank God you could make it, Torrance." Jane was so relieved, she hung her head down for a split second and then flung it back and loosened her shoulders. Spartak copied Jane and smiled again.

Jane pointed to Spartak and then pointed to Torrance. "Peace and Love, OK?" she said to Spartak. He nodded yes again.

Jane then took Torrance aside in the small amount of space that her office allowed and started whispering to her quietly. "OK...look," Jane said. "I think this man is Russian. So I need you to translate. I'm not sure where we're going with all this, so let's keep to a tight script here. I want to use what he doesn't know to our advantage if need be, because he may be up to no good. Bernie Pushaw found him over at Environmental Fields this morning and apparently he was digging something up in the fields. I mean, in a field full of human crap, that alone is weird behavior. And Bernie doesn't know what the guy was trying to accomplish, so we need to tread carefully. OK...you ready?"

Torrance nodded. She was her usual imperturbable self and prepared to follow Jane's lead.

"OK. Tell him, oh, tell him something like you're the most revered doctor in the whole state of Maine...and parts of Coney Island."

"What?! That's nuts, Jane!" Torrance blurted, while trying to maintain their whispering. Spartak's eyes turned wary.

"No...tell him that. Everyone's heard of Coney Island, especially Russians. He's got to think we can be helpful," Jane said, smiling confidently at Spartak. "We need his cooperation. Then ask him if he's OK. Bernie told me he tried to taser this guy, so we might as well be sure he's OK so he can't come back at us later. But wait a minute." Jane stepped out into the main office. She came back with the stethoscope Dr. Leckman kept at the PSO in case of emergencies. She handed it to Torrance.

Torrance looked at Jane with a crazy smile. Then she started up her Russian and began speaking to Spartak. He immediately seemed more relaxed.

"He says he was having trouble breathing, but now he feels much better."

"OK...um...use the stethoscope and act like you're checking his lungs," Jane suggested. Torrance thought back to her own last physical for inspiration. She had Spartak take off his coat. She popped the listening prongs into her ears and asked him to take deep breaths. She moved the stethoscope disc to various places on his chest and tapped him in what she hoped looked like legitimate places. She turned to his back and repeated the steps again.

"Now ask him what he was doing in the fields this morning," Jane said.

Torrance tried to get an answer to this question, but Spartak would not budge.

"OK. We've got to crank things up. Tell him he was in a very poisonous place this morning...a place full of rotting human crap, which will definitely make him very ill, especially his penis. Tell him that."

DON'T TOUCH MY COCKTAIL!

"Jane, are you sure? Isn't this kind of unethical?" Torrance asked with hesitation.

"Just tell him that. We need to shake him up a bit to find out what's going on," Jane said.

Torrance elaborated as Jane told her, but Spartak still shook his head no.

"OK, tell him we can give him important medicine to help him, so his penis won't fall off in a few hours. But if he doesn't tell us why he was in the fields, we can't help him."

Torrance kept on with Jane's scheme. She even elaborated on the terrible shape he'd be in, all the oozing, the throbbing, the burning sensations...to the point that Spartak began to whimper. Then he bent down crying and put his head in his hands on his knees.

"Oh, God. Now this? Ask him why he's crying," Jane said.

Torrance asked the question. Spartak looked up at them with red, soaked eyes and moaned "lustabread! me lustabread!" plus a flood of other words that Torrance began to translate.

"He's saying 'lustabread! me lustabread! She won't want me if my penis is broken! She's waiting to meet me at Buddy's, but now I can't meet her with a dying penis! What can I do?' followed by more sobbing and snuffling and mumbling in Russian about Buddy's."

Torrance looked at Jane. "What's all this about lustabread? What can he mean?"

"Lustabread? Lustabread?...Oh, as I live and breathe..." Jane smacked her forehead and sat down in her chair. "I can't believe it! Lustabread...of course! Of course it is! Lustabread...he's saying Lobster Bride! This can't be happening. What planet are we on? OK. Torrance. Listen. This guy must have logged onto this new website called Lobster Brides!" Spartak looked up at the last two words and started shaking his head yes.

Jane explained further. "A woman named Gluella Trott was just in here earlier today, telling me all about this site she's running to attract wealthy foreign men who are looking for brides along the coast of Maine. If you can believe it. And she insisted her clientele would only be wealthy men. But look at this poor sucker! Don't tell me he's a Russian oligarch! For God's sake. I knew there were holes in Gluella's game plan!"

Torrance thought for a moment. "Well, he keeps saying his Lobster Bride! and a whole bunch of other Lobster Brides! are going to meet him and his fellow Russians at Buddy's. You know Buddy's, Jane? ...That bar and grill on the mainland? I have an idea. Maybe we should ask him when he's meeting her. I can tell him I'll give him the medicine to help him, but it's important to know when he's meeting his Lobster Bride! to be sure the medicine will have enough time to cure his problem. That way you can go look for all these mysterious Russians at Buddy's at the chosen time and maybe find out what's going on that way?"

"Torrance Balankoff! That is brilliant!" Jane exclaimed. "That's a great idea! Do it...ask him."

Torrance quizzed Spartak and promised him the medicine and got the day and time out of him. "Spartak says they'll meet at Buddy's this coming Tuesday at 3 PM. But now we need some sort of fake medicine to give to him, Jane. What'll it be? Have you got some aspirin lying around here?"

DON'T TOUCH MY COCKTAIL!

"Well that should be easy, compared to what we've just been through," Jane laughed. "Go ask Helen for a few tablets and then we can wrap it up with this character. When he first came in, Helen said he needed to make a phone call. I can let him use my phone, but if he knows you're listening, he might not make the call. So just stand outside the door when you come back with the aspirin. If you hear him on the phone, listen carefully and don't come back in until he's done. OK?"

Torrance went out to see Helen and then returned to Jane's door and held her ear close while Spartak spoke. When he was done, she waited a few seconds, then knocked and entered Jane's office. She handed the "important medicine" to Spartak and carefully explained that he should take one pill each day for the next two days and that should solve any problems he might have with his best friend downstairs. She went so far as to write down the instructions in Russian for him, which lent a genuine stroke to the whole performance.

Jane offered her hand to Spartak and said to him again, "Peace and Love." He raised her hand to kiss it and said the same words back to her. He thanked Dr. Balankoff with all his heart...in Russian. The three "comrades" walked out of Jane's office, the women said farewell to the stranger, and off he went.

"So what did he say on the phone, Torrance?" Jane asked, once Spartak was gone.

"I think it's still a mystery, Jane," Torrance said, shaking her head. "He was talking to someone he called 'Egor.' Spartak told him to pick him up as planned. He said he had proof about the black Chinese...or the Chinese

65

black...or maybe the blackened Chinese? I could not quite get that last part. Didn't make sense."

"Jeez, there is more to this than I can figure out right now," Jane said. "But you have saved our butts, Torrance! Do you think you could go with me to Buddy's this Tuesday? I really need you to translate."

"I'll check my calendar. It sounds doable at the moment, but I'll have to get back to you and confirm."

"OK...and really, TB, thanks a million for dropping everything to come help us. You're wonderful...just like your brother!"

After Torrance left, Jane walked around in the office, trying to justify letting Spartak go. She reasoned that this was her first step towards catching up with the whole Russian gang at Buddy's on Tuesday when she would have them all in her grasp...to get to the bottom of this bizarre encounter. To figure out why Spartak had been rummaging around in Environmental Fields, of all places. She was beginning to hatch a plan.

16
Friday, December 13
Early Evening

"God, I hope we can exterminate the vermin who did this to Troy." Jane was fuming as she sat down with Storm and Israel at the PSO table for a recap of the beaten man found on the beach. "What is happening to St. Frewin's Island? We can't have thugs going around smashing people up. And we can't have Russians crawling all over, trying to cart off our women."

"What's this about Russians, Jane?" Storm said.

"Oh, I haven't wanted to bother you about them. We had a recent incident...some unknown alien traipsing around the island septage recycling fields. And it looks like he may be one of a bunch of Russian sailors hoping to hook up with some island girls on a new dating website. It's ridiculous. I'll fill you in another time."

"OK—whatever," Storm said. "So, according to the boatyard staff, Troy Overlock owned a cellphone. We spoke to management and Troy's colleagues, but no one has seen the phone. Israel and I searched the boatyard buildings and grounds, but we found nothing."

Jane stood up and walked over to the whiteboard to begin taking notes on their thoughts.

"What does this mean?" Storm said. "Maybe the boatyard is not telling us the truth. Or, did Troy's attacker take his phone? Or maybe his stuff is squirreled away at home. Maybe Troy hid his cellphone for some reason.

Could this be related to his attack? And will he be in any shape soon to talk to us about it?"

"I'd hate to think the boatyard is lying or that they have something to hide," Jane said. "All you hear is what a reputable place it is, how hard and carefully they work."

Israel spoke next. "Well, did Troy have dangerous or incriminating information on his cellphone that had nothing to do with the boatyard? And who cared? Who stood to be exposed or to lose something? What was his personal connection with his attacker?"

"Keep the questions coming, men. And until we can speak with Troy, we need to get a list of his friends and colleagues and start interviewing them beyond the scope of the cell phone matter. Why would someone hurt him? Does he have enemies? Does he have secrets? Was he up to no good?" Jane asked, adding more detail to the board.

"As for Troy the person, the boatyard staff said the same thing over and over," Israel said. "He's a gentle giant. Wouldn't hurt a living thing if he could help it. Always willing to lend a hand to help others."

"And remember, Jane. You may find that people won't want to say much to you, at least not at first. Or they won't recall details," Storm said. "If you have to, go back to them more than once. It can take time for the truth to come crawling out."

Jane looked at all the questions they had produced. "Storm, you have the Crimes Unit looking into Troy's bank account?"

"That's right. We'll hear from them soon," Storm said.

"OK. Israel and I will track down Troy's people and start talking to them first thing Monday. I'll try to be diplomatic and patient. But I can't promise! And now it's getting late. You better hurry to catch your last ferry."

DON'T TOUCH MY COCKTAIL!

"You want to walk me out to my car, Jane?" Storm said, nodding his head towards the door.

"Sure...let me get my parka."

They strolled together to Storm's Subaru.

"So, everything OK with you, Storm? Homicide busy on the mainland? Your family?" said Jane.

"All good, Jane. I was just wondering how you've been. Helen said you were in Switzerland recently."

"Yah...a quick trip over. The Alps are incredible," Jane said.

"Family over there?"

"No, no family. I was visiting Konstantin Balankoff at his chalet."

"Konstantin Balankoff? How'd that happen?"

"Storm, are you being nosey? What is this? An interrogation?" Jane laughed, looking at him with a big question mark on her face.

"Nah. Never mind. Don't listen to me. I'm just surprised he's your type, that's all."

"Well, what can I say to that? Maybe we've both said too much. Anyway, have a safe trip home. I'll report to you on Troy next week. Maybe we can talk to him in a few days. I'll get an update from the hospital."

"Sounds good, Jane. Take care," said Storm. He got into his car and drove off.

17
Saturday, December 14

Chanson Pratt closed out her computer map of Lowell, Massachusetts when she heard her cellphone buzzing. She was more than curious about Zen-Ti and his environs. The internet was bare...few relevant details and no images under his name. What was his stomping ground like? His day to day? Where did he live? Who did he live with? But here was Samantha Lloyd calling from Maine to discuss Chanson's menu for the upcoming New Year's Eve party....

"Let's run down your menu one last time. OK, Chanson? You're sure you want the big pig roast?" Sam asked. She was envisioning the mess she knew it would be to set up the equipment outside in the winter cold. They would fire up the portable spit rotisserie, keep roasting, roasting, roasting the pig for hours, and then break it all down when the pig was done and devoured. Gooey debris all over every inch of the rotisserie and cooking utensils—such a massive, sticky pain to clean up.

If that was what Chanson wanted, Sam would have to stock up on her cleaning supplies—salt, vinegar, baking soda, ammonia—anything to cut through all that grease. "It's going to take some extra infrastructure and two to three people dedicated to standing around in the cold to babysit the pig for eight hours while it cooks. You're OK with paying for those extras, Chanson? We could do a pulled pork dish instead, prepped ahead in my catering kitchen. What do you think?"

DON'T TOUCH MY COCKTAIL!

"You know, Sam, I definitely want the real deal. And I think Salem is willing to monitor the pig roast at least part of the time. It's just so Texan and homey to have the whole roast turning round and round, which makes the meat so juicy. I know it's a huge chore, but we're willing to pay, so let's stick with the whole pig roast...OK?"

"You got it, Chanson. I'll order you a nice Berkshire pig. Well, make that two pigs, about fifty pounds each, to feed about one hundred guests. Now how about the rest? My notes show black-eyed peas, white rice, collard greens, corn bread, pecan pie, grapefruit pot de crème, eight crates of champagne, a routine bartender set-up, and Texas Rattlesnake Bites, Armadillo Eggs, and Chicken Enchilada Puffs for appetizers. Are you all set with that?"

"It sounds soooo gooood, Sam! I'm starving already! This party's going to be a lot of fun. You've lined up the folks who will set up the thousand helium balloons in the great room, right?"

"Yes. The Party Hearty people will take care of getting everything blown up, arranged under the tarp, and ready to release into the air at the stroke of midnight. It's a festive idea, Chanson!"

"I get so crazy every year getting ready for this thing, Sam, but it's really worth it. Also, I wanted to let you know, I've lined up some extra help to assist with the cleaning at the end and taking everything down. I hope it'll help lighten our load."

"Oh yeah? Who'd you hire?" Sam said. "I only ask because St. Frewin's is swamped with parties that night. I think anyone on the island who's vertical is going to be working one party or another."

"Well, interestingly, this group is from Lowell, Massachusetts, if you can believe it."

"Hey, I know Lowell. My cousins lived near there. That poor city. It wasn't safe when we were young and visited them, but they say things have calmed down a lot since."

"So, Sam!" Chanson said as she hastened to wrap things up. "We're squared away on the food. And you've checked with the Public Safety Office about keeping the roads clear down on the point, so I guess we're finished here. Thank you so much for all your help. I'll see you in Maine late morning on December 31. Have a nice holiday in the meantime!"

"You, too, Chanson. Have a good trip up to the island!"

Chanson was satisfied to end the call right there. She probably should not have mentioned where the extra help was from...especially when Sam had a connection to Lowell! Big Mistake. And she hadn't meant to jump off the phone so rudely, but she didn't want to wait around for Sam to ask why Chanson would hire a clean-up crew from way down in Massachusetts.

18
Saturday, December 14
Afternoon

The cartilage in her right ear felt deformed and on fire. In about thirty seconds, she was certain that ear would become a permanent part of the floor boards. The weight her "attacker" was applying with his large hand over her left ear effectively pinned her entire head and body to the floor. No matter how frantically she scuttled her legs along the floor's surface or tried to buck her body, she could not break his grip. And her flailing arms were useless...two skinny noodles flopping in the air. She felt like a juvenile soft-shell crab skittering for its life under the palm of some Arnold Schwarzenegger wannabee.

Her "attacker" continued to hold her head down firmly, meanwhile talking matter-of-factly to the other women in the room. Because her ears were more or less plugged, she heard very little dialogue. But she could smell everything about him. A puff of sweaty BO, a whiff of detergent, and oregano...lots of oregano. It didn't have the typical pungency found on a spice rack. This oregano was denser, male, and steaming out of his armpits. Maybe it wasn't oregano? She could no longer keep it bottled in. She started laughing her head off, or as much as her head could crow, considering how her skull was fused to the floor.

And then she got angry. "Hamidi, cut the crap!" Jane yelled. "I think you can let me go now, OK?" She had to shout, to make the Cypriot organic farmer from the north end of the island release her from his simulated "attack."

Hamidi Louca leaped up from the crouched position he had staged to pin Jane's head down on the floor. He had enthusiastically agreed to show Jane and her friends eight basic self-defense moves. Jane thought it would be a good idea in dealing with the Russians. But now Jane was miffed as she tried to pull herself up gracefully on numb limbs. "I was hoping you would show us some real, honest-to-goodness self-defense tactics, Hamidi...but I don't think we're making much progress when you insist on sitting on top of my head on the floor."

"Sorry, Jane. I was explaining to the other women how a victim in your position could kick the legs upward to break out of the stronghold, but you were my guinea pig for illustration purposes only. Won't happen again," Hamidi assured Jane.

"Well, it was good of you to come down here and help us, but we'll give it a rest for now. I'll call you if we need your help in the future, OK?" Jane said.

"Sure, Jane. No harm intended. You were a real sport!" Hamidi assured her.

....

"OK. That's it for the self-defense, folks," Jane said, taking deep breaths and frowning at the five women in the Public Safety Office. "Thanks a lot for coming to my rescue, you guys," she growled in jest. Grace Cleveland, the owner of her own homemade pie business, Apple π, stood next to Maggie Banner, the owner of the Grand Harbor Inn, and her assistant India Barton. Cora Gould, who waitressed at Connor Mulroy's pub, was off to the side with Torrance Balankoff. They all laughed it off.

DON'T TOUCH MY COCKTAIL!

Jane directed everyone to take a seat at the Public Safety Office table so they could go over her plan to ensnare Spartak Volkov and his fellow Russian yahoos. On Tuesday, Jane and her four volunteers would pile into one car, take the ferry to the mainland, and drive over to Buddy's Bar and Grill in downtown Graniteville for their "Russian research." Torrance Balankoff would come along as translator.

"Thank you all for helping me on this mission," Jane began. "We're going to engage in some social interaction with these Russians who have been seen on St. Frewin's recently...in particular, the Environmental Fields on the north end of the island. So," Jane went on, "our goal will be to find out why the Russians are here. What were they doing in the Environmental Fields? Are they here for any other reasons? And how are they getting on and off the island when they don't use our public transportation?"

"I feel like I'm in some kind of spy ring...pies to spies!" Grace Cleveland whispered to India Barton. This escapade would give Grace a good excuse to take a much-needed break from the holiday baking orders pouring into her shop.

"One thing we know is that one or more of these Russians are here to meet women they've contacted on the website called Lobster Brides! Now I heard two of you are actually signed up with Lobster Brides! Could you please remind me who is a Lobster Bride!?" Jane asked.

"Please don't think any less of us, Jane," India spoke up. "But Cora Gould and I both joined Gluella's site. Probably it will all end up as a lark."

Jane looked at India and Cora and said, "I don't mean to be nosey, you guys, but I guess I am being nosey. Why did you sign up for Lobster Brides! when you have so many other website choices available?"

"Oh, that's easy," India volunteered. "We are so sick and tired—fed up to here," she was flinging her hand high over her head, "with all the tried-and-true sites...all the usual American guys. Do you realize how many flannel-shirted, book-reading men are out there who love to laugh, go to MOFGA fairs, hike in the woods, canoe and kayak and bike, watch great movies at night, and work the grill? Gawd. If you're a single woman, you could easily get buried alive by this same old nonsense for the next fifteen years! We want someone exotic, spicy, unknown. Someone challenging who grew up on other food, in other languages, on other continents."

"Besides," Cora added, "you meet up with these promising New England studs and they look nothing like the pictures they've posted...repeatedly! Never! Then you have to sit there, sipping on your piña colada, and listen to the homely real-life dud yammer on for more than an hour about some great trip he took to Costa Rica with his ex-wife, or the woman he just broke up with. And he never gets around to asking you about yourself. No give and take. You're just a scoreboard for him to tally his old successes and good times."

India added, "At least with Lobster Brides!, we'll meet foreigners for one, and they'll have money, so we won't have to pay for lunch after they claim they left their wallets at home. Believe me, there are some very lame American men out there, Jane."

"OK. I believe you. I get it. So, a few pointers before we head over to Buddy's Bar and Grill to meet these folks," Jane said. "Based on what little we know, these men are apt to be rough, smelly, not too bright, and they don't know much English, which is where Torrance will be a big help."

"Wait a minute, Jane," India interrupted. "I don't understand. And I also don't know why you had Hamidi giving us self-defense tips. Gluella Trott assured us repeatedly that her clients are all wealthy, well-educated, accomplished men from other countries. I specifically asked her about language barriers, because to be honest, I don't have the time to learn five foreign languages before I find the right man. And I certainly don't want him to attack me in the process!"

"Ditto, I'll say!" Cora added. "Are you sure about these Russian guys? Sounds like this might not be worth our time if we're going to be scraping the bottom of the barrel."

"Look, India, Cora...I'm sorry, but I can't speak for this Gluey and her Lobster Brides! You need to talk to her directly. She's the boss on her end. All I know is that one of these so-called Russian suitors was in the Public Safety Office yesterday, and he struck me as a lower-income Russian gofer who knew next to no English."

"Well, that's great...just great," India fumed. "What are you thinking, Cora? Should we talk to Gluella? Should we alert the other women who plan to attend the hook-up? Should we just back out altogether?" Cora steered India to the far side of the main office to discuss their dilemma further in private.

"Anyway," Jane said to the other women, "while they're thinking things through, here are my thoughts. These guys are up to no good, I suspect. But some of them are also here for romance and a chance to meet someone special. We, however, want hard information from them.

So when we meet these Russians, let's focus on making them think they are totally appealing. Words more than action. You don't have to sit in their laps. You shouldn't start making out with them. No groping body parts. Our goal is simply to compliment them on how sexy they are...verbally."

"Like what, Jane?" Grace Cleveland asked.

"OK. Try to turn their negatives into plusses," Jane said. "You know...compliment them on their smelly undershirts. Tell them you love men who don't shave, you love their scent of boiled beets and engine room oil...kind of play with the concept. Then when they're feeling on top of the world, you slip in the questions I mentioned—Why are they here? Why Environmental Fields? How are they getting to the island? But keep your inquiring sensual, so the answers will just slide out of them. Does this make sense?"

"Jane, will Torrance be able to keep up with all this?" Maggie Banner wondered.

Jane let Torrance answer. "I think if you get a big table at Buddy's, or a couple of tables near each other, and we generally stay together, I'll just hop from couple to couple," Torrance said. "I'll make my way around our group discreetly and do my best. So I'm guessing we'll be OK."

India and Cora returned to the table. Jane thought they had positive looks on their faces.

"So, Jane, are these guys dangerous or not? Should we be worried about our safety?" was India's question.

"You know, I was just trying to cover all the bases, including self-defense. I'm sure we'll be fine, India. It never hurts to have some advance precautions," Jane answered.

DON'T TOUCH MY COCKTAIL!

"OK, well, we've decided to come along for the ride, Jane. It should be a riot and an adventure, if nothing else," India told them. "And it's a quiet time of the year at both the Inn and the pub, so we can spare the afternoon. But we're definitely presenting a complaint to Gluella. It may be she's not even aware that some lowlifes have high-jacked her site."

"Um...about Gluella," Jane was hesitating.... "If you could hold off on your complaint till after we've seen the Russians, that would be helpful, India. In fact, I also need you to do a really big favor if we're going to pull off this meeting with the Russians at all, without a huge mix-up."

"What's that, Jane?" India asked.

"Well, we don't want too many real Lobster Brides! showing up at Buddy's next Tuesday. So I need you to ask around and tell any other women who have signed up on Gluella's site that the meeting at Buddy's has been canceled due to unforeseen circumstances. That way the six of us can get together with the Russians without too much interference from the actual Lobster Brides! What do you say?"

"If I do that, what about Gluella? Won't she get angry?" India pointed out.

"What does Gluella care once she's put everyone male in touch with everyone female at any one location? You're all your own bosses, right? She won't be pulling any more strings will she?"

"I guess that's a good point," India conceded. "But I'm still curious if she realizes she's got suspicious characters interfacing with her website."

"That I don't know. It's an issue maybe we can address down the road. Anyway, I'm really glad you two will help us with this important part of the task. And by the way, you should all feel free to wear a disguise if you want to," Jane suggested. "We don't know whom we might run into at Buddy's...you may not want to be identified in the clutches of a bunch of Russian hobos."

"And we'll gather here at 1:30 PM, Jane, and drive to the ferry together?" Grace asked.

"That's right. One or maybe two cars. So, I'll see you all here on Tuesday," Jane said. And that concluded their strategy meeting.

19
Saturday, December 14
Evening

Bernie Pushaw was sitting on a stool in his garage that night and staring at the thirty-two heavy-duty garbage bags he'd hauled back home in his truck from Environmental Fields. There weren't many guys like him on this island that would have put up with all the shit it took to dig that chunky Chinese dreck out of the crap and salty goo in the trench at Environmental Fields...AND wash the crap and goo off the nuggets afterwards. It was a bitch of a job.

Bernie took three showers to get rid of all the stench and muck coating his own self...one shower with his clothes on, two showers without. Afterwards, he made sure to leave the shower stall as he found it. No use turning the bathroom into a toxic dump and driving his wife, Noreen, crazy with all that crap. It didn't take much imagination on his part to hear her screaming at him...yet again.

So what was all the excitement about these little black nuggets? Bernie tipped his glass of Rebel Yell and took a soothing sip. He looked at a few of the nuggets resting on top of one of the garbage bags. He took a nugget and started rolling it around in his right hand. Absent-mindedly, as a joke all his own, he tossed the nugget into his Rebel Yell and raised a toast to himself.

What happened next, he never expected. The nugget started to sizzle on its surface, as though it was getting fried in Bernie's drink. Bernie saw black flecks start to

81

float off the little chunk, and that god damn little fuckin' chunk started to look like it was turning into gold! *God damn that little chunk! It WAS gold! GOD DAMN! That was it! GOLD!! Bernie, You Genius Penis!!* Everything started to make sense. And Bernie could not shut his mouth for gaping in wonder.

After he sat for a few moments to make sure he wasn't going to black out, Bernie's tired brain stepped on the accelerator. He knew exactly who was out to claim these god damn nuggets. That Russian Star Trek guy and probably all his Star Trek buddies were going to invade St. Frewin's if they could and steal it all away, Bernie surmised. Hell, he had to hide his booty fast. Where and how?

And the answer was smack in front of his face. Of course! That's it! The dairy farm! Son of a gun. Bernie was supposed to babysit Stan Helmstadt's cows for the next few days while Stan and Frieda were over to New Hampshire to hear a famous medium speak and to attend an "Elvis" concert. "Brain culcha" was what Stan called it. And Frieda, Stan said, was hoping the spiritual medium would help her to contact her late father, who had been on the brink of telling her something important years ago when he collapsed in his death bed and was gone. Frieda figured her father had had enough time by now in the afterlife to pull it all together and finish his sentence, and she hoped the medium would be able to help draw him out.

So that's what Bernie would do. He would re-bag the gold into a bunch of smaller trash bags to make carrying them easier on his back. Then he would bury his trash bags in Stan's manure storage pile until this whole Russkie thing blew over. And the quicker Bernie got the gold out of his house, the safer he'd feel. He didn't need any foreigners shootin' through his living room in the middle of the night and gettin' Noreen all pissed. God knows what she'd do if a Commie caught her in her flannel nightgown.

20
Saturday, December 14
Afternoon

The 9:59 AM American Airlines flight from Washington, D.C. to Portland, Maine's Jetport had landed with more than enough time for Geneva Pratt to rent her weekend car and make her way north along the coast in daylight. What a relief it was to be back on Route One and soon to be boarding the ferry to St. Frewin's Island. She was breathing real air again...fresh oxygen! For a few days, no sucking on the tailpipe of D.C. No canned, federal urban exhaust turning her lungs into tarry sponge.

As Geneva drove along, she marveled, like always, at the kooky, bizarre entrepreneurial contrasts Maine had to offer along Route One's narrow two-lane highway. On one side an elegant kitchen design center where no one walked out without slapping down tens of thousands of dollars for a chef's temple. Across the road, gritty rural Maine in all its bravado: "Steak Bombs—$10.00!" and a scrappy little dispensary advertising "Medical CBD, Vape."

She slowed down a bit to catch today's billboard at her favorite fresh fish store on the mainland, which proclaimed, "SEX SELLS. TOO BAD WE SELL LOBSTERS. RELISH TODAY, KETCHUP TOMORROW!" Down the road a stretch Geneva passed the modest woven goods outfit where beautiful, soft, woolen blankets in the deepest of blues cost an arm and a leg. And a mile later, there stood the weathered old farm housing the "New England School of Clinical Hypnotherapy."

Geneva went over in her mind her plan to investigate the Environmental Fields on St. Frewin's, whose notorious trenches she had last viewed via video in Senator McGill's office this past Thursday. She intended to drive over to the Fields and take a look at all that muck for herself.

"Any thought of going up to your parents' island home this weekend, Geneva?" the Senator had asked casually on Friday afternoon. Geneva had lied. The less he knew, the better.

....

Of course it's disappeared, Geneva said to herself when she finally located the gouged-out furrow area. She juggled the anger and confusion in her brain as she kicked the frozen earth. How had it happened? Had someone scooped up all the Chinese gold and removed it from Environmental Fields? Could it be the Russians? She booted the ground again. She had no idea. And contrary to what she had told Senator McGill, Geneva had conveniently let the end of the week slip away without calling "Egor" back on behalf of the Senator. McGill had been swamped with legislative conundrums and skirmishes that kept cropping up, which distracted him from inquiring into Geneva's progress. She would, of course, "remember" to make the call on Monday. After all, what could possibly happen for another few days to a row of Chinese gold frozen in a slushie of ruined caviar and human waste?

But something had happened to the gold. Fortunately, no one had seen her drive into Environmental Fields in the late Saturday afternoon sunset, and no crew was present to wonder what the hell she was doing poking around in the frozen cesspool. She walked back to her car and drove to her family's home.

She was intent on solving this mystery. It wasn't a question of helping the Senator to claw back his goodies. It wasn't a question of greed on her part. Rather, an ulterior motive had taken form in her mind over the past forty-eight hours, after she had done the startling math and realized that a ten-gallon barrel held about 23,467 troy ounces, and the price of gold was hovering around $1842.24 per troy ounce, which meant more than forty-three million dollars of gold nuggets had somehow disappeared since Thursday afternoon.

....

Geneva smooshed the last of her Indian poori bread in the swirl of lamb rogan josh and mango chutney at the bottom of her bowl and devoured the heavenly combo. How fortunate for St. Frewin's that the new Indian restaurant offered takeout six days a week. Everyone on the island had heard about Rajiv Basrak, the investigator from the State crime lab who had worked on the Ruth Farrow murder case. Now he was one of them, dishing out exotic happiness night after night at his colorful little joint, Curry in a Hurry, for people like Geneva who didn't have the ingredients or the time to make dinner.

21
Saturday, December 14
Late Evening

Later on in the evening, Geneva happened to look out the bathroom window on the third floor of her parents' home. Was someone driving into Stan Helmstadt's dairy farm across the road? Geneva saw outside lights turn on near one of the barns on the property. While she couldn't be sure, what she saw didn't feel right. Why any activity way down in the cow fields at this time of night, in early December?

She went to a cabinet in the hallway, took out her father's astronomy telescope, and set it up facing the Helmstadt farm. The scope was powerful enough to enable her to study the area near the barn. As she adjusted the knobs on the telescope, she could see someone out there sharpening into her view. Who was that messing around on what looked like a mini ski slope? She thought it might be that dopey guy who had been spreading the caviar and gold in the video she had watched with the Senator. She wondered what on earth he was doing out there in the cold. The view through the telescope did not suffice to satisfy her curiosity.

Geneva headed downstairs and pulled on her hat, down coat, gloves, heavy socks, and a pair of snow-claw boots. She left the house...it was time to investigate...no matter the frigid temperature, the heavy falling snow, the dark hour. *Thou shalt not covet thy neighbor's house, nor his farm, nor his cattle, nor anything that is his.* Well, she wasn't about to trample on the Tenth Commandment...she just wanted to take a peek under that Bible.

Geneva walked down her parents' long driveway to the main road. The clarity of the stars was a shock to her city eyes...stars so bright against the black December sky and the moon flooding the snow fields with plumes of fluorescent-like light. Amazing. She turned right and hiked towards the Helmstadt farm across the street. Apparently the Mr. and Mrs. were away—no lights were on in the house—only down near the barn.

Geneva treaded with ease, the snowfall covering her tracks as she closed in on the barn scene. From a distance, she could see Bernie grunting while shoveling a wide hole in the steamy ski slope, which she now realized was a manure pile. She ducked unseen behind a shed.

She watched Bernie trot down the mound and grab what looked like a small garbage bag, which seemed to drag him backwards as much as he was dragging it forward. He strained to move up the mound and finally dropped the bag in the hole. He did this numerous times...she nearly lost count...maybe fifty bags in all? He was huffing with deep pants...wheezing and coughing in gags.

Bernie finally and exhaustedly dropped his last bag in the hole and covered up his treasure with more dung and snow. He tossed his shovel down to the ground. Geneva watched him make the sign of the cross, and then he stumbled downward. He slowly walked over to turn off the barn lights, then headed towards his truck and took off.

She waited at the side of the shed for about five minutes while he drove away. She listened for the sound of anyone else in the cold silence of the night...anything else. Falling snow. Nothing else. It was now or never, she told herself as she scaled the foul mountain before her, with Bernie's shovel in hand. She leaned over to begin excavating his mystery bags...just one for now...just one look.

In her hand she saw nuggets. She pressed on them. They were hard. And of course, of course it all began to come together. All so very logical. Senator McGill's mysterious blackened gold had resurfaced...and now it would become Geneva's pot, at the end of a most curious rainbow. She quickly descended the slope, exited the farm, and walked home for more garbage bags of her own.

....

Back on the mound, like Bernie before her, Geneva exerted herself with concentrated force...but now she reverse-engineered Bernie's task and yanked the first bag of nuggets free from its hiding place and guided it down towards the ground, to the garbage bags and toboggan she had brought along to haul home her catch. She soothed her slightly rattled state of mind with the thought of the long, hot shower that would soon wash away this clinging grime. She had to stay focused and not pay attention to the stinking gobs and blobs that were beginning to coat her gloves and coat, her face, her hair. She was doing this for her family, and they were never going to know. But obviously, she totally recognized the incongruous stew she'd plunged herself into. Quite an outlandish task. Maybe years from now she would give a TED talk! ..."The Price of Economic Gain"—one cow patty at a time.

At bag number three, she paused to philosophize on her actions. How many times could stolen goods be stolen again before the thieving at any one stage became simply a transfer of wealth? Possibly neutralizing the crime free of any remaining hint of wrongdoing? Seriously, hers was no crime. Laundering precious metal? Perhaps. Stealing? No. This was a Rescue Plan. And no one would ever know she had been here—in and then gone...stealthy...like a fog bank silently on the move. She was thrilling to the silken simplicity of her goal...she could appreciate the adrenalin of suspense. She would look back on this night as the night she became The Phantom.

22
Saturday, December 14
Later in the Evening

Bernie was humming along to some country music and driving back to the Helmstadt barn when he pulled in and jerked with a start at the "Apparition" in his high beams. He'd forgotten his shovel, but dang it all if right there before him wasn't a Holy Saint! For a moment, Bernie was transfixed. His truck lights outlined a beautiful young shepherdess standing on high in a very fancy, silvery down coat, like some shiny creature from heaven.

Bernie could not understand what he was seeing. He rubbed his eyes more than once. Maybe it was all that Rebel Yell he had been drinking in his garage before he drove over the first time to bury his gold.

He started prayin' to God that this weren't no miracle hatchin' up on Stan's dung pile. Bernie was wiped out from dealin' with all these Holy Smokes that kept poppin' up on St. Frewin's. He couldn't take much more, and a miracle was the last thing on earth he needed. And now he was gettin' the CNN willies, 'cause next thing you know them TV news people would be houndin' him day and night and crawlin' all over Stan's property to take a look at this——what? Living Virgin Mary in a ski jacket? For fuck's sake! Or was it Lady Madonna? The Statue of Liberty? Who was suddenly appearing to Bernie Pushaw, of all people!

But HELL. Bernie knew how to handle his liquor, even if his farts were blowin' 0.8 right now. And Bernie was no longer in a mystical mood. So he started roaring. "Hold it right there, you up there! You may be beamin' up. You may be beamin' down. But you jus' park your beams right there! Don't move an inch, ya hear me?!"

Bernie scrambled, slipping and sliding, towards Geneva, who was crowning the manure mound, a weighty garbage bag in her arms. She was so absolutely stunned by his appearance and interruption, she lost her footing and came tumbling down, landing on top of him in the grimy snow below.

They seemed to intend to struggle, but it was more of a "getting to know you" moment of tussling, when in a split second, Geneva felt Bernie let go of her garbage bag and disappear from sight, from her grasp, from the surface of the earth, gone to the underworld for all she could tell. She was dizzily perplexed. The snow kept falling.

"HELP!!! OH, MOTHER OF GOD!!!! MY EFFEN ANKLE!!!" was what Geneva heard next. Bernie's panicked yelling was rising up from the bowels of the earth. She very cautiously moved back from the source of the sound and made sure she was on solid ground before she attempted to stand up.

She noticed some kind of metal grating installed over a huge hole located near the side of the cow dung mound where they'd fallen. She looked downward and could see, very faintly, something dumpy, that had somehow landed in the subterranean pit. "Hang on there, sir. Just a minute," Geneva called out calmly to the blubbering Bernie. She remembered her flashlight in her down coat pocket and pulled it out to investigate Bernie's fall from grace.

"Don't just stand there gapin'!" came the bellowing from below.

DON'T TOUCH MY COCKTAIL!

Her flashlight was shining down on a scrappy looking fellow, kind of a cute cross between Jeffrey Dean Morgan and a troll doll. It was that Dopey character again. He must have fallen through an inconspicuous hole in the grating that had corroded over time until it was big enough to swallow him whole. Which meant he was stuck in this underground holding tank below the cow dung. Really stuck...and immobile at the moment.

"Are you OK? Are you hurt?" Geneva called down with genuine concern.

"Ma'am, I got no idea who you are, or why you're here. But you gotta get me out of this pit right away," was all Bernie could think to say.

Geneva analyzed the scene before her—fast. She knew this was the Environmental Fields employee who had filled the furrows in the video she watched with Senator McGill. And she was certain this employee knew exactly what was in the garbage bags—why else would he snatch the goods and then bury them on this farm? Well, she wanted IN, and she was in control at the moment, which was something she needed to use to her advantage, without being a totally greedy pig. She decided it was time to take command. Time to reshuffle the cards Fate had just dealt her. This moment would never come again.

"Look, I'm going to be honest, sir," Geneva began. "You and I both know what's in those garbage bags you buried in the cow dung. And we know it's not yours. But we can move past that wrinkle and come to a win-win solution. So here's what we're going to do."

Bernie cut her off and drilled into her. "How in God's name do you know what's in my garbage bags?" he groused. "And what is your God damn name anyway,

93

since it sounds like we're about to do business. And you're standin' ten feet above my head while I'm stuck down here with a bum ankle in a puddle of crap."

"Sir, you don't need the answers to any of those questions right now. Not ever, in fact. What you need is *me*, because you've just gone and snatched defeat from the jaws of victory tonight. But I'm here to save you. And it's starting to freeze. So this is the plan." Bernie seemed ready to pay attention.

Geneva crossed her puffy parka arms and took charge. "You are going to sit tight down in that pit until I dig out twenty-five of those fifty bags you've buried. And then I'm going to haul them away. A classic Solomonic split, and it's going to have to do. I'm sorry it will all take some time, and I'm sorry you're in pain. But I'll leave the rest of those bags in that manure for you to keep. You do with them what you want. I'll never tell a soul."

Smoke was coming out of Bernie's ears right about now. He couldn't believe this Tinkerbell in Gore-Tex was goin' for his gold. But one thing he did understand—he was talkin' to the butcher, not the block. And at least she weren't no Russian. She looked and sounded American as far as he could tell. And he was willing to agree his life must be worth twenty-five bags of gold. Plus, he was no idiot. So that was it. He acquiesced.

"Hey, you're the boss, Mystery Woman. Do what you gotta do, and then get me the hell out of here. I'm pretty sure Stan Helmstadt's got a ladder in his barn, so you can go fetch it and get me outta this pit. But you gotta promise me...promise me now."

Geneva couldn't help but suspect this guy was half-baked, but it didn't matter. She smiled down at him and said "I promise" in all sincerity, and then she added,

DON'T TOUCH MY COCKTAIL!

"Once we get you back on terra firma, you will drive away in your truck and I will disappear into the night. We are never going to speak again. Don't even try to find me, or ask around about me. Or I will ruin this one chance you have for a rich and happy life. Any questions?"

23
Saturday, December 14
Night

Within two hours, Geneva returned to Bernie's living hell with Stan's ladder, a rope she'd brought from home, and—Sweet Angel in this moment—a stretchy bandage Bernie could use to wrap his swollen ankle. She secured the rope to the bull bar of Bernie's truck. Then she lowered the ladder down into the holding tank and threw in the rest of the rope and the bandage after it.

Bernie bound up his ankle and hobbled to a standing position on his good leg while leaning against the ladder. He wrapped the rope round and round his chest and knotted the rope to create a sort of sling. Geneva started to pull Bernie upward in his rope sling, as he pulled himself up the ladder with his arms while his good foot reached and steadied on the first rung.

"Uh! WAIT! Hold on there, Girl! You're crushin' my chest...and all my Alfie Olays! Go easy, go easy. I ain't no sack of potatoes you know."

"OK, OK...let's go slower. But I have no idea what you're talking about. Alfie Olays?" Geneva asked.

"Sounds like you're not so smart as you think, hey, Stranger? Or should we call you 'Princess' or 'Lady Madonna'?—whoever you are. 'Alfie Olays' are those little squirts in your lungs that suck in the air and let out the exhaust. Didn't they teach you that in school?"

"Oh...Alveoli? Good God. Just forget it," Geneva said dismissively. "Shut up and let me get you out of there."

DON'T TOUCH MY COCKTAIL!

She pulled the rope again to raise Bernie to the next rung. He signaled for her to rest.

"You know, Stranger, I got high blood pressure and high cholesterol, so you better hope I don't faint or have a heart attack while you're manhandling me here," Bernie threw in for good measure.

"WHAT is your PROBLEM?!" Geneva knew she wouldn't lose it, but she imagined she would have liked to. "Why are you harassing your Good Samaritan in this hour of reckoning?" She glared down at Bernie in aggravated wonder. "Do you think I have nothing better to do than listen to your whining about your clogged arteries?"

"Yah, well, you owe it to me to listen, Nameless One. You're cuttin' my gross national product in half by takin' twenty-five bags. What gives you the right to do that to Bernie Pushaw?"

"Oh...so you're Bernie? Nice to meet you, Bernie," Geneva started laughing and flipped him a friendly wave. She coiled the rope around her crooked arm again, to be sure it stayed taut.

"At least you're bein' pretty pleasant about all this bull shit," Bernie had to admit as he clung to his perch. "Some duds on this island, they see Bernie walkin' towards them, and all they can say is a flat Hi. And that's it. Now maybe I didn't turn out to be no captain o' industry, but these duds known me all their life and all they can come up with is one word? And it doesn't even have any flavor! What's so hard with 'Hi, Bernie. Whatcha been up to these days?' What am I? Dirt?" Bernie sputtered and began coughing again.

"Listen to that cough of yours. I bet you've inhaled enough Marlboros to kill an elephant herd," Geneva chided as she hoisted Bernie up another rung.

"Heh, Marlboros," Bernie chuckled. "You got that right. I'm even part of their Rewards Program." He gained another rung.

One had to wonder if such a thing as a cigarette Rewards Program even existed. Geneva could not believe this guy. Half clod and slightly endearing. But he had punctured her dream for a perfect getaway. The Phantom was pissed. She yelled down, "That explains the shape your Alfie Olays are in! You probably have the lung capacity of a raisin!"

"Now don't you go tryin' to cheer me up, Secret Agent Woman. I'm just about at the end of my rope."

"Well, that makes two of us," Geneva observed, and she heaved him forward one last time so he could crawl out of the hole and onto firm ground.

24
Sunday, December 15

Diane Savoy turned off the engine key and added a dash of Lancôme to her rutted lips. Look at that face—raked with runnels, her exhausted skin hitchhiking south and dragging her eyelids down the pike. Why did it all have to pile up at her chin line in two ridiculous mittens of flesh that disappeared only when she smiled? She blamed it all on sun, smoking, loss of hormones, soap, gravity, time, herself. Anything else to add to that list?

But today her concern could not be loss of face. It was her husband, Wilton Savoy. He needed serious reining in. And this was the first step. This Boston connection.

To her amusement, it had been simple...a call here; a call there. Before long, she was talking to an entrepreneur out of Revere, Massachusetts, who handled "Events Planning." Diane was impressed at how smoothly the meeting had been arranged. And now, after a three-hour drive from Maine, here she was in Boston, ready to talk to Ray Bun, the Chief Events Planner, who would help her put into play the spiteful deed she wanted done. Nothing violent, mind you. Just a jolt, embarrassing as all hell...to send a certain message to a certain someone.

....

"So here's what I envision, Ray Bun," Diane Savoy said to the man strolling beside her in Boston's Faneuil Hall. Her small dark blue winter pea coat was a minnow swimming next to Ray Bun's whale of a black bulging hoodie and swollen woolen team jacket. "I want to hire you to overwhelm one Chanson Pratt at her upcoming New Year's Eve party. This will be at her house on St. Frewin's Island off the coast of Maine. I'll give you the address when we're done here. I'm thinking you'll probably want to drug her—just slightly—to avoid a scuffle...you know what I mean," Diane said, lowering her voice.

She stopped and drew closer to Ray Bun for a private exchange, motioning him to lower his head towards hers. She continued in a conspiratorial voice—as if the Sunday tourists in the surrounding food courts would give a hoot about Diane Savoy and the handsome Black Superman at her side. "Then you'll hang a sign around her neck that reads WHORE and sit her limp body in a chair under a huge tarp that's going to be on her living room floor." She resumed her brisk walking.

"Mrs. Savoy—One moment, please," Ray Bun said. "Could you tell me more about this tarp on the floor? Why will Mrs. Pratt have a tarp on the floor at her big party?"

"You know. It's silly, but while we're talking business here, I'd prefer it if you would call her Whore, OK? Can you do that for me? 'Mrs. Pratt' sounds too respectful, and take it from me, Ray Bun, this woman deserves no respect. So where was I? Yes, OK. My informant tells me the Pratts will have a stash of helium party balloons under the tarp in their great room, which they'll pull off to release the balloons at midnight. So you'll want to have the Whore all doped up and on her little throne under that tarp before midnight. Then when the tarp comes up and the balloons float away, everyone will see her sitting there in a heap with the sign WHORE around her neck. A big sign. Do you get the picture?"

"It's making sense, Mrs. Savoy. Your goal is clear. But a little more intelligence would be helpful. Do you have a floorplan of the Pratt residence? Do you know if they will have security for the party?"

"For heaven's sake, Ray Bun! It's up to you to do your own due diligence. Isn't that what I'm paying you for? I don't give a damn how many square feet the Pratts have. How should I know if there will be armed guards? That's for you to find out."

"If you say so, Mrs. Savoy. It will all get rolled into the final price of the job. But whatever logistical details our clients can provide us in advance usually translates into a lower invoice."

"Well that's exactly what I want to discuss with you next, Ray Bun. Do you offer a lay-away plan for payment? And do you have a brochure that spells out your terms of service? Like penalties for delays, or no shows? Botched events? And what about malpractice insurance? Do you carry malpractice insurance?" Diane Savoy had drawn up a long list of practical inquiries.

"Uh, Mrs. Savoy, may I remind you. We're from Revere. And over in Revere, there is no such thing as a lay-away plan for our events. I mean, think about it. We stage violent events, Mrs. Savoy. We deliver chaos to the unsuspecting. We orchestrate occasions Martha Stewart wouldn't go near with a ten-foot cheese ball. She's been to prison. She knows better."

"Well, I'm not about to pay you totally up front if I have no assurances that you'll get the job done," Diane objected.

Ray Bun reached in and unbuttoned the top button of his Oxford shirt underneath his team jacket. The muscles in his tree trunk of a neck were seizing up on him. "Mrs. Savoy, let's be calm now. My team and I work very hard to deliver professionally. I'd give you our references, but they change a lot, you see? Some happy customers of ours just aren't here anymore to praise our work. Some are away for a long time, or they're unavailable to comment, generally speaking."

"Well, as you must know, Ray Bun, if you screw up my job, I can always report you to the Better Business Bureau. So I have consumer protection going for me."

"Mrs. Savoy, I'm afraid you don't appreciate what kind of an environment we're working in. The Better Business Bureau doesn't want to know that my company exists. Our area of expertise is way outside their parameters. And I don't want to get into all the nitty gritty, but we are not members of the Elks Club, you know? We don't do United Way. And the Chamber of Commerce would probably shit on their brochures if they saw us coming. Are you getting my drift?"

"Oh, never mind all that. Just tell me how your payment scheme works." Diane was getting a tad peevish. She glanced down at Ray Bun's feet. On a man his size, his white sneakers looked like two styrofoam packing corners that had just come off a new fridge.

"Like I said, Mrs. Savoy. We help you, the client, carry out highly irregular events, so it's not prudent for us to have to stay in touch with you afterward to track month-to-month payments on any final amount due for our efforts. We always require full payment up front at least ten days in advance of completion of our assignment. I can put you in touch today with our collections intermediary. He's a man by the name of Tony Abanditono."

"That sounds like total bull to me, Ray Bun." Diane stood in his path and glared upward at his sunglasses.

DON'T TOUCH MY COCKTAIL!

"How are you staying competitive with those inflexible terms?"

"Competitive, Mrs. Savoy?! Are you joking? Do you think you're going to find even one other professional firm to slip this whore a mickey and stuff her under a blanket at her own big blowout? This whole routine with the 'disco biscuit' angle, out of state, on an island, during the winter, with lots of people standing around, well, this calls for an experienced crew. Do you think you can just go look up that kind of muscle on Craig's List?"

"Oh, now you're talking about a crew?! How many people do you intend to transport up to Maine on my dime, Ray Bun? It doesn't take a village!" Diane wasn't about to let him snooker her.

"Well, for your kind of misdeed, Mrs. Savoy, I'm thinking of scheduling Jay Bun, Man Bun, Van Bun, and Tiny Bun. We need two people to subdue the subject, one person to handle the logistics, one person to create diversions as needed, and myself to keep command of the situation. You can never have too much manpower in these situations, especially with all the OSHA requirements."

"OSHA? OSHA! What kind of clap trap are you feeding me, Ray Bun? Do you and all those other Buns want my job, or not?" Diane could not believe her ears. She searched around the shopping complex for a bar. She needed a drink...in a hurry.

"Look, why don't we head over to Ned Devine's Bar and I'll treat you to something refreshing," Ray Bun suggested. "Maybe a gin and tonic? You've probably had a long day so far and it'd be good to sit down. What do you say, Mrs. Savoy?"

Carol Chen

Her onslaught of questions was churning Ray Bun's stomach acids into a virulent concoction. He hadn't anticipated the bravado of this jowly-faced, little pipsqueak who called his office out of the blue last week and was now drenching him with her venom. But Ray had been in this business long enough to identify Mrs. Savoy's likely vexation...the entanglement of one Chanson Pratt and Mrs. Savoy's husband. It was often the same old, sorry story.

"That's very thoughtful of you, Ray Bun. An excellent idea," said Diane Savoy, already envisioning a possible way to wrap this vendor of hers around her fist. "And by the way, this Bun business, your last name. Where does that come from?"

"Yes, Bun is my last name, Mrs. Savoy. It's Cambodian. I'm half Black and half Cambodian."

"My goodness. You're not kidding me, are you? What kind of combination is that? Do you feel at home anywhere?"

"Sure, I do. I feel at home in Revere."

"Revere? That's not what I meant."

"Well, that's what I mean, Mrs. Savoy," Ray Bun said, and he gave her a big smile.

....

"Hey, Zen-Ti, my man. How are you doing, you up and coming King?" Tony Abanditono oozed into his cellphone, laying on the praise. He considered Zen-Ti and his Lowell gang as very able men climbing the ladder of success. "I'm just checking in about a funny coincidence. You have an upcoming job on St. Frewin's Island in Maine, right? Night of New Year's Eve?"

DON'T TOUCH MY COCKTAIL!

"Yo, Tony! Good to hear from you, my old Money Bags! And you said it. You're going to be my go-between on the Chanson Pratt round-robin hubby nabbing on New Year's Eve...and yes, sir, we're talking St. Frewin's Island in Maine. Why are you asking, Señor Tony?"

"Well, Zen-Ti—I just wanted to know if you realized there's another hustle that same place, same night. And if that doesn't knock your socks off, my man, then you are already barefoot!"

"Now that's news to me, Tony. How come this place way out there in outer space is getting so much traffic? Do you have any juicy details you can spare for free?" Zen-Ti was quite curious now.

"I don't know much, Zen-Ti. Something about a Ray Bun—I think he's Revere material. And he's got some gig over at the Pratt complex, same as you. Something about revenge due to a hubby stuffing some gal's cannoli? I don't know details."

"I'll be damned, Tony...I'll be damned. And now I am forewarned, Bro. You're the man!"

....

Zen-Ti sat and stared at his honeycombed office wall, still in need of a mega patching job. He was scouring his cerebral crystal ball about this Ray Bun. It could only mean trouble, no matter what might come. He took a few minutes to surf the web and then made a few discreet phone calls.

"Hey, ZM!" Zen-Ti yelled a while later to his cousin and colleague. "I need you to run over to the warehouse and grab me a female gang outfit with the hairy blond wig.

Carol Chen

Make sure we pack it up for our job on the Maine island. OK? Gracias, Bro."

25
Monday, December 16

Jane waited alone in the manager's dark paneled office at Calderwood Boatyard. Long enough to recognize the manly eau de toilette of cigarette smoke, engine oil, and good old BO. As she concentrated on ignoring the fumes, she could see photographs of clients' boats hanging on two walls. Several large scheduling grids for ongoing work covered other walls. Uniform black lettering filled the grids, showing winter was the time to tackle maintenance and overhauls of everything from dinghies to 200-footers. Clearly Calderwood's was busy, and Jane had to admit...it didn't look like an outfit that would block out time to beat up an employee, such as the unfortunate Troy Overlock.

Jane glanced down at the Manager's desk. What she did not see peaked her interest...no family photos. The rest fit the mood: BOSOX pen holder, piles of paperwork, a dish of small wing clips, an unopened Mr. Goodbar. Jane backed away and straightened up when she heard the door open.

"Thanks for dropping by, Officer Roberts. How can we help?" Jerome Williams said as he walked into the office. Jane was surprised to see him in a navy blazer. That struck her as fairly fancy attire for a winter's day in a remote island boatyard.

"Hi, Mr. Williams. Thanks for meeting with me. I'm here to ask you a few more questions about Troy Overlock. And I wanted to let you know the hospital said he's doing much better...might even be able to talk later this week."

"I'm glad to hear that, Jane. We're all shocked about what happened to Troy. It doesn't make sense. Now, what would you like to know?"

"Do you have any idea why Troy's cellphone is missing? Was there anything at all that he was working on for the boatyard that could have been a threat to someone? And does Troy seem to be the kind of person who has dark secrets in his life? Or enemies? Maybe drug dealings?"

"Hold on there, Jane. So many questions. I don't have all day," said Williams, patting three of his paperwork towers.

"Oh, apologies. I'm just trying to find answers to explain what happened to Troy."

"Honestly, Jane, I must admit I don't really know Troy on much of a personal level. I mean, I know him to look at him. Big, burly guy...like a walking walrus," Williams chuckled. "That's how the guys kid him."

"Right. We helped him on the beach. I saw him in person," Jane said. If Williams was trying to joke about Troy, that certainly qualified as rude.

"As for a dark side to his life," Williams continued, "Well, what can I say? I'm not his confessor. Not his therapist. And I'm not around the crews much when they're talking to each other about whatever they talk about. I suppose if there was something threatening being discussed, it might filter back to me. But enemies and dark secrets? Drugs? That's a bit rich, don't you think, Officer Roberts?"

"Maybe, maybe not. We've got a man who was beaten within a yard of the pearly gates. I think it makes sense to consider the worst."

DON'T TOUCH MY COCKTAIL!

"Well, I can't imagine there's anything mysterious about the work he does for Calderwood. He handles incoming boats, readies boats for delivery to customers, does some small craft deliveries, that kind of thing. Not really turf for Harry Bosch or NCIS, if you get my drift."

Jane ignored the jab. "So, it sounds like you don't know anything that could help us solve why Troy was beaten, Mr. Williams?"

"That's right. But my secretary did prepare a list of his close associates here at the boatyard, which your receptionist requested when she set up this appointment. I hope it's of some help. However, I'd rather you talk to the men outside of the work day. We're on a lot of deadlines right now and can't really spare the time for interviews until after 4 PM."

"OK. I understand, Mr. Williams. Thank you for the list. And please call the PSO if you think of anything that might be important to the case. I'll give you a call if I have more questions, OK?"

"Sounds good, Officer Roberts. Nice to meet you."

"Thanks! Same here, Mr. Williams."

Jane gritted her teeth as she walked away. She had not taken a liking to Jerry Baby. Back at the office, she looked up the telephone numbers for Troy's associates and left them messages that she would like to talk with them about the attack. The sooner the better—today, tomorrow, or Wednesday—they should drop by the PSO between 5 and 6 PM. Jane was counting on them, for Troy's sake.

"Helen, what can you tell me about these people?" Jane pointed to the list of Troy's friends on the whiteboard. "Ralph so and so, Norm so and so , Joe and so on, Randy, Todd, Spencer...."

109

"Let's see. They all work at Calderwood's, right? I'd say most of them are in their thirties. Everyone but Joe Miller grew up on St. Frewin's. I'm not sure who Joe Miller is. Todd had a seafood truck a while back. Can't remember the details. Some kind of uproar around that food truck."

....

"Hi, Randy. Come on in and have a seat at the table. Thanks for taking the time to talk to me," Jane said to the boatyard employee. He sat down in his three layers of sweat shirts and thick canvas overalls, all of it streaked with paint and grease.

"Sure, yah, no problem. Help if I can."

"We're trying to figure out who beat up Troy Overlock and why, pure and simple. Do you have any ideas?" Jane said. The stubble on Randy's face was like the stubble on his head. Sharp, hard barbs that looked like they would leave a sore path in their wake if he kissed someone.

"Uh, not sure. What do you want to know?"

"Well, like I said, we're focusing on who beat up Troy and why. Is there anything you can share about what happened to Troy?"

"Hell, wish I knew to tell you, Officer Roberts. Troy's the sweetest guy on the planet. Why would anyone do such a thing? Pains me to think about it."

"So you don't really have any information that might help us? Or maybe I should be more specific. Is Troy involved in anything around the boatyard that could get him in trouble? What do you think?"

"You mean like the guys who deal drugs? Selling us meth and coke? Doubt it. Troy isn't into illegal stuff. He's like a lamb, you know? A huge, chunky lamb. Nothing bad about him."

"A huge, chunky lamb? Why do people keep talking about how big Troy is?"

"Well it ain't my place to go on about his weight. Or how cranky it makes him. That's his own business."

"Can you tell me more about that? About Troy being mad about his weight?" Jane asked.

"Nah. I've done said enough, Officer. Maybe one of the other guys can help you...I really don't know anything about Troy and that girl he broke up with. They say she got tired of him getting bigger and bigger, but like I said, what do I know?"

"Um, Randy, one more thing. Could you fill me in a bit more about meth and coke sales at the ship yard? Is there a lot of that going on?" Jane said.

"Did I say that?" Randy looked at her with a question mark in his eyes.

"Yes, you did," Jane said.

"Oh, crazy me. That was just like...a hypothetical. Isn't that what they call it? I was just talkin' about a 'what if.' You know. Nothin' for real." Randy smiled and shook his stubbled cheeks.

"You're sure about that?" Jane asked.

"Sure as you and me sittin' here."

26
Wednesday, December 18

"Come right in and have a seat, Todd. Thanks for agreeing to speak with us. Our receptionist, Helen, mentioned you used to have a food truck. That was before my time. How'd you like being your own boss back then?" Jane asked.

"Whoa. Didn't expect you to start out our meeting with that, Officer Jane. It's ancient history at this point. And I squared things away with the Maine DEA a few years back, as far as my cook goes. You're not gonna open that can of worms up again, are you? I thought I was doing you and Troy a favor coming down here." Todd's dark, heavily lashed eyes blinked repeatedly at Jane, his thick, spiky hair ready to jump off his head.

"I apologize, Todd. Just making small talk. Didn't mean to go poking into any old wounds."

"Hah, wounds. You said it. That scum bag short-order cook of mine got it into his head to sell drugs out of *my* seafood truck. Talk about lying. That piece of shit lied all right. He lied to me. He lied to the Food Inspectors. He lied to the fucking clams!"

"OK, OK. Ahh, let's move on to the topic of Troy. We're looking for his cellphone as part of our investigation. Do you have a guess as to what might have happened to it?"

"Cellphone? Let me think. Troy usually kept it in his truck, so he'd have it when he got to the Wi-Fi at the ferry terminal on the mainland. But that detective Storm Nosmot and his sidekick looked all over the boatyard for that cellphone when they were at Calderwood's. No luck. So I say, try Troy's house? Maybe his parents know something?"

"Thanks. We'll check. Now, do you know if Troy had any secrets or enemies...anything that could explain why he was attacked?"

"Jesus, Officer Roberts. Enemies? You know, you're still kind of new on this island. We don't really know who you are. You can't expect all of us to go spilling Troy's personal beans. Why would we feel comfortable telling you about his disappointing love life and all his frustrations? We can't go into his weight problems. You need to go easy on what you're asking. Things take time."

"So you're saying Troy was disappointed in love? And worried about his weight?" Jane said.

"I'm not saying that exactly. Go easy is all I'm saying."

....

"Helen, do you know what I mean if I say people on this island are driving me crazy with how they answer questions?" Jane stretched her head back and forth and drank from a large glass of water. "Out of one side of the mouth, everyone keeps trying to hold back from giving me any insights. At the same time, out of the other side of the mouth, they're gushing with hints and tidbits. What is that all about?"

"Have you ever heard of human nature, Jane?" Helen gave her the smile of an oracle. "Didn't Storm warn you it will take time to get down to the truth? People are funny, Jane. You know that."

....

"So how long have you worked at Calderwood's, Spencer?" Jane asked the tall man in russet-colored coveralls. His entire body was one hard muscle from his large, shaved-bald head down into his heavy work boots. He looked at her intensely from across the PSO table.

"I've been in and out of there over the years," he said, his bright smile catching Jane with its whiteness. "They're good to me. They always take me back. See, now and then, my inner spirit pulls me North towards Mt. Katahdin. I got a cabin up there where I hang out from time to time."

"Sounds nice. God's country," said Jane.

"Sure is. Almost enough to keep you sane. So, what do you want to know, Officer Roberts?"

"Well, this beating of Troy Overlock. Are you as astonished as I am? I've been telling everyone we can't have this kind of thing on St. Frewin's Island, right? Someone attacked to within an inch of his life? What kind of impact is this going to have on our daily lives? What about our tourism?" Jane could see Spencer was starting to look towards Helen for rescue from Jane's heat. "Oh, wait. I'm sorry, Spencer. I'm too wound up. I've been talking to so many of you about this and trying to get a grip on answers. Sorry...."

"Hah. Venting! I get it. I come down from the woods and my mother starts right in venting at me. I'm not back here five minutes and she starts coming at me, roaring about all this stuff that's driving her crazy. People do that. Drive someone else crazy, so you feel less crazy yourself. Go ahead. You can vent. I'm used to it. I'm a sponge for venting...Ha ha!!"

"Venting...funny. So, where was I?" Jane said.

"Hold it a minute, if it's OK with you, Officer. They say you used to be a lawyer, and I got a real estate question.

DON'T TOUCH MY COCKTAIL!

Could I run that by you, before I tell you exactly who whacked our Triple-Quarter-Pounder Troy?"

Did he just say "You used to be a lawyer?" Oh, boy. My speckled past...Jane, the "Lawyer." Who wandered in the legal desert for forty months, living on quantum and meruit until she found the Promised Land...which never happened. Sometimes you're brave enough to say goodbye to something you never really wanted. That's what happened to Esquire Jane.

"You know who whacked Troy?" Jane said.

"Nah. Just joshing you. But seriously, one real estate question?"

"Well, ask your question and I'll let you know if I can answer," Jane said.

"So I got this piece of land. It ain't square." Spencer paused as if in thought. "And it ain't round. And I want to sell some pieces of it with my cousin. Can I do that without some kind of permission?"

"What's your cousin got to do with your land?" Jane asked.

"Well some of my land might be on my cousin's land."

"Then, first you need to be sure your land isn't on your cousin's land," said Jane.

"Of course I do. I don't want to sell something that isn't there."

Jane reminded her head not to spin. "I tell you what, Spencer. After we're done here, I'll give you the names of some real estate lawyers and you can call them about your land."

....

Jane sat in her side office to ponder the innuendos she had picked up from Troy's friends. By now, everyone but Joe Miller had stopped in to talk.

Why was it those two details kept surfacing? ...Troy's weight and its bad impact on his search for love. Impossible to find love. Jane thought back to a funeral she had attended years ago for a colleague who had taken his own life. When the minister spread his arms and called out to the sorrowful crowd, "What do people want?" Jane had waited in suspense, wondering where the minister would go with his answer. He looked around at everyone and said to them, "What do people *want*? They want to be *loved*."

Well, that's what Troy wanted. Jane, too.

27
Thursday, December 19

"What have you got planned for Christmas?" Jane asked Helen and Israel Tenner while they sat at the PSO table and began opening up their cartons from Rajiv's Indian takeout. Jane was so relieved it had been a calm day thus far. No cars skidding into ditches. No passengers falling off the State ferry. No 911 calls. Such a luxury to have a desultory afternoon to reboot her energy.

"Oh, it'll be small this year," Helen said. "John Leckman will be with me most of the time. And we hope to make a trip to visit Josiah in prison. I guess that's about it. How about you, Jane?"

"Sounds good, Helen. Since I'm scheduled to cover the office through the holidays, Mom and Dad and my sister, Desdemona, will come over on Christmas Eve and stay a few days at my place. We haven't had a Christmas with Desdemona for a long time, so it should be fun."

Israel chimed in next. "If the weather cooperates, I'll probably drive to Stowe on Christmas day to spend a few days with my parents and the rest of my family. We're a big crowd...brothers, sisters, cousins, lots of kids, grandparents.

Jane looked over at Israel and gave him a quick wink. She wasn't apt to say it out loud, but Israel's presence on their team had been an improvement...a plus. For all kinds of reasons, Jane was more comfortable around him than she had been around Zeke Pendleton. Relief from Zeke's misplaced cockney lilt and all his Zen paraphernalia.

Carol Chen

The phone started ringing and Helen picked up. "Yes, she's here, Gluella. How can we help you?" Helen looked at Jane with a question mark on her face and grabbed Jane's appointment calendar. "You and your attorney would like to meet with Jane ASAP? OK. Please hang on and let me check her schedule." Helen pressed the HOLD button. "What do you want to do, Jane?"

"Oh, great," Jane said, stuffing a piece of chicken tikka into her mouth before her next words. "It didn't take long for Gluelulu to get wind of our Russian summit at Buddy's Bar and Grill. OK. Let's plug her in for Monday afternoon. And please find out who's she bringing as her lawyer."

28
Friday, December 20

"It may be a giant puzzle. That's what we've got to figure out, Israel. Try to see any possible connections between all these crazy pieces on the table." Jane and Israel were driving along Route One to Abenaki County General Hospital to visit Troy Overlock.

"Meaning," Israel said, "we have Troy's attack, the interviews with his co-workers, we want to know why the Russians are on the island and why are they interested in Environmental Fields. And you haven't said yet. How did your hook-up with the Russians go? Did you get thrown out of Buddy's?"

"We had a wild time—but not booted out," Jane said. "And despite the language barrier, my Mata Haris and I picked up on a few details. After spending all afternoon pretending we were Lobster Brides!"

"Don't keep me in suspense."

"OK. Number One: The Russians are bunked on a ship out in the Atlantic Ocean. Number Two: They weren't able to name a single fish, which suggested to us the Russians are not here to catch seafood."

Jane turned into the visitors' parking lot at the hospital. She drove around until they found a space.

"That's all you got?" Israel said.

"Like you could have done better," Jane sniffed.

Storm was there to meet them near the hospital's main entrance. Troy had improved during the week, and the doctors told the officers they could speak with him...fifteen minutes max.

....

Jane took one look at the human mound of gauze and purple blotches and hoped it didn't show that she was about to flee the room. Storm and Israel walked right over to Troy and gave him the high five while they introduced themselves.

"Are you OK with all of us hovering around you, Troy?" Jane said. She dug inside her bag to find her notepad with her important questions for Troy. No use trying to do it off the top of her head when she was so distracted by the shape he was in.

"Do you mind if we ask you a few questions? You can say no. Whatever you're comfortable with," said Storm.

"S'okay, you guys. Not sure about my memory," said Troy.

"Do you know who did this to you?" Jane asked.

"Never saw it coming," Troy said. "Don't know."

"Any idea why someone would hurt you?"

"Can't really say." Troy turned his head to look out his hospital room window. He left his head resting just so.

The uneventful interview went on like that until their fifteen minutes were up. No question bore fruit. No fruit was ripe. They might as well not have driven over in the first place. Jane was frustrated they would walk away with nothing. She wondered if Troy was holding back what he knew. And she wondered why. It occurred to her that their leaving without his telling them was an important part of understanding what had happened to him. If Troy could, but refused to divulge the truth, it might be because he remained terrified of his attacker...or more likely, attackers. Because he knew who they were. And he was still under their thumb.

29
Monday, December 23

"So, Jane, Gluella's attorney is someone by the name of Gaspard Pariballou," Helen said, reading from her phone notes the following Monday.

"You know as well as I do, Helen, that I am not looking forward to this meeting with Gluey and Attorney So and So," Jane complained out loud, minutes before the designated time. "But I love, no—make that *relish*—yanking on her chain and raining on her parade at the same time. Who's that attorney again?"

"Gaspard Pariballou."

"Pariballou...Pariballou, OK, got it," Jane said under her breath, attempting to lock in the name.

"Remember, Jane. Her name is Gluella. And I don't know that her website is all that bad," Helen said. "You hear how people meet and get married all the time now, thanks to online dating sites. It can be a useful approach. Gluella's just another entrepreneur doing her thing."

"Well, in her case, she's trying to maneuver within an extremely narrow set of human expectations, and I think it'll lead to disaster. I doubt she can deliver what she's advertising. But I'm psyched to do this. Pariballou—with a 'P.' Pariballou. I won't let Gluey get to me, even if she is a revolting cocktail of corn syrup and vinegar." Jane scrunched up her face and watched Helen shaking her head.

....

The unlikely trio sat down at the PSO table. The pit bull in Jane's brain strained against her civilized upbringing. Gluella looked like her teeth weren't going to unlock today. And Gaspard Pariballou, a hairy little man who moved quickly, was busy fluffing his notes and several legal volumes...like a gerbil scuffing up shreds of bedding before snuggling into its nest.

He finally looked up and began. "My client's position, Officer Roberts, is simply this. *You* have tortiously interfered with client contracts in her business known as Lobster Brides!"

"I highly doubt that, Attorney um...," Jane responded with a slight toss of her head. "Could you please elaborate?"

"That's Pariballou, Ms. Roberts," he said calmly. "So, yes. Let's begin with Buddy's Bar and Grill last Tuesday. First, you took it upon yourself to cancel a legitimate meeting between Ms. Trott's actual Lobster Brides! candidates and her visiting overseas clientele. Then you marched your troop of fraudulent Lobster Brides! into Buddy's for an introductory meeting with Ms. Trott's clients."

"I don't know why you think I masterminded this escapade of yours, but go ahead, I'm listening," Jane said.

Pariballou continued. "What began as a social gathering quickly escalated to women lounging on men's laps, then couples intimately intertwined, to the point that local law enforcement had to be called in to quell, in Officer Finn Gallinen's own words, 'overtly nymphomaniacal behavior.' The fallout from that meeting has severely disrupted Ms. Trott's ability to provide complete client satisfaction. As I said, we are in pure tort territory."

DON'T TOUCH MY COCKTAIL!

Jane was pleased to think she had opted for an elaborate disguise. Finn had never caught on. Why was he still such a thorn in Jane's PSO badge? It had all started with the Ruth Farrow case. In Jane's mind, Finn was all chip...didn't even need his own shoulder.

As she sat there, digesting Pariballou's critique, she saw something in his eyes that reminded her of little black peanuts. When he spoke, the small ruddy pouches he had for cheeks puffed in and out like mini bagpipes. She finally pegged him. He was a gerbil juris doctor, and a bona fide moron.

"Look, Attorney Paralegal..." Jane began.

Pariballou's eyebrows shot up.

"You're talking about female potboilers hooking up with wealthy foreigners in the State of Maine. What's that got to do with torts? Maybe you mean 'tarts?' " Jane suggested merrily and grinned at Gluella.

"It's Pariballou, Officer Roberts." He frowned. "I also refer you to the Maine Unfair Trade Practices Act. Your antics have exposed Ms. Trott to the possibility of being charged with material misrepresentation and dealing in a mislabeled commodity."

"Oh," Jane slapped her hand down on the table and grabbed the lawyer with her eyeballs. "Are you saying these women are Gluelulu's commodities? And that Gluelu may be accused of misleading her clients? Well, may I point out to both of you that it is a false statement of a material fact to pull in these commodities—these WOMEN—with the possibility of marriage to wealthy, educated foreigners who speak English. From what I've heard, all Glueall has dredged up thus far are a bunch of zombie Russians who crawled out of a Russian trawler with ten words of English stuffed in their underwear. And God knows if they're handing out HIV/AIDS and tuberculosis on their way to the altar."

"If you continue in this vein, Officer Roberts, we may have to inject libel and slander into the complaint we're poised to file in Abenaki County Superior Court," said Attorney Pariballou, stabbing his pen in Jane's direction.

"Ha ha!! Aren't you the tease, Attorney Paribooloo!" Jane's face lit up and she rested her chin in her upheld palm. "What I'd love to know is, how did these post-Soviet washouts make it onto Gluelu's client list in the first place. I recall her emphasizing the enormously steep entry fee to Lobster Brides! What am I missing here?"

Gluella seemed to go pale for a moment. She leaned towards Pariballou to whisper into his whiskery ears for about three long minutes, taking deep breaths between each minute. Jane was fascinated by the exchange. It was like watching one of those big-lip damsel fish conferring with a professional rodent.

Pariballou stared intently at Jane while he answered her question. "As the creator of Lobster Brides!, Ms. Trott has a wide range of latitude with her fee scale. From time to time, to accommodate a large group that plans to sign up with Lobster Brides!, Ms. Trott is in a position to offer a bulk discount on the entry fee. She will have to check her records, but it is possible the Russian clientele you met at Buddy's Bar and Grill were recipients of such a bulk discount."

Jane knew a gas bag when she saw one, and there he was now, right in front of her eyes. Obviously the Russians had hardly paid jack shit to roar up to St. Frewin's Island and start racing around looking for babes they could dip into melted butter.

DON'T TOUCH MY COCKTAIL!

Jane revved up her saucy motor. "Well, well, Attorney Paripillow. That explains how Mrs. Trotter has succeeded in misleading the women who signed up to become Lobster Brides! And I'm beginning to doubt any of these men could survive the deep algorithmic vetting process she claims to require for each new male candidate. I may have to look into pulling the plug on this entire, insane operation," Jane said tersely.

"Hold on, Officer Roberts. We have you on the hook concerning additional egregious behavior. Might you be so kind as to listen to this recording of statements made by your outlaw brides to Ms. Trott's Russian clients?" Pariballou clicked on a small tape recorder he had pulled out of his briefcase.

"Oooooo, Spartak, you Big Pirozhki! Where did you get those loooooong nose hairs sprouting out of your schnoz? They're so sexy...I bet you would love to tickle my woo-woo box with those bristly little buggers, wouldn't you?"

Gluella interrupted the tape and started seething at Jane. "Did you hear that? How am I supposed to run my business when I'm hounded by scammers like you and your girlfriends out there treating my unsuspecting clients like fools? They're furious at me. They're demanding their money back. I'm not going to let you off the hook for any of this, Jane!"

"It's Officer Roberts to you," Jane corrected Gluella pointedly. "Now I'm not saying I was at this alleged hook-up, and I'm not saying I know anything at all about your complaints," Jane stated firmly. "But if these Russian men you're talking about are so unhappy, why don't you refund their money...or explain it was all a big mistake? It's not like they qualify for your website. And if they don't know much English, how could they be insulted? You need more proof and substance before you can hang me out to dry, Gluelulu."

"Enough of these men know enough English to make the difference," Gluella yipped back. "Attorney Pariballou, please play the other comments. Officer Roberts needs to hear this."

Jane swiftly snapped her hand upward in a STOP sign. "Really, that's enough. You're wasting my time with your drivel."

"Then I'll cut to the chase, Officer Roberts. We are prepared to take you to court if you interfere any further with Ms. Trott's business dealings, on St. Frewin's or on the mainland. Consider yourself warned."

"Warned? Take me to court?" Jane exclaimed as she stood up from the table and began wagging both index fingers at her audience. "Now you listen to me, Parabeagles. When are you two going to wake up and smell some reality? Have you even confirmed whether these Slavic plug uglies have their necessary US B1/B2 Visas to be on this island at all?"

Gluella shot a searing, accusatory facial missile at Attorney Pariballou. He cleared his throat and took a limp stab at responding. "That is a work in progress, Officer Roberts. You needn't worry. All in good time."

"In other words, NO on the visas, right?" Jane asked. "OK, you two. We're calling it quits here. And I'm only giving you my advice this one time, Gluten. Take your sticky business and get out of St. Frewin's pristine zip code. The Cold War may be over, but if any more of your suspicious clientele set foot on this island, they're going to get a very frosty reception, I can assure you," Jane said, glowering at Gluella and her lawyer. "A frosty reception...as in Federal ICE!"

30
Christmas Week

Wobbly strands of tiny purple and yellow lights were flickering across the mess room of the good ship *Valentina Petrovna*, swinging askew with every swell of the Penobscot Bay undulating beneath her hull. Egor, Yaroslav, and their motley Russian crew spooned into their huge bowls of cold sour milk soup, boiled turnips, radishes, and sinewy chicken legs. Their favorite rapper, LL Cool J, someone they could all agree on, was playing in the background.

Smiling down from huge posters on the mess room walls were the heroic three—Kobe Bryant, Kareem Abdul-Jabbar, and Michael Jordan, where ideally pictures of Putin should have been on display. Bold yellow and purple banners and blankets embroidered with "Los Angeles LAKERS" in big, happy letters rounded out the sports merchandise decorating the mess room.

The men's conversations were in Russian of course, but the metaphors tended heavily towards basketball. That's what the Russian crew lived and breathed...basketball...and women and American rap. Curiously, the men didn't give a hoot about Russia's own rappers—Oxxxymiron, Big Baby Tape, Face—none of them. Here, in the land of the free and the brave, LL Cool J was their man.

"Did you hear how much those Lobster Brides! love us all just the way we are?" Spartak asked his friend Dimitri over their curdled soup. "My girl told me my stinking undershirt was driving her wild. And she loved it

128

that I've never used a Q-tip in my life. She said that was evident, but it showed how manly I was."

"But did they mean what they said, Spartak?" Dimitri said. "Think about it. One gal wanted to take a bath with me in vodka and boiled potatoes. Who does that? And why did the women have so many questions about why we were on their island? They were hammering on us— What did we want? What about Environmental Fields? Why were we in Maine at all? Very strange. Maybe they're defected KGB."

Egor and Yaroslav, the ship's managers, knew enough to give this crew the leeway they needed to keep functioning. Like paying the discounted entry fee for any of them who wanted to sign onto some kooky American website called Lobster Brides! Egor had done a particularly good job at twisting that Trott woman's arm until she agreed to lower her exorbitant price. While these boat bosses considered every man on their crew expendable in the end, they were content to keep each man happy as long as he continued to be useful.

But "useful" had proven a fleeting goal lately. Egor was admonishing the men about all the fucking "airballs" they had lobbed on St. Frewin's Island to date. So many missed shots and balls that failed to get the necessary results for the "Beeg Boss" back in their home city of Makhachkala on the Caspian Sea.

"Fadeaways" were what they needed most now—those miracle shots and miracle baskets in the game, when your momentum and balance were pulling you away from the net...like the *Valentina Petrovna* would eventually begin pulling and moving away from this God damn island with its peculiar, thwarting population...those local people constantly mucking up the works and interfering with the Russians' schemes. Like that taser guy at Environmental Fields...and that Officer Jane...such thorns in the side of Mother Russia...the kind of people who made America a jungle.

So, the Russian crew was getting one final chance to make good. The pressure was off on retrieving all that ruined Premier Beluga Caviar and the disappeared Chinese gold—both meant for some drunk loser slob of a Senator, "Beeg McGill," in Washington, D.C. What was done was done. Let it go. After all, the Soviets had lost a million civilians in the Siege of Leningrad...lost a million comrades in the Siege of Stalingrad. What was one barrel of caviar or one barrel of Chinese gold? Enough nonsense.

Now their new assignment was to kidnap a man named Salem Pratt, who was drowning in debt to his Russian creditors, due to recent, stunning losses in his semiconductor business. Salem was nearly wiped out. Kidnap the man and threaten his life properly, until he figured out how to pay down his multi-million-dollar debt. Those were their orders. Then release him, dead or alive.

And lucky for the Russian crew, this Salem Pratt was planning to be on St. Frewin's Island over the Christmas and New Year holidays. Forcing Pratt to pay up would ensure the crew their return passage to their home port. Or else. They were expendable.

31
Monday, December 23
Afternoon

"Come right in. Don't worry about the snow. Just stamp your boots outside." Jane was shepherding a man making his way into the PSO.

"Thanks. You must be Officer Jane Roberts. I'm Joe Miller. Nice to meet you," he said, giving Jane's hand a hearty shake. "I'm on my way to the ferry and thought I better follow up first on your telephone message about Troy Overlock."

"Right, that's great. Have a seat, Joe, and we can talk," Jane said. "Would you like some coffee?"

"No thanks. I'm all set."

"I appreciate you showing up so close to Christmas. Busy time of year."

"Not a problem. My family and I begin celebrating Hanukkah tonight, so that was another reason to check in with you before I run out of free time."

"Someone mentioned you're new to St. Frewin's?" Jane said.

"Yes...moved here last year from Brooklyn. What an incredible place this is! Really happy I took the big step— you know," Joe wiggled his fingers in quotes, "Juban descendant carves out new life as Maine boat carpenter."

"Juban descendant? What are you saying?" Jane asked.

"That's me...I'm a Juban...maybe you don't know. I'm a Cuban Jew."

"No kidding. A Juban? That's the first I've ever heard the term. Interesting. I had no idea there was a Jewish connection with Cuba," Jane said.

"It is interesting. My family goes back quite a way in Cuba. And we take pride in being Jubans."

"Well, you're going to have to fill me in when you have more time. It sounds fascinating...really."

"I see you're a swirl baby yourself," Joe said, looking over Jane's face.

"Excuse me?" Jane was surprised at his directness. It was true she sprang from a clash of civilizations in a New Jersey suburb. But she didn't think about it much...didn't dwell on being half Peking duck and half kielbasa.

"You know, a little of this, a little of that," said Joe. "That's a swirl baby. In fact, I've noticed you around town. Kind of refreshing to see someone sort of ethnic."

"Tell me you've never been accused of being blunt," said Jane.

"Hah. All the time. Sorry. I'll back off. Just trying to break the ice."

"OK. Let's switch to what happened to Troy. In a nutshell, do you have any idea why someone would beat him up?"

"If I knew, Jane—OK if I call you Jane?—I would have phoned you right away. None of us knows what happened to Troy. We're all shaking our heads."

"OK. How about this. Three things people focus on when talking about Troy—how nice he is, how big he is, and that he can't find love. Do you have anything to add to that?" Jane said.

"All true. But listen. As far as his size, we know it's hard on him. But it's his own private matter to deal with.

Psychologically and practically. We can't go there. It only belongs to Troy. Does that make sense?"

"Fine. And I can see it may be a dead end for me to explore. It's just popped up so much, I can't help but wonder how important it is...to him...maybe even to why he was attacked. OK. Enough."

"If anything occurs to me, I will definitely call you, Jane. I hate to think I left the Mafia in Brooklyn, only to find another version of them running around on an island in Maine."

32
Monday, December 23
Late Afternoon

Jane stood staring at the white board in the PSO office. She uncapped her magic marker and began adding more column headings, next to the notes for "Troy Overlock Assault"...adding acronyms and so forth...ICE, Lobster Brides!, Russians, FBI, CIA....

Jane disliked acronyms. Useful as they were, they were also often meant to numb the pain. Take IED...the worst. Improvised Explosive Device. She didn't even like the complete term. Terms like IED could be deliberate disguises—to whitewash violent content. Make it easier to skirt around the horrors. Just dish out a sentence about IEDs, and your audience would blink past the fact that you were really talking about home-made bombs full of vicious stuff like nails, screws, darts, razors, bolts, glass, marbles, and ball bearings—all blasting at you more than 450 feet per second.

Calling them IEDs resulted in just another visual symbol instead of the real weapon and what it was meant to do—to dig into all the soft human tissue possible and fuck someone up for life. And the words "improvised" and "device"? They sounded like something out of Silicon Valley or a James Bond movie. Enough with the window dressing. Jane wanted mankind to refer to homemade shrapnel bombs as just that. Call a bomb a bomb. Ditch the squeaky-clean acronyms.

DON'T TOUCH MY COCKTAIL!

She sighed and added more columns for "Environmental Fields" and "Stan Helmstadt Ruffled Manure Pile."

The office door opened and closed with a monster of cold air. Israel walked in from his routine island inspection. "I thought you wanted Helen to rip down that skanky pink cellophane and those cans on the front door," Israel said, pulling off his parka. "The stuff's definitely gotten trashed by the wind and snow."

"You think it looks like a strumpet's dirty nightie?" Jane grumbled. "So do I. But Helen pointed out that stepping on Trudy Moody's toes and her decorations would not be good for island politics."

"Well, I'm glad I'm getting to know who the real power brokers are around here," Israel laughed. He looked at what Jane had written on the white board. "What's with Stan's ruffled manure pile? That's sounds challenging, Jane."

"Ya, ha ha. How'd it go out on the roads? No accidents, I hope," Jane said before answering his question.

"We're good...roads are passable...not too slippery."

"So," Jane said, "I'll get to Stan's manure pile in a minute. But first of all, I think we have a problem. All those puzzle pieces I mentioned earlier? Well, they suggest to me that something fishy is happening on this island...like St. Frewin's is possessed...something weird. I know that's not very technical, but look at this," and she began dissecting each of the columns, beginning with ICE, Lobster Brides!, and Russians.

"First of all, we've got Lobster Brides!, Gluella Trott's dating site. She's pulling in foreigners without proper visas, like our Russian friends. She knows it, and she isn't doing much about it. Now I don't know if Immigration and Customs Enforcement cares, but I alerted them anyway after Gluella's visit earlier today. They'd like to send a representative to look into the situation, but it'll have to wait until after Christmas."

"I read somewhere that ICE has an annual budget of about eight billion dollars...more than enough dough in there to treat themselves to a quick trip to Maine in winter, you'd think," Israel said.

"We'll see. On top of that," Jane continued, "my alerting the ICE officials must have set off some alarms, because then I got calls from the FBI and the CIA. Can you believe it? They told me they're cooperating on some kind of surveillance concerning St. Frewin's right now, but they refused to give me any details. Even though it's our turf! I find that kind of insulting."

"Sounds like something big might be coming down, Jane?" Israel guessed.

"Yeah, well we'll be the last to know. If they bother to tell us. Anyway, next column. Environmental Fields has to be linked to all of this, because we know the Russians were interested enough in Environmental Fields to send that sailor Spartak to scope it out. Why all the focus on this septage recycling field on our little island? It's strange." Jane added a note under Environmental Fields. "But we don't know the connection. We only know they're out in the ocean on a ship, and they don't fish.

"Then there's Troy Overlock," Jane said. "Is his assault linked to his employment? No one I spoke to thinks so. Are the Russians involved? Does Troy have anything to do with Environmental Fields? And why does everyone mention Troy's weight problem?" Jane scribbled on the whiteboard.

Israel spoke up. "And Helen said MCU-Central finally called. They found nothing of interest in Troy's bank account."

"Right," Jane said. "So we should speak with his family. Finally, about Stan Helmstadt...he called the other day to complain he was away a few weekends ago and came home to find his manure pile 'ruffled and all dug into' as he described it. He said he thought it was totally suspicious. And he and his wife wondered if it had anything to do with Spartak showing up at the PSO a few days earlier. So that's another question mark."

"Gee, how do these people make a connection like that last one?" Israel asked with skepticism.

"I guess they're simply trying to make sense out of a mystery. Anyway, let's look at all of this. What do you think?" Jane said.

They pondered the white board for a few minutes. "OK...so let's see. You've got...." Israel was talking to himself as he looked back and forth through the headers. "The topic, or two topics, that seem to blow everything up into something bigger, or link everything, are the FBI and the CIA. The FBI covers primarily national crime; the CIA focuses on international intelligence. And we know we have Russian actors. So there appears to be some kind of situation involving a possible crime on our island with an international angle as well, which is where the Russians might come in. And maybe Troy is also in there somewhere."

"That might make sense, Israel. I like that. And it's helping me to focus. Because one person who may know more about the Russian element is Bernie Pushaw. He came in here to alert me about Spartak...Bernie found him wandering around at Environmental Fields. And I never did ask Bernie what happened. That's something I need to do."

"And what about Stan Helmstadt, Jane? If he was away for the weekend, who took care of his cows? Did someone come and go who might have seen something, or who knows something? We should talk to Stan as well."

"OK. Let me add notes about these points to the white board." Jane stepped back and studied their trail of thoughts. "The one sad topic that doesn't seem to fit is poor Troy Overlock. Why was he attacked? How could his beating possibly be related to a criminal situation with an international angle?"

"Well, we've managed to come up with a few assignments. Do you want me to go talk to Bernie and Stan...or the Overlocks?" Israel asked. "Or should we split up the visits...whatever you think best, Jane."

"You can handle Stan and I'll deal with Bernie," Jane decided. "We'll both go see the Overlocks. If we can reach all these people by the end of tomorrow, maybe we'll have more to ponder over the holidays."

33
Tuesday, December 24
Morning

"So, Bernie, can you remember the spot where you first found that Russian guy Spartak? Do you have any idea what he was doing in Environmental Fields?" Jane was hoping Bernie would have total recall and the answers to all her questions. She knew she should know better.

"Jeez, Jane. What can I say? Just look at this mess," Bernie said, basking in his complaining. He and Jane were crunching along on uneven swaths of frozen, crappy ice at Environmental Fields, which seemed to stretch on forever. "I mean we try to recycle this here septage in what the State DEP likes to call an 'orderly manner.' But hell, the DEP's way up in Augusta, an' I'm way down here in this crud, day after day, tryin' to unload it in an orderly DEP manner. And tryin' to keep me and my co-worker, Jason Coombs, from catchin' some kind o' bug or germ that's gonna make our eyes cave in an' our noses fall off. I do what I can, you know? I do what I can."

"So can you answer my question, Bernie?" Jane looked at him somewhat exasperated.

"What question is that?" Bernie said.

"This Spartak character. What can you tell me about him?"

"Oh, him. You mean Star Trek? Yeah, well he jus' kinda appeared outta nowhere, like from a space ship or somethin' and I was callin' him to halt, and he jus' took off like a Russian bullet. That's about it, Jane."

"But where did you first see him, Bernie?"

"Well, like I was sayin', Jane, it's such a mess out here, wha' do you think? It ain't like it's a Monopoly board with street names every which way, is it?" Bernie scoffed. "Jus' a bunch o' rows o' shit in a giant ice cube tray, far as I can tell."

"So there was nothing you could see in Environmental Fields, anywhere on the ground, or in the furrows maybe, that interested Spartak? Nothing out of the ordinary? Nothing that stood out?"

"Well now you're goin' roun' in circles, Jane. That ain't a good sign. You can't make up what ain't there, right?"

"But I seem to recall you were very concerned about Spartak the day you saw him. You came into the Public Safety Office talking about how he should be arrested or something like that. What's changed since then? You're willing to write it all off now?" Jane wondered.

"Darned if I can even think that far back, Jane," Bernie said sheepishly. "You know me...ripe case of CRS."

"CRS? I hate acronyms. What's CRS?" Jane said.

"You know, Can't Remember Shit."

....

"It's just the most gaw-danged thing I ever seen, Israel," Stan Helmstadt said as the two men walked through greasy strands of snow towards the manure pile on Stan's dairy farm. "If it ain't someone horsin' around, then I'm chalkin' it up to a UFO. Plain and simple. What other 'xplanation could there be?"

"Well, show me what you've got, Stan. I'll take down your information. Maybe Jane and I can come up with an answer for you. You never know. We might get lucky," Israel suggested.

DON'T TOUCH MY COCKTAIL!

"Where'd you say you come from?" Stan asked as they stepped around some patches of ice.

"I'm from Vermont," Israel said.

"Vermont, hey? Skiin' and syrup, right? We got them, too, but we also got the ocean an' seafood. Ain't no ocean an' seafood in Vermont, is there?" Stan's throat rattled out a long, corrugated chuckle.

"So looky here," Stan said, pointing to the huge pile of dung, distinctly cratered on its surface. "Look at all this excavatin' in the top of my manure. What the hell are all those holes dug out for, Israel? If I can't make heads or tails of it, and you and Jane can't, then maybe it's eggs from outer space that some critter buried. And then they gone an' hatched themselves and crawled away. Makes about as much sense as anything I can think o'...like turtles layin' their eggs in a pile o' dirt and then hittin' the road to leave the little buggers to figure it all out on theyah own. Naycha at work, right?"

"That's quite an interesting idea, Stan," Israel said at his level best.

"We got any bettah answers, son?" Stan asked. Then he started walking carefully towards the underground holding pit near the manure pile. "Lemme show you anothah thing whiles yer here. Careful there that you don' fall in. Damn grate cover's gone an' rusted out in that spot. Now here's our second mystery...see down theyah in the pit?"

"What is this area for, Stan?" Israel asked.

"It's the holdin' pit for excess manure and runoff in a stohm. But look close down theyah. See that dirty white thing? That's one of them stretchy bandages for when you bust up your ribs. So's I ask you...what the hell is one of

141

them stretchy things doin' down in my pit? How'd it git theyah? You got any ideas?"

"It certainly seems strange, Stan. I can see why you called the Public Safety Office. Is there any way to fish that thing out? Do you have a long pole? Or how about a ladder? I can climb down in there and collect the wrap as evidence," Israel offered.

"Makes sense to me. Let's go to the shed and we can rustle up a ladder for yah. Heh, heh," Stan began cackling. "Bet you didn' think you'd be crawlin' 'round in a shit pit when you signed up for St. Frewin's, didya?"

"All in a day's work, Stan. No problem at all," Israel assured him.

34
Tuesday, December 24
Afternoon

Jane and Israel sat down with the Overlocks at their worn and scarred dining table. Their large, open kitchen was scrubbed clean and minimal, lacking the homey clutter of many island farmhouse kitchens. Mrs. Overlock placed a photograph of Troy in the center of the table—Troy looking out at all of them with his hearty smile and biblical beard. "I just want him to be here in spirit while we're talking about him, Jane. If Troy was strong enough to tell you, I'm sure he'd appreciate the work you're doing to find his attacker," Mrs. Overlock said, her saddened eyes resting on her son's image.

"Mr. and Mrs. Overlock, I'm so sorry we're here at all—again. How are you doing?"

"It's damn quiet, for sure," Mr. Overlock said. "We just have to get on with it and hope for his recovery. Nothing else to do."

"Well, thank you for letting us come over to ask you a few more questions. We don't know yet what led to Troy's attack. Maybe you can help us," Jane said. "Did he seem tense or different in the days or weeks before he was beaten? Did he seem like he was keeping anything bottled up inside?"

"Troy seemed himself," Mrs. Overlock said. "As I look back, maybe he was on his walkie talkie a little more than usual, but that was probably because an unexpected bunch of boats arrived late in the season, at the end of

November. Troy had to organize getting them cleaned out, lined up for storage, and shrink-wrapped for the winter."

"Did you know that for a fact, Mrs. Overlock? Or did Troy just tell you that?" Israel asked.

"When you put it that way, it sounds so...so accusatory. I had no reason to question anything Troy was telling me. Why would I?"

"OK. Well, did Troy go anywhere or see anyone out of his ordinary routine?" Jane asked next.

Mr. Overlock shook his head. "Nope. Nothing struck us as unusual. And you have to remember, Troy is his own person, with a busy job. He has his own part of the house, and there's no need to keep tabs on him."

"So nothing comes to mind that was out of the ordinary," Jane thought aloud. Troy's parents shook their heads no. "You mentioned Troy on his walkie talkie. Would we be able to take a look at the walkie talkie?"

The Overlocks turned to one another and then to Jane and Israel. Mr. Overlock spoke. "You know, Jane. We never thought about the walkie talkie. I don't think we've come across it."

"And there's still no sign of his cell phone?" Jane said.

"Not at all," Mrs. Overlock confirmed. "If Troy didn't have his phone on him when you found him, I guess that is strange."

"Well, I'm wondering if Troy's attacker had a reason to dump both his phone and his walkie talkie. Or maybe they're stashed somewhere in your home? Would you mind if we looked around a bit."

Troy's mother massaged her worn and knuckled hands and looked at her husband. "OK for them to search, Frank?"

"Fine with me. Help yourself," said Mr. Overlock.

"And just one rather personal question before we take a look," Jane said. "Most of Troy's fellow workers mentioned that Troy's weight really bothered him. Was that an issue for him?"

"I guess I'd answer that by saying he hadn't learned yet to live with who he is," said Mr. Overlock. "He's a big man, and that's who he is in God's eyes. But I'm not sure Troy could accept that."

"Oh, Frank. You know it was hard on Troy. What's God got to do with it?" said Mrs. Overlock.

Jane didn't know what to say, and she realized saying nothing would go a long way. "OK...well, Israel and I will take a quick look around and then be going. Thank you again, and we're hoping the best for Troy."

....

"So, what did you think, Israel?" Jane asked when they were driving away after they had carried out a general search of the Overlock home and garage for Troy's phone and walkie talkie...Zilch.

"About the Overlocks?"

"Yes. Did they pass muster this time?"

"Sad and tired are the words that come to mind," said Israel.

"Hmm. Did you notice how they didn't have many questions for us, and they didn't seem very energized when they were answering ours? Pretty resigned to what happened to Troy...but is that natural? I'll have to think about that."

"They seemed to have two different takes on Troy's weight."

"They sure did. It is what it is, per the father. But the mother was more sensitive about the issue. I wonder...." Jane said.

"I almost forgot to tell you. Stan Helmstadt said Bernie Pushaw kept an eye on the cows when Stan and his wife were away that weekend."

"Really?" Jane shook her head. "Bernie again. He keeps cropping up, but he doesn't seem to know a thing lately. Nothing helpful. What is it with that guy? Is he dense, or is he lying?"

....

Mrs. Overlock sat looking off into the empty spaces of her kitchen. She and Mr. Overlock had stayed seated at the table after Jane and Israel left. "What are you thinking, Frank?"

"Nothing. Nothing at all. Why? Should I be thinking about something?" her husband said.

"No. No, you're fine. But I can't help feeling guilty. We haven't told anyone...about Troy's cash. Maybe we should say something. I know money is money. But what if all that money he has might have something to do with his beating? What then?"

"How can I answer that, Lorraine? Knowing why Troy got attacked is not going to heal his face overnight. Reporting the fact of the money isn't going to spring him out of the hospital any time soon."

"But what about justice, and punishing whoever went after our Troy?"

"What about it? That's not our job."

....

DON'T TOUCH MY COCKTAIL!

The Pushaw home telephone rang and rang until Bernie's recorded voice advised: "Leave a message. If it's very, very urgent, call me back when it isn't." Jane asked Bernie to call her, which he did several minutes later.

He always seemed to be in the thick of things. But cross his heart over the telephone, he had nothing to report on the weekend he looked after Stan's cows. In fact, he was offended that Jane acted as though he was not telling her the whole story. She gave him no details, and he stuck to his guns. "It's like they say, Jane. No good deed goes unpunished. Here I was doin' Stan and Frieda a big fayvah checkin' in on their farm, and now you're actin' like I was jumpin' around in their manure pile or somethin'. That's pointin' the fingah at me, Jane, without no grounds or nothin'."

Jane's ears caught the fast ball. "Wait a minute, Bernie. What about their manure pile? I didn't say anything to you about the manure pile."

"Ha! I'm jus' pullin' yer leg, Jane. Don't get so uptight. Maybe you need yuhself a little vacation," Bernie suggested. "Have a Merry Christmas. Get off the island and go shoppin' or see a movie."

35
Friday, December 27

Christmas blew in with more snow and was gone. And all Jane felt was emptiness. Emptiness...despite Trudy Moody's holiday pastiche clogging the PSO, and Jane's own chubby wreaths and strands of tiny white lights glowing round her house. Plus tres leches hot cocoa on Christmas Eve; and Mom, Dad, and Desdemona laughing over goofy gifts; and roasted apple cider and soy sauce pork with rice on Christmas Day, Nigella's Christmas pudding, and clove-studded oranges in bowls everywhere.

Mom's gift of a SpyGuy recorder pen for Jane was certainly unexpected. God knows how it would ever come in handy while Jane was measuring clams, chasing dogs, and keeping the peace. Nevertheless, she threw it into her hobo bag, just in case.

But her torpor of loneliness still smothered the tidings of comfort and joy. Because Konstantin was not there, stuck as he was in some Indonesian port while he wrapped up his latest inspection of an industrial fishing fleet. He was all Jane could think about when she wasn't obsessing about Troy's beating. Or why Storm had opined Konstantin was not her type. Or why Jerome Williams had no family photos on his desk at the boatyard. Or what Bernie Pushaw was not telling her about what he knew. It had been that kind of Christmas, and SAT phone calls with your lover were no substitute for a night-long embrace. Jane hoped getting back to work would feel better than trying to celebrate a hollow holiday.

DON'T TOUCH MY COCKTAIL!

....

Back in the office on Friday, Jane found solace in all the unanswered questions waiting for her. She picked up her phone. The boatyard might be open.

"Hi, Mr. Williams. Jane Roberts here. I have a few more questions I wanted to run by you." Jane could picture Jerry Baby at his desk, breathing in the stale male air and biting into Mr. Goodbar.

"That's fine, Jane," said Williams.

"This past fall, did you have an unusually large number of boats delivered in late November? And was Troy Overlock busy dealing with the intake?"

"Let me check our records here...OK, for late November, I'd say we had the usual stragglers showing up, but nothing noticeable...not a large number. And none in December."

"OK. Umm...Troy's parents mentioned his walkie talkie that he used for work. Has anyone found the walkie talkie at the boatyard since Troy's attack?"

"You're right. He does have a work walkie talkie. But nothing's been turned in, as far as I've heard."

"Well, I guess that's it, Mr. Williams. Thanks again, and if anyone happens to find Troy's phone or walkie talkie, please let me know."

Jane wanted to review this news with Mrs. Overlock. Not Mr. Overlock. He wasn't the book Jane needed to open. Mrs. Overlock was that book. But Jane didn't want to upset her either, didn't want to turn one page too many.

....

"Listen, Jane. I hear what you're saying about not many boats arriving in November. I'd like to come down to your

149

office, to talk more, if that's all right with you?" Lorraine Overlock gripped her telephone and hoped to God her husband wasn't about to walk into the house.

"You can definitely come over, Mrs. Overlock. I'll be waiting right here for you," Jane said, a tingling feeling telling her that some kind of break-through about what had happened to Troy was about to happen...finally, maybe?

....

Twenty minutes later, Mrs. Overlock was seated with Jane at the PSO table, a cup of tea in her hand. "He'd be really angry if he knew I came down, Jane, so please...not a word to my husband."

"I understand your need for this to be confidential, Mrs. Overlock. Right now, I don't know why we can't keep it that way. But if anything has to come out, I'll let you know first. That's the best I can offer."

"Well, I appreciate your frankness, Jane. I know things always end up in the open somehow, but for now, let's keep the lid on."

"OK," said Jane.

Lorraine Overlock let out her nervous breath. "I didn't bring the money with me. I left it where Frank hid it. And I can't say just where that is. But you need to know Troy has about five thousand dollars in cash, and we—his own parents—don't know where it came from."

"When did you find out?" Jane said. The ice was thawing....

"The day after Troy was attacked, and you came by to tell us in person, well, after you left, Frank went straight into Troy's room to look around for anything that might explain someone beating up our son. All Frank found was the money. And he hid it."

"So you knew about the hidden money when Israel and I returned to ask more questions the other day?"

"That's right, Jane."

"Have you asked Troy about the money, now that he can talk again?"

"Frank and I thought it would be better not to bring it up. Troy's in such a state. We figured talking about the money might upset him more. He's got to focus on getting stronger and better. He's got to heal, Jane."

"I understand. OK. Look, I'll keep all of this in my head. At least we now know Troy had money from somewhere. Do you have any idea what he was going to do with the money?"

"None at all, Jane. He didn't say a word to us about any of this."

"Well, I'll keep plugging away. We'll try to solve where the money came from, and whether it was linked to his beating."

"I hope everything I said here today will help to catch the attacker."

"It's important information, Mrs. Overlock. You definitely did the right thing...especially for Troy."

After Mrs. Overlock left the office, Jane went over to the whiteboard and added a dollar sign and question mark, $?, to Troy's column. She knew what she meant, and it probably would not attract attention.

PART TWO

36
Tuesday, New Year's Eve
Morning

"Yo, Jane, Sonny Mannix here. Sorry about all the static in the background. I'm calling you from the ferry—must be atmospheric conditions. A storm's coming in!" he yelled into his mic.

"That's fine, Sonny. Go ahead, I can hear you," Jane said. She leaned towards the window in her office to see the condition of the noon sky...one heavy gray lid, no sun in sight.

"Well, between the earlier boatload and this boatload, we've seen an awful lot of what I guess you might call Russian heavies and some sort of Black guys who look like gang types from out of state. Pretty strange traffic for a day like New Year's Eve, don't you think? Just thought you'd like to know," Sonny said.

"Sonny, come on. Why do I always end up lecturing you? Though in the one case, I'm actually interested to hear about the Russians, concerning something we're looking into. So tell me more about them. But about the so-called gang types you mentioned, you really have to be careful about racial profiling. Just because you have a bunch of Black people on your boat doesn't mean they're a gang. What prompts you to say that anyway? And what does 'sort of Black' mean?"

"Well, come down here and see for yourself, Jane. We're pulling in to St. Frewin's in about ten minutes. You be the judge. But right now, out here on the ocean, these guys I'm looking at are all wearing these fancy matching jackets with the name 'Forbidden Fruits' embroidered on them. And they keep whipping off those jackets and strutting around flexing their muscles at each other and talking in some kind of code. I guess that doesn't mean a thing necessarily, but when they started howling at the waves in unison, I just thought you might want to know. Hell, you're the Public Safety Officer, not me."

"Sonny, do you have even one politically correct bone in your body, let alone your brain? These antics you're describing, well, they sound like guys having crazy fun. Guys of a certain stripe just having fun out on the ocean. What if they were white guys? You'd probably chalk it up to frat boys and forget about it. And besides, what do you expect me to do? Race down to the ferry and grill them about their forbidden fruits? Whatever happened to America?—the land of the good and brotherhood...innocent until proven guilty? Give me a break."

"Up to you, Jane. It's just my good citizen BOLO for the day."

"OK...Never mind, I appreciate your report. Now tell me more about the Russians. How did they strike you? And how did you know they were Russian?"

"The Russians, Jane, were on the earlier ship. They spoke Russian, which is how I know. I know a little Russian, OK? And they all wore black balaclavas, which anyone will tell you was kind of intimidating, despite the cold weather. I mean we've got mothers and kids filling up the ferry and then all of a sudden, this swarm of foreign-talking guys who look like hit men comes stomping on board. And while I'm no expert, I was in the military, and I think I can tell when a guy is packing knives on him."

"How can you tell that?" Jane wondered.

"Meet me for drinks some afternoon when I'm off work, and I'll educate you, Jane. How's that?"

"Very funny. No thank you."

37
New Year's Eve
Midmorning

Samantha Lloyd's team descended through the snowy plains to Young's Neck midmorning, to begin setting up for the party at the Pratt estate. Driving along the white plowed road, the caterers could see the incongruous mansion ahead of them...a playful architectural igloo of icy glass cubes, anchored in snow and shot full of sun.

Samantha parked her catering trailer at a service entrance parking area outside the main kitchen, which was a glass cube unto itself. For the pig roast, the crew set up two motorized rotisseries on a canvas tarp covered with sand on a patio area located through a breezeway on the other side of the kitchen. The crew carried the pigs, a metal tub, bags of ice, and a work table to the patio. Bales of hay were stacked to provide outside seating for curious guests. Chanson wanted to present any interested guests with the unusual cultural experience of watching how pork was roasted on an open spit...in Maine...in winter.

"Now, Hamidi, Torrance, Grace, India, Cora...and OK, there's Bernie Pushaw," said Samantha.

"Hey there, Sam, ladies, gent," Bernie greeted everyone as he sashayed into the kitchen, while cracking his wide, minty-smelling smile and snapping his hand in a sharp salute. "Glad to be on board. Any time."

Sam looked at Bernie, their Local Hero. She reluctantly saluted back at him, slightly annoyed and feeling like she was his anointed baby-sitter. He would have been better off attending a marathon Alcoholics Anonymous all-nighter, instead of this tanked-up bacchanal. But his wife Noreen didn't want him to miss out on the fun, and she hoped keeping Bernie busy would be a good alternative approach.

"Thank you all for pitching in," Sam began. "We're short on staff with all the parties on the island tonight, so I really appreciate your help. I've also hired some Cypriot workers from the Party Hearty company to help as waiters. They should be arriving later on, and Hamidi Louca will be in charge of translating for those people, as necessary."

"Sam, sorry to interrupt. But will we also clean up at the end of the party?" Grace Cleveland asked.

"If you want to stay to work on that, Grace, you'll be paid. But Chanson has hired another group who will assist with breaking down the party, so we should be all set," Sam told them.

"So," Sam continued, "remember our goals at all times. Perfect orchestration down to the last detail. Nobody gets aggravated. Don't argue with the guests. Keep things tidy. No nibbling when no one's looking. Polite deference and congeniality towards everyone. If you run into any problems, let me know. Got that?"

"Sam, I don't mean to be a whiner, but every party has its skirt-chasers and guys trying to pinch our butts...how do you want us to handle that sort of behavior?" India asked.

"If you feel harassed, come right back to the kitchen and arrange for one of the male servers to trade places with you. Or let me know and I'll do the reassignment. Don't stick around in an uncomfortable situation."

Samantha looked for other questions, but there were none.

"OK. During the course of the party, some of you will haul food and fixings from the catering trailer into the kitchen here. Some of you will finalize the side dishes. We'll arrange platters of appetizers and circulate at 10 PM to serve them to guests...and then another pass with appetizers at 10:30 PM.

"After the appetizers, we'll pull together the roast pork and side dishes and set them up on the tables in the gathering room and the dining room. Guests will be eating buffet style starting around 11:30 PM, so we don't have to worry about sit-down service. As long as we have food, let's keep bringing it out until midnight. And if you need the bathroom, there's one to the left over there, off to the side of the kitchen."

Sam looked around at her audience to try and remember if she was forgetting anything. "Oh, FYI, Chanson said her husband, Salem, would step in, now and then, to help us tend the fire and babysit the roasting pigs during the afternoon and early evening. After the meat is done and has rested for thirty minutes, Salem will help us carve it up.

"Bernie, your wife, Noreen, has already volunteered you to assist with the pigs. So, Cora and Bernie, you can help Hamidi fire up the coals, organize the pigs on the rotisseries, and start the basting. Torrance, if you could help them set up and then switch later on to serving appetizers, that would be great. And remember, this roast pork is the heart of Chanson's party tonight, so let's do our best! Thank you."

"What's on the menu, Sam, besides roast pork?" asked Cora.

"OK...tonight we'll be serving Chanson's favorite Texas appetizers—Texas Rattlesnake Bites, Armadillo Eggs, and Chicken Enchilada Puffs. Nathan Herinton and some of his friends will man the bar, which is in the gathering room. Lots of margaritas and tequila sunrises on tap there. And champagne, of course. For side dishes, there's white rice, black-eyed peas, collard greens, coleslaw, and corn bread. And for dessert, grapefruit pot de crème, chocolate bourbon pecan pie, and churros. "

Everyone was nodding and sighing enthusiastically. A great menu!

"In case anyone asks you, the Texas Rattlesnake Bites are battered and deep-fried cheese and jalapeño balls. And the Armadillo Eggs are baked cheese, pepper, and sausage balls. So," Sam said, "let's get started with the pigs and the appetizer prep and we'll continue from there."

38
New Year's Eve
Midafternoon

Once the coals in the rotisserie fuel pans had turned gray and were hot and quiet, Hamidi and Torrance pulled the thick tarp off the long metal tub, filled with a million ice cubes and two pigs. They lifted out the first pig and put it on the prep table. Sam had already rubbed each pig with salt and pepper, stuffed the main cavity with herbs, oranges and a few onions, and sewn the skin closed for the roasting.

"OK, Cora and Bernie," Hamidi began, "we're going to need you to help us skewer the pigs on the spit rods and secure them with spikes. Come on over here and I'll show you what we do."

"Oh, Jesus," Bernie started to stumble and sob. "I don' know if I got the stomach for all this torture, Hamidi. Even if it is legal an' edible, you're still rammin' spikes through these little piggies. Please don' tell Noreen or Sam...but maybe I can just sort of keep watch for you guys?"

"That's fine. Look away and keep an eye on the coals," said Hamidi. He eyed Torrance with a glance that silently asked "Has Bernie had one too many already?"

Once the pigs were securely loaded on the spit rods over the hot coals, Hamidi and Torrance covered the pig ears with big flaps of folded foil to prevent them from burning. They then turned on the automatic rotisserie motors to begin the rotation process. Cora stood at the prep table, ready with large vats of basting juices—one pig would be slathered with a Texan barbecue sauce; the other, with a Cuban-style mojo sauce.

Try as he might, it was too tempting for Bernie to avoid sneaking a look at the pigs and the ordeal they were undergoing. He hesitatingly joined Cora to stare at the mesmerizing turning of the forms...on their uneasy, magical transformation from pig to pork.

Heading back to the kitchen to continue with prep, Torrance could see tears running down Bernie's face. Was he looking at the shrinking, darkening bodies and feeling horror...or was he sensing the ancient echo of primitive hunger?

Bernie could no longer contain himself. "I can't help it. All I keep seein' is two little dead Won Tons. And why in God's name did you go stickin' those flying saucers on either side of their heads? It's makin' me sick and heart-brokin'!"

Cora was leaning toward Pig #1 and carefully basting it with the mojo sauce. "What are you talking about, Bernie? Those are pig ears wrapped in foil...to keep them from burning and making a mess."

"But you remember Won Ton, don't you, Cora? He was Jason Coombs' pit bull who drowned in the ocean last year. Poor little guy—came bobbin' up all bloated and pale...lookin' a lot like these little doggies here in front of us, 'cept they're all crucified and gettin' fried right under our noses. It's too sad. I can't take this."

Cora switched to the Texan barbecue sauce and was swabbing it generously over Pig #2.

"God, just look at what you're doin', Cora, puttin' all that soupy stuff all over that porker. Looks jus' like Jason when he had to dump tomato juice all over little Won Ton after he got skunked in the woods."

"Bernie, maybe it would help you to stop thinking about Won Ton right now," Cora suggested. "Maybe you should take a break. I bet Won Ton would want you to do that, don't you think?"

"You know, Cora, after Jason fished his poor pup outta the ocean and we buried him good, we was both so stricken, we hadda figure out how to honor poor Won Ton. I mean dog is man's best friend, and Jason's dog was dead, right? So Jason took to wearin' Won Ton's State o' Maine dog tag on his neck, and me, well I had to stand by Jason...show 'im support, you know?"

"So what did you do to show your support?" asked Cora.

"Me? Well I wore that little rascal's rabies tag...."

Bernie suddenly started growling low and pawing the air in front of Cora's face. "GRRRR!!!! RRRaaaa...GRRRrrrrr!!!! Heh, heh...fooled yah there, didn' I, Cora? But I gotta tell yah...wearin' Won Ton's dog tags sure did help us get through the dark times, if you know what I mean."

Cora gazed back at Bernie. She was totally unfazed. Bernie looked away and began wiping his tears. "I'm gonna take a break now. It might be a liquid break at the bar they're settin' up, but I'll be back," and Bernie sauntered away.

39
New Year's Eve
Near Dusk

ZK made a slow turn into the Grand Harbor Inn so all
three of them in the car—Zen-Ti, ZM, and ZK, the
Forbidden Fruits trio—could get a drive-by glimpse of the
beautiful old establishment. They had spent the late
afternoon cruising around the island and chatting it up
with the few owners of stores and cafes that were about
to close up shop for the winter.

ZM remarked how nice the Mainers seemed. Zen-Ti
took a more cynical stance. "Of course these Maine folks
are nice to you, Ding Bat. That's because they're all sitting
here like one big bag of white flour, and you come along
and you're this EX-O-TIQUE chunk of brown sugar in
soy sauce to them for about five minutes. And then they
assume you're going to head back home where you come
from, or maybe get hauled off to the one-way hotel.
Because basically they see you as Black Asian and there
isn't anything you can do to change that."

"Well," countered ZM, "you've got to start somewhere
with good people."

"Look, Zen-Mo" said Zen-Ti, "the US of A has been
trying to change things since Abraham Lincoln. That's 250
years ago, ZM. You think you're going to make a
difference after five hours in Maine?? Go smoke that,
Bro."

"Yah, but Zen-Ti, did you see how short they are on
everything? They don't have any hot sauce on this island

is my for instance to you. Except for that Indian curry joint. Hell, I could open up a little Oriental bodega and make a killing!"

"What makes you think they want your Sichuan hot sauce, Boy?" ZK threw in his two cents. "Are you trying to save the white man from his own grub?"

"Ah, you bad guys. Just let me smoke my own dream pipe, that's all," said ZM. "And why don't you run down tonight's plan for us again, Zen-Ti, so we remember what we've got to do."

"OK...As you all know, this is no 'shoot and scoot.' We're just here to shake things up a bit."

"Details, man, details," urged ZK.

"So, tonight we're doing a hubby snatch—grab and go. Once we dump him in the car, that's it. Pure and simple," Zen-Ti explained. "I'll give you the signal when the time's right. We'll be looking for Salem Pratt, the man of the house in his silver and gold striped jacket...."

"But why do we have the blonde wig and the female gang getup if this is just a hubby snatch?" ZM asked.

Zen-Ti took on a professorial air. "ZM, every operation's got to have a Plan B, besides a Plan A. Don't you know that by now, Bro?"

They were chuckling as they slowed down to take a closer look at the Inn's front façade, when Zen-Ti suddenly hissed, "Get down, Zen-Kan! Get us out of here pronto!"

ZK did as he was told. Back on the main road, everyone glommed on to Zen-Ti with the same question. What just happened back there?

"Well Boys, looks like Plan B has popped into first place. God damn! Keep driving ZK and put some tar between us and that Inn."

"You have to tell us what you're talking about, Zen-Ti. You need us. And we need to know," ZM complained. ZK started grumbling as well.

"Hey! Kill that noise, and cut the crazy bad. I need you to be sweet bad. I just saw Ray Bun and what looks like a couple of his dudes through the big front window of that Inn. You know Ray...he's that diesel from Revere. Looks like they may be staying at that Inn. Sure living large. And I'd say how can that be, except Tony Abanditono called me about this guy a few weeks ago. They're here for real. Which means there may be trouble at our party tonight. So, listen up. We've got to pow-wow right now."

40
New Year's Eve
Evening

Samantha was beginning to feel that whirligig dizziness in her head...everything about food happening at once, topped by a thousand questions. "Hamidi, any sign yet of our Cypriot waiters? Oh, they're trooping in right now. OK. Great! Torrance, how are the pigs doing? And do you think Bernie's avoiding the booze...or at least enough not to ruin the pigs?"

Torrance gave Sam a half-hearted look. "I left Cora basting the pork, Sam. I'll go back and see how she's doing. I think Bernie wandered off somewhere. I don't mean to badmouth him, Sam. But he's not the most reliable pig roaster I've ever seen. He was about to lick one of the pigs when I caught him in the act and barked at him. That's when he wandered off."

"Oh, he is such a guaranteed fuck wad. Is there even one wave left in his brain? But never mind...let's get the Cypriots in here so we can start them on plating the appetizers."

....

The island taxi had deposited three Cypriot men at Chanson and Salem's service entry. As they were walking towards the kitchen door, four other men in white jackets and black pants stepped out of the darkness, dropped their cigarettes to the ground to grind them out with their shoes, and then joined the Cypriots as if joining the work party. The men in the white jackets signaled hello to the Cypriots and entered with them through the kitchen door.

Hamidi looked up. In Greek he said, "Come in, come in. What have we here? You're the guys from Party Hearty, right?" The Cypriots all nodded. Hamidi looked at the other four waiters in white jackets. "Who are these guys?"

The Cypriots shrugged. What did they know? They didn't know anything. One of them guessed. "They're waiters, too?"

"OK, OK, maybe too many waiters, but that's fine," Hamidi said. And to Sam, he explained that Party Hearty had apparently sent more help than needed, but he would square it away with the company next week. It was too dark and too cold to turn away the extra guys right now, and it looked like Chanson had an overflow of guests, so the added hands would work out well.

Sam agreed, welcomed her expanded crew inside, and started to explain their appetizer tasks, with Hamidi translating. Sam noticed signs of a lack of comprehension on the faces of the white jackets. She asked them if everything was all right. They began mumbling and said something about Russian.

Sam took a hard look at the white jackets. She realized they did not look like the three Cypriots. She sputtered an exasperated expletive and thought about grabbing a drink. She strode over to the western patio and stuck her head out the door. She braced herself in the cold air. "Torrance! Could you please come help...I think we need a Russian translator."

Torrance reappeared inside the kitchen and looked at the crowd that had gathered since she had gone to check on the pig. Sam spoke to Torrance. "Tell them we'll need them to serve the appetizers and prep the food. See if they comprehend any of that."

Torrance translated at Sam's directions. The white jackets started laughing and nodding yes with their heads. "OK, Sam. I can handle these guys...they're Russian. Not to worry."

But Torrance was worried. She didn't let on, but she was 110% certain one of the waiters was the mysterious Spartak who had appeared at the Public Safety Office. If he recognized Torrance, he didn't show it. And she thought the other three Russians looked familiar too, from the hook-up at Buddy's. None of them seemed to realize who she was. Torrance credited the short red-haired wig and fishnet stockings she had donned for that crazy gathering of partly fake Lobster Brides!

The white jackets began a quiet, but heated discussion among themselves. Torrance quietly moved over to prep some food trays near them while trying to eavesdrop on their conversation. One of them was growling about having to act like waiters when they should concentrate on kidnapping the "Rhinestone Cowboy" and then get the hell out of there. Torrance casually walked back towards Sam and signaled with her eyes that they should head to the side passageway.

Out in the hallway, Torrance alerted Sam to the situation. "I've just overheard the Russian waiters talking about how they're supposed to kidnap the 'Rhinestone Cowboy.' What do you think they mean, Sam? Should we find Jane and report it to her? She's been concerned about other inexplicable Russian activity on the island these past few weeks."

"Torrance! Did you see the mob out there? We're getting swamped by a hundred guests who are blowing in from the cold and Texas—starving for food and booze. We cannot let Chanson down. You're going to march right back into that kitchen with me and translate my every last syllable. Come on. Let's go!"

Sam lit into the waiter crew. "I don't care if you're Russian operatives, Latvian mafia, or Chechen gangsters!" Sam's long hair came undone with her outburst. Before she clipped it back in place, she began running her hands through her hair and making fists at the waiters with clumps of hair in her hands. "I don't care if you're here to grab the Rhinestone Cowboy, the Lone Ranger, Daniel Boone, or whoever. I don't give a damn if you want to bring down the entire United States Government! Just not on my watch!"

Torrance was about to slam Sam's comments back at the white jackets in their native tongue. But she paused a wise moment and chose a softer touch without clearing it with Sam. In Russian, Torrance explained, "Sam the head caterer appreciates very much that you are here to kidnap the Rhinestone Cowboy. She also encourages you to chase after Beyoncé and Taylor Swift while you're in America. But she would greatly appreciate your help with the catering tonight, and as thanks, she will pack up two bags of delicious food for you to take on your journey." The Russians' eyes grew wide in amazement.

"Now let's heat up these fucking Texas Rattlesnake Bites," Sam grabbed one and shook it at the Russians, "and these shitty Armadillo Eggs." She grabbed one of those and shoved it towards the men. "And then you're marching out into that party and serve them to the guests. No more questions!"

DON'T TOUCH MY COCKTAIL!

Hamidi, meanwhile, was doing his best to translate the relevant information to the Cypriots, which resulted in a kind of chaotic United Nations of the Kitchen. Everyone was chattering away in three different languages, when one of the Russians actually tried to complain to Sam. Torrance translated. "Sam, he says if they don't do what their big boss told them to do, they will get killed. They are expendable."

"Expendable?! I'll give them EXPENDABLE!" Sam had that telling murderous caterer look in her eyes. "Torrance, you warn them. If they don't do as I TELL THEM...I'll...I'll, OH, FOR CRYING OUT LOUD. Really, what am I trying to accomplish here? Forget about it. Just forget it! We're going to IGNORE them."

41
Public Safety Office
New Year's Eve—Earlier That Day
2:30 PM

Jane stretched her arms wide and rippled her spine where she sat. She looked out her office window. She looked through her door to the main room of the PSO. Yup. Sheer being and nothingness all right. It was time to face facts. Her career was moldering...nothing brilliant in sight...no X Factor...all the Zs had fallen off her pizazz.

Granted, she was juggling a few juicy morsels—like slowly pulling the curtain to reveal Troy's attacker, and writing out her grocery list. Ha ha!! Plus, who knows what criminal undercurrents were luring the FBI and the CIA to St. Frewin's Island. And thanks to Sonny Mannix and the State ferry, as of late morning, it sounded like urban and Slavic troops were storming the island with fruits and nuts.

But still...she would talk it over with Helen and Israel. There had to be something they could do to shake things up, make their office world sizzle in the new year.

Her intercom abruptly buzzed to life. "Jane, hard to believe, but I've got the FBI on hold for you," Helen said.

"That's amazing, Helen. Maybe they're calling to give me a clue," Jane snickered as she punched in the call. "Hello, Jane Roberts here."

"Officer Roberts—Jane Roberts. This is Alex Champus from the FBI. Do you have a few minutes? I wanted to expand on our recent communication and discuss some cooperative measures with you."

"My goodness, Mr. Champus. Nice to hear from you. We definitely have time to talk. I'm just sitting here counting the waves go by...." Jane faked a cheesy grin on her face and bobbled her head back and forth.

"Great. I'll give you a rundown on our operation and then maybe we can agree on a plan. FYI, I interface with and straddle both HSI and ERO...."

Jane heard a string of letters rattle around in her head as he droned on. She gripped her desk and nearly fainted. "Whoa there, Mr. Champus. Where you're concerned, do I need to be concerned? I mean about the meaning...of all those acronyms you're, well, as you say, *straddling?*"

"Ah, right. Well, OK. FYI means For Your Information."

"Really now, Mr. Champus. Are we straddling or *sneering?*" Jane said. She took a peek a boo stance and threw her imaginary Champus a check hook.

"Let me continue, if you don't mind. HSI stands for Homeland Security Investigations and ERO stands for Enforcement and Removal Operations...." Once again, Jane could feel a flood of capital letters washing over her.

"...at the CIA, which—God help you, Jane—means Central Intelligence Agency. Are we ready to move on now?"

Jane fanned herself hard and tried to bite her tongue. "OK. I think I've got it. You are focusing on a security investigation. You are an enforcer who shanghais crooks by their nuts and chucks them to the ends of the earth. With some central intelligence sprinkled on top. How am I doing?"

"Irreverent, Ms. Roberts. Rather irreverent. Will that interfere with our working together?" Champus asked.

"Relax, Mr. Champus. Let me know what you have in mind, and I'll let you know if I can handle it." Jane snatched a pen off her desk and aimed it at her grocery list with a rollicking flourish.

"Very well. ICE, the FBI, and the CIA are cooperating on a combined operation on St. Frewin's. Our debarkation is scheduled to commence at approximately zero zero zero zero hours tonight." Jane scribbled madly. Champus poured it on. "Ground zero is the Pratt residence on Young's Point."

"Are you serious?!" Jane yelped in half. "Salem and Chanson? You're not saying they're zeros, are you?"

"Ms. Roberts, the less flippancy, the better. Now, listen up. This is where you come in. If willing and able, you will be our scout in a pre-mission reconnaissance and surveillance platform. With insertion at approximately twenty-two hundred hours. Actual stealth will not be necessary. The engagement criteria will be the least possible."

"What the...?!" Jane balked and watched her head topple off and roll around on her desk. "What are you saying, Champus? Give it to me in layman's terms, for God's sake."

"Look, Jane," Champus fumed. "What don't you understand?" She could hear his molars colliding.

"How about NONE of it? How about you drop the constipated jargon and talk to me like you're a human being? Remember, I'm just a little old Public Safety Officer on a podunk island."

"That's absurd. But I'll give it a shot. You are going to head to the Pratts' God damn party and keep a sharp eye on everybody for us, without looking like you're anybody but a party-goer, starting at 10 PM. So wear a fucking evening gown—no uniform. Be discreet. No need to introduce yourself. Keep it down to one drink—no falling into your cups. And don't get caught up in yackety-yack-yack with anyone. NOT allowed. If anything strikes you as *unusual behavior* for a New Year's Eve party, keep a log and call it in to us at twenty-three forty-five hours...sorry, eleven forty-five PM tonight."

"And your number?" Jane said.

"Got paper and pencil?" Champus asked.

"HOOAH!" Jane threw her arms up in the air and let out a shriek.

"What was that?"

"Nothing," Jane said.

"OK...Take this down...TOO ZE RO TOO, NIN ER FIFE AIT, SIX TREE WUN FOW ER."

"Say again," Jane said.

"Damn it, Jane. I said (202) 958-6314."

"10-4."

"So, the FBI is counting on you to help KEEP AMERICA SAFE, Jane," Champus said, tightly boxing his words.

She grabbed her imaginary slingshot and marbles. "Not so fast, Alphabet Boy. About that 'fucking' evening gown...."

"What about it?"

"I don't own an evening gown."

"Then improvise. That's part of your assignment."

"Can't I expense one on the federal budget?"

"Never overburden the taxpayers' dollars, Jane."

"For crying out loud, Champus. You waltz into my phone and shamelessly nudge me into becoming your Jane Wayne at the last minute. And you can't squeeze a little dough out of the Feds for a party dress?"

"Jane, we're not here to pass out beans and bullets to just anyone."

"Wait a second...I heard ICE has eight billion dollars to throw around. The FBI must have billions more. You could even pay someone official to provide surveillance. Why me?"

"We heard you were cheap and easy. Anyway, I've got to go now, Jane. The White House is on the other line."

....

"Sam," Chanson Pratt was calling her name from the hallway. "There's a call for you from Jane Roberts down at the PSO. Can you talk?"

Sam picked up the Pratts' kitchen phone. "Wait, slow down, Jane. I think I understand you. You need to attend the Pratt party to provide some low-keyed law enforcement presence...new regulations? Well, sure, I'll let Chanson know so she's not surprised when you show up. And what? You need one of my evening gowns? For Chrissakes, Jane, I'm in the middle of prepping Chanson's food. OK, OK. Just go in my closet in the spare bedroom and take whatever you need. ...if the door is locked? Well ring up Nathan Herinton and he'll let you in. Yes, he'll be happy to. ...Look, Jane. He's a good guy. Let up on him already. What? ...Don't be ridiculous. I can't do a thing about the fact that my bust is bigger than yours. Just try everything on and use the one that fits best. Right. Right. Look. I've got to go. Good Luck. See you when I see you!" Sam hung up the phone.

DON'T TOUCH MY COCKTAIL!

....

Deep inside the swanky side of Sam's closet, Jane swished through drycleaner bags protecting her friend's collection of gowns. So many pastels, too much summer, a few sequin numbers, but nothing that caught Jane's eye. Until she raised the leather dress off the closet bar and held it in the light. Wow. Black, long, racy, spaghetti straps...perfect for a vampire's girlfriend. Perfect for the cheap and easy (hiss!) Jayne Wayne, who was out to tell the world she despised authority, enforcement, official lingo, and all its turkey dressing. That did it. Jane grabbed the gown and took off.

42
New Year's Eve Party
9:45 PM

"Oh my god...," Trudy Moody announced as her eyes bounced like super balls inside the Pratts' vast, angular palace, where small random apertures interrupted broad, stark white sweeps of cliffs defining the interior space.

"I swear to you, Frieda, this is what happens when you let some professional hotshots go hog wild with rulers and protractors and a load o' drywall. The more you pay, the worse it gets. Look at this living room, if that's what they're callin' it. It does not say 'St. Frewin's Island and New England' to me. It does not say 'Welcome Home, Honey.' I mean, really, would you want to relax in this, this...flossy, glassy WAREHOUSE...after a hard day at work?"

Trudy Moody and Frieda Helmstadt had arrived at the Pratt's New Year's Eve party slightly before right on the dot—9:45 PM—before any other guests were in sight. They were touring the main living room while their husbands wandered off to look for holiday spirits.

Trudy's head swiveled atop her neck to take in the hard surfaces and the starkness. "Look at all this white, and all these windows. Since when did just one nice picture window go out of style? This whole place is a picture window every which way you look. I tell you, it must let in way too much sunlight during the day. Can you imagine all that sunlight? Especially now during the winter?"

"Trudy, you are so full of it. And don't be so loud. Chanson might hear you," Frieda shushed.

"But Frieda, you walk through this room on a sunny day in January, and you're liable to go blind and get skin cancer all at once! But if these people can pay someone to come up with a house that looks like they're livin' inside a three-story, see-through filing cabinet, they can probably afford to pay the doctor to get rid of their cancer."

"I wouldn't go that far, Trudy," Frieda countered. "It's all so refreshing in a way...I like the light and space. An exciting change from your typical low ceilings and small ordinary windows."

"God almighty, is that supposed to be furniture?" Trudy was appalled. "Those couches look like a bunch of giant white Chiclets! How can you sit on them things without fallin' right off at the same time? You know...I am sorry. But this place is not my idea of comfy...."

....

At 10:15 PM, Chanson and Salem stationed themselves in their front hallway to greet their guests as they entered. Chanson's fluid cerise gown rippled over her trim torso at the slightest breeze. Salem wore his silver and gold striped tuxedo as anticipated. "So good to see you, Maggie," Chanson bubbled as she shook hands with Maggie Banner from the Grand Harbor Inn. "And this charming young man?"

"Yes, Chanson, this is Ryan Young, my loan officer from Abenaki County Bank." To Ryan, Maggie said, "This is Chanson's husband, Salem." And to the Pratts, she added, "We're really looking forward to your pig roast. It's all I've heard about for days around the island."

"Well, we wanted to share a bit of Texas with you tonight. So do enjoy!" Maggie and Ryan moved forward into the party and Chanson welcomed her next troop of guests.

"Winnifred, so glad you and Kenmore could make it tonight. And I see you have with you Wilton and Diane Savoy...Hello, welcome to our home!" Chanson never skipped a beat. Neither did Diane Savoy. Wilton turned his head away from both of them.

Winnifred Billings bringing *both* of the Savoys along to the party was news to Chanson. Should she be peeved? But who cared if the Savoys were here together. Who gave a hoot, honestly? So what if she, Chanson, was getting laid by Wilton—frequently. It had no bearing on this New Year's Eve party, or anything, for that matter. And Chanson got a nasty satisfaction from seeing Diane's face as cracked and weathered as an old cowboy boot. She knew Diane and Wilton shared the same bed. But really, how could Wilton bear to wake up each day with that wrinkled snakeskin inches from his face? And what was Winnifred saying just now? Winnifred invited Diane Savoy along because Winnifred and Diane go way back...sorority sisters or something? With this next guest, Harriet Buxton, as well? All three of them in the same sorority...or so Winnifred was explaining....

"And this is—Oh, yes, Harriet Buxton of the Maine State Police. How wonderful you could attend," Chanson welcomed her. "You know I think Officer Jane Roberts will be here tonight, so be sure to keep your eye out for her."

Chanson patted herself on the back for not jumping out of her own skin. She could not believe she was finally face to face with the infamous Harriet Buxton...the

DON'T TOUCH MY COCKTAIL!

Director of Human Resources at the Maine State Police. Harriet was the one who had insisted on appearing in J. T. Karl's Wild Open upcoming spring catalog if Chanson's dear friend Zara Billings was going to be featured as the main model.

Poor Zara, no longer living on St. Frewin's Island...now stuck in State prison for the recent death of her husband, Kendall Billings. Kendall died under suspicious circumstances during the course of the investigation of the recent Ruth Farrow murder. And Zara was now a poster wife for when marriage went sour, and the wife went shopping...for fentanyl.

But Zara was not festering! As a Director of J. T. Karl's Wild Open, Chanson Pratt had convinced Wilton Savoy, the marketing director, to snatch Zara up to become the face for a new line of prison-inspired clothing. And to Chanson's relief, J. T. Karl's Wild Open was showcasing Zara in the catalog, which meant she was being pampered in prison so she could keep up her ravishing good looks.

But that Harriet Buxton! To think she had dared to threaten J. T. Karl's Wild Open with income tax review if the company did not put her in the catalog as well. All due to prison inmates, such as Zara, falling under Harriet Buxton's jurisdiction as the Director of Human Resources for the Maine State Police. The gall of that woman.

Chanson wondered if Harriet had made the connection...that she and Chanson had spoken, that Chanson was on J. T. Karl's board. That Chanson had advocated for Zara. It did not look like it. But one never knew. These old goats could be pretty cagey and poker-faced. Chanson heaved her chest. She could not wait for this night to be over and it had hardly begun.

179

Chanson turned next to the gentleman at Winnifred's side. "Are you going to introduce us, Winnifred?"

"Oh, my dear, yes. This is Lieutenant Joseph Adderley also of the Maine State Police. He lost his wife this past fall, and we thought it might be good for him to get out of the house. Good to be with people on New Year's Eve here on St. Frewin's Island with the rest of us." Mrs. Billings smiled warmly at the Lieutenant. She had taken a shine to the Lieutenant over the past summer, ever since he had handled the investigation of the death of her son, Kendall Billings.

Chanson smiled back at them all. "Well, Salem and I want you to make yourselves at home and have a wonderful evening. The bartenders are straight ahead in the gathering room, and you'll find waiters just about everywhere armed with trays of Texas appetizers. Please party up!"

Chanson leaned against her husband. "Great to see our islanders here tonight. And enough law enforcement to boot. But what about all our Texans...do you think they'll make it in time? Any update on their flight?"

"Yes," Salem said. "I got a call from Hitch a half hour ago. They landed earlier today and wanted to prowl around Freeport first. He should be arriving any time now with the other cowboys and cowgirls. But you know, Chanson, Hitch started to launch into some questions about the Environmental Fields outfit here and did I know anything about the place. Seemed strange to me, his sudden interest in a septage recycling operation. Not sure what that was all about. But don't worry about a thing, Honey. You always get a good turnout."

....

DON'T TOUCH MY COCKTAIL!

The mainland ferry terminal lights began blinking to signal closing time for the passenger waiting room. The boats would continue to run their holiday special schedule until 3:00 AM, but at 10:15 PM this New Year's Eve night, it would soon be lights out in the waiting room where the computers for public use were located. Geneva Pratt rushed to finish her transactions. A few more account numbers, a few more clicks, and The Phantom concluded the precious metals liquidation she had plotted out since the night she had dragged home the garbage bags of gold. Basking in the glow of salvation, she could hardly believe it herself. It would be her secret—her eternal secret. She winked to no one in particular. She winked to herself.

43
New Year's Eve Party
10:30 PM

India made a point of stopping by the roasting headquarters to see how Cora was holding up. India could hear the sizzling sounds of burning fat, and she saw and smelled the dense, smoky haze of charred meat and cracklings thickening the air of the patio. "God, Cora. Look at you in the hot fat zone! How can you stand watching these carcasses go round and round?" India puckered up her face at the pig pyre.

"Oh, it's not that bad," Cora said. "The turning of the meat is kind of like the ocean tide...sort of hypnotic and soothing...repetitive. Doesn't really bother me." She dunked her basting brush into the mojo sauce and swiped zig zags down the pig skin. "How about you, India? Appetizers still going strong?"

India looked through the glass expanse at the throngs of partiers. "They've got the usuals in there tonight...islanders and summer people gobbling everything off our trays. And then there's this bunch from Texas...they seem to be watching what they eat. Lots of tummy control going on."

While the women were conversing, Cora noticed a waiter quietly approaching India from behind. India in turn could see a white-jacketed man walking towards Cora. As the men moved closer, both women looked at the men and then at one another. In an instant, the emotions surrounding the quartet began crackling like the fat dripping from the pigs and hissing on the hot coals below. India could not believe this was happening. The Russians were here. And they recognized both women.

"Injun, Injun! I can't beleef it is you!" Spartak was calling out with glee, his grin so wide, it devoured both his ears. "It is Spartak. Remember your Spartak...from Buddy Bar party? How is your woo-woo box, Injun?"

India braced herself. She looked at Spartak. His enthusiasm did seem genuine, and he really was adorable in a foreign greaser kind of way. But what to do about him? About the Russians? Here and now? This was going to take some quick thinking. She hesitated to answer, to give herself enough time to come up with the perfect response.

Meanwhile, Cora could hear Dimitri cooing into her ear "Hey, Sexy Lady. You still want take bath with Dimitri in hot vodka and potatoes? Maybe we go find bath tub in beeg house here? Never too late!"

And then it came to India. "Oh, we thank the Russian Orthodox God that you two are here!" she exclaimed enthusiastically. "Can you please help us finish the final, hardest part of roasting the pigs?" She contorted her face into a beseeching look.

"Peeg?" said Dimitri with a broad smile. "We know peeg...we do peeg in Russia. No prublum." He and Spartak immediately stepped closer to the rotisseries to study the pigs...and smell the basting sauces.

Cora took up her basting tool again and was dipping into the thick Texas barbecue sauce when Spartak gently stopped her hand. "No, no bbq...no bbq. Too theek. Won't walk into peeg. Need this one," he said, pointing to the thinner mojo sauce. "Thees good. Thees one walk into peeg and make eet sing. Very good, da singing peeg."

India sidled over to Cora and leaned in closely to murmur, "Just go along with them, Cora. Do what they say as far as the pigs. We've got to keep them busy until I can find Jane." As she walked away, India assured the Russians, "I'll be right back!"

Bernie was busy fetching and feeding new briquettes into the burning coals, along the sides of the roasting trays. He acted like he was oblivious to the Russians' presence, and he kept his head down, but he listened as intently as an inebriated individual could. And what he overheard jerked him into high gear. Bernie's brain was shouting out "Holy Shit!" Because every time one of the Commies got a little spark on him from the pig fire, he yelled out "PIZ DETS."

PIZ DETS! "*Well, Hello Professor Pushaw,*" Bernie was telling himself. He knew a PIZ DET when he heard one, and he had heard more than a couple of them already this winter. Like on his God damn walkie talkie that night he had to rush down to the boatyard for that weirdo shit pick-up. PIZ DETS his ass. He had been an idiot for thinking it was Jason talking about a PIZZA DIET. Fuck that. If these Commies recognized Bernie now, they would grab him in no time. And what about Bernie's gold? Secret Agent Woman had gone and run off with half of it. Bernie didn't need any Commies coming for his other half. Bernie knew he was standing next to some Deep Shit. And Jane Roberts needed to know what was going on.

As India walked past Salem, who was hurrying over to help with the pigs, she asked quietly if he had seen Jane Roberts tonight. Salem had not, so India headed away from the kitchen to enter through a separate passageway.

DON'T TOUCH MY COCKTAIL!

She could not afford scowls from Samantha. India knew she had to find Jane.

....

Bernie ducked around the scurrying bodies and trays of food in the kitchen and finally found a scratch pad on a far countertop. He grabbed a nearby pen and headed straight for the bathroom off to the side. He didn't have time to track down Jane Roberts tonight. But he had to tell her everything he knew about them PIZ DETS Russians. Well not everything. But nearly everything. He would write it down on paper before he forgot. He knew to do that much. Hell. At this point, he could be a spy! Hah! He was a spy!

When the note was all done, Bernie used his highly diluted thinking cap and tucked his note to Jane into a safe place, right there in the kitchen. A place where someone would find it later and hand it over to her. He had to have faith in that. He had to count on it. And now the pork needed him, so he headed back outside to help Cora.

....

Salem had arrived at the pigs to pull together the grand finale. His buddy Hitch McGill was tagging along to help cut and plate the meat. Salem could see Bernie returning to the roasting scene and he had some kind of violent red stain all over the front of his jacket. Bernie admitted he looked a mess and Salem thought so too. "Here, take off your jacket, Bernie—let's set it aside to clean it up later. You can use my coat for the time being. We'll run upstairs and get another coat for you. Meanwhile, you'll look like a million dollars while you're guarding the pigs." Bernie

185

donned Salem's flamboyant gold and silver striped jacket as he was told. Salem and Hitch then entered a side passage and hurried off to retrieve another coat.

Cora had noticed the Russians becoming distracted by Salem and Hitch's arrival at the scene. But now Spartak and Dimitri were focused on the pig pit, and their arms were busy lifting the slippery bulk of the cooked pork off the spit supports and placing the finished product on the prep table. They removed the metal spikes from their huge, crisp, pungent, honey-colored cargo—roast pork for a hundred mouths. But as soon as the second bulk of meat hit the table top, she heard the two men call out Dasvidaniya!, and they raced off in the direction Salem and Hitch had taken. All of which left Cora confused and alone with Bernie in the smoky clutches of the pork.

She knew enough, though, to stick to her assignment and keep the pork on track. "OK, Bernie, like it or not, it's up to you and me to save Chanson's main course here. We are going to break up these hunks and get everything ready for Salem to cut up when he gets back."

"I hear ya, Cora. And I can help ya now that the Won Ton twins don' look like themselves no more." Bernie shoved up the sleeves of the silver and gold dinner jacket and moved forward to tackle the pigs.

Before he touched the pork, his momentum was thrown off course. There through the kitchen glass wall...who the hell did he see? What the hell was Secret Agent Woman doin' at this damn party? The door to the kitchen swung open as several waiters trooped out to bring appetizers to a crowd that had gathered to watch the pig roast. Bernie could hear the women inside conversing. "Mom...." That's what he heard. Secret Agent Woman, Mystery Woman, was sayin' Mom to Chanson inside.

DON'T TOUCH MY COCKTAIL!

How the hell could Chanson Pratt be Secret Agent Woman's Mom?

Secret Agent Woman stepped out to the kitchen patio for a quick look at her mother's frozen version of a luau. Banks of snow formed a wintry corral, and steaming clouds of vapor rose from the mounds of hot coals. Fire and ice. A study in contrasts—that was her mother all right. But Geneva suddenly blanched at the site of the man in the silver and gold tuxedo. That man again! In her father's tux? It didn't make sense...neither the tux, nor the man. She glared fiercely at Bernie as if to say "Don't you dare," and swung around and left.

....

Dimitri and Spartak looked both ways down the long passageway. No Rhinestone Cowboy in either direction. Salem Pratt had melted into his own home. Should Dimitri and Spartak attempt to race around in this maze of an ice palace, or get back to an inside cube, where the Rhinestone Cowboy would eventually reappear? Returning inside made the most sense. They headed to the kitchen for the time being, to help "Beeg Sam Woman" with her side dishes.

44
New Year's Eve Party
10:45 PM

Salem and Hitch were walking along the side passageway past several cubes until they could reach the first of two sets of stairs and two passageways leading up to Salem's office on the third floor. Hitch had downed more than his fair share of Diablo Margaritas and it showed in his gait.

"I have to say, Salem, you and Chanson have got yourselves quite a crowd out there tonight. Lots of good-looking fillies in fact," Hitched observed with a knowing leer in his eyes. "Lot of nice, long tails on some of those women. You can see how they like to flick those tales as they move."

Over their long years of friendship, Salem had often heard Hitch voicing his proclivity toward younger females, but he had never bothered to point out to him any inappropriateness. Now he had reason to see things in a different light.

"I'd love to slap of few of them on the rear to see if they'll start bucking," Hitch chuckled aloud. "There's nothing like riding them hard in a rodeo, if you get my drift, Old Boy."

Salem shot a sour look at his fellow Texan. "You know, Hitch," Salem started to object, "don't you think it's about time you cooled down some? Your overt interest in women and the younger set is really growing thin."

"Well, speaking of younger women, Salem, your Geneva has certainly turned out awfully fine. She has a lovely head of hair." Hitch looked at Salem with boozy eyes.

"Hitch, I mean it. You've got to tread carefully. Geneva is my daughter, and you know it. Strictly off limits...to you anyway."

"Hold on now," Hitch said, backing off. "You know me...I'm just a firm admirer of the opposite sex. And seeing this bunch of fillies out there tonight, well, hell. I'd like to lasso a few of them...pull 'em in...up close and personal, that's all."

"That's what I'm afraid of, you raunchy old longhorn. But listen, I just remembered I've got to make a few calls before I bring Bernie another coat, so I'm going to hurry on ahead of you." Salem started rushing, taking the steps two at a time. Hitch fell back and did not try to keep up with him.

Salem had two important calls on his mind...one to his corporate CFO and one to his private finance manager. They both knew to be ready to hear from Salem tonight. He had to have answers about his semiconductor empire. He needed to know if he was going down, or had bought more time, or if impossibly good fortune had lifted him and all his silicon chips out of the fucking void. Just a few calls, and then back to the pigs, and keeping Chanson happy, and trying to get through this night.

45
New Year's Eve Party
11:00 PM

"OK, My Heroes," Zen-Ti spoke low to his fellow Forbidden Fruits once they entered one of the large glass cubes past the entry hall. "We're a little early here, so let's fan out to keep from getting too much attention. Settle in good. If anyone asks you why you're here, you just say you're on Miss Chanson's party crew."

The team of three flowed into the crowd of people entering the Pratt party, and now it was time to go to work. Earlier they had replaced their Forbidden Fruits jackets with a variety of simple, black zip-up fleeces. Unassuming; raised no questions. They swept the surroundings and the guests with their knowing, urban eyes, their Bay State eyes. Zen-Ti had warned them earlier—no jiving, no kicking back and having fun in all this dope, and no making time with the ladies.

And now, Zen-Ti reviewed their goal one last time. "Our one and only gig tonight is to find Cigarette Man in the silver and gold stripes. Whoever gets to him first, just keep him talking...all friendly...all normal. And steer him towards that closet we scoped out near the kitchen service entry. Just stand there with him and keep him talking. Don't let him get away from you. We'll catch up with you to subdue the dude...then toss him in the car and book it out of here and back to Massachusetts. Got that?"

"I'll tell you what I've got, Zen-Ti. I've got a boohoo on my chest," ZM started up. "How the hell are we going to bag this dude without our cellies? We can't call each other while we're looking for Cigarette Man. We can't call each other to say we found Cigarette Man. We can't call Tony Abanditono to release our moolah for getting Cigarette Man. I say we've got to charge Miss Chanson a premium for our services."

"ZM, you should have practiced up by watching old shows o' *Hawaii five-0*," ZK teased.

ZM scoffed. "*Hawaii five-0*? Hawaii? It's fuckin' twenty-five degrees outside, Man! I say more like *Gunsmoke*. That's what I should have watched. Antique TV, you know?"

"OK, my home boys," Zen-Ti said, breaking it up. "Let's bounce."

....

Samantha headed back out to her catering truck to keep the side dishes moving along. She was stirring and dishing out food when she heard a knock on the trailer door. She opened the door and let out a huge laugh.

"Konstantin!...You made it after all! This is fantastic. Jane will flip when she sees you. She has no idea!" Sam was ecstatic for Jane. She deserved to be happy in love, and Konstantin was the solution. He had been in cahoots with Sam about his plan to surprise Jane at the end of the year, which suddenly turned out to be now, tonight, at this New Year's Eve celebration. "I don't know if she's arrived yet, but you can hide yourself somewhere, anywhere, and sneak up on her when you think the time is right."

"Not a word, Sam..." and Konstantin left the trailer and disappeared through a door that led to a side passageway.

....

"Excuse me...yes, thank you. I'm just trying to get a better look at those waiters in white jackets who just walked in. Do they look Russian to you?" Jane asked the woman who was jammed into Jane's armpit in the densely crowded gathering room of the Pratt party. "Do you think they look at all funny?"

"Russian? Who can tell? Funny? They all look funny. I'm sorry, but I really can't help you. I can't even move, it's so damned packed in here. I need some air. I'm going to push past you." The woman groaned as she rammed Jane into four other guests. Jane took a quick Statue of Liberty stance to keep her drink from flipping onto the heads around her.

"Hi there. Pardon the pushing." Jane smiled generously at the wall of humanity being held back by her elbow. "This woman is trying to head out for some air. Oh, sorry, my leg—should I pull it in for you? There you go." Jane swallowed the rest of her drink and signaled a waiter for a refill—"Another Aunt Roberta! No ice. Thanks!"

"So tell me," Jane began casually speaking to two men whose breast pockets she was unintentionally half-clambering up due to the crush of the throng. "Have you noticed these Greco-Roman gods here tonight passing out hors d'oeuvres? Bad boys, do you think? Kind of dangerous?"

Several faces in the wall of humanity looked at Jane like she was nuts. But one elderly gent whispered to her, "I believe they're staff hired for tonight's party. At least that's what I gathered when I ran into two of them in the bathroom. And don't tell anyone, but I think they were snorting cocaine."

DON'T TOUCH MY COCKTAIL!

"For shame!" Jane said. "Really. Drug-free help is so hard to find these days." She handed him her business card and wiggled and shimmied her way towards the opening that led to the next glass cube. She thought maybe she had caught sight of some of the urban visitors Sonny Mannix saw on the ferry earlier in the day.

"Sir? Sir...I have a question," Jane yelled at a giant of a man in a ten-gallon hat. The decibels in this cube were killing her ears and cranking up her voice. She observed he wasn't going near the hors d'oeuvres. "Do you have any idea who those men in black fleece are? Maybe friends of the Pratts from Texas?"

"Haven't a clue, Ma'am," the tall hatter bellowed back. "I'm from Graniteville just down the road on the mainland. My company installed all the toilets in this house."

Useless, Jane thought, as she handed him her business card. She kept barreling ahead, trying not to snag buttons or jewelry or dress straps. Through the field of gowns and tails and talking heads, Jane had noticed Chanson waving her over. Jane started elbowing towards her hostess when she heard a male voice coaxing her from behind.

"Love that leather sheath, Jane Roberts. Could you be Dracula's fiancée?"

Jane turned to look back at the voice moving forward out of the crowd. Son of a gun. Michael Corleone in his perfect black suit...with those cheekbones that could turn a woman inside out. Pick any of *The Godfather* scenes in Sicily, didn't matter which one. There he was. Joe Miller from the boatyard.

"What are you doing here, Jane?"

"Joe Miller!" she shouted. "What are *you* doing here?"

"I asked you first."

They inched and swerved and poured themselves towards one another.

"You certainly get around fast for a boy from Brooklyn," Jane said.

"You think so? My sister went to college with Geneva, the Pratts' daughter. So she invited me tonight. What are you drinking, Jane? Can I get you another?"

"Sure. Make it an Aunt Roberta."

"Good God...you're not wasting any time. But, seriously. What are you up to tonight, Jane?" Joe leaned towards a passing waiter and put in the order.

"Oh, a little of this and that, a little *ESSSS...pionaaage.*"

"Really? What are you looking for?"

"Unusual behavior, Joe. Any kind of *unusual behavior*, and I'm right on top of it. Go, Jane Wayne! But where you're concerned, tell me something. What do you think Troy Overlock would do if he got his hands on a lot of moola?"

"Moola? Are you trying to be groovy, Jane?"

"It's secret code, Miller! This place is crawling with acronyms and code...you gotta be on your toes, Joe. So whats about Troy, huh?"

"Well, since you're so ravishing in those party skins, Draculina, and nearly as shellacked, maybe I'll let you in on a secret. But we could do with a little razzle dazzle first, don't you think?"

"What would that be?"

"Something like this?" Joe kissed Jane quick—just a neutral, asexual, lips-on-the-cheek number; no passion, slurpiness, sighs, or pressing.

"And what's that get me?" Jane shouted above the party noise.

DON'T TOUCH MY COCKTAIL!

"Troy wants a tu...mmmmmr tu...kkkkkkk."

"Tanya Tucker?" Jane said.

"A TUMMY TUCK!" Joe yelled.

"A TUMMY TUCK?!" Jane's jaw dropped.

"Yes."

"No...."

"Yes."

"No! For a guy? Isn't that, too, too, you know?" Jane splayed her fingers across her midriff. "Too cut and paste? On a guy?"

"Why not?"

"No."

"Yes!"

Joe grabbed Jane. Jane grabbed Joe. They both crumpled in laughter and missed colliding with the waiter and Jane's Aunt Roberta by the width of a twist of lemon.

"Oh, give me that quick. I need to drown my inhibitions," Jane said, grabbing her glass off the tray. "Joe, please elaborate."

"This is all confidential, Jane. You cannot tell anyone I told you. You cannot go asking Troy about it."

"Sure, Joe. What—Ever—You—Say." Jane took a long gulp of her cocktail. Confidential. So much was confidential. Confidential? Who confidential?

"You already know Troy is obsessed about his weight problem. For months he's been talking about saving up to pay for a tummy tuck. It's as simple as that, Jane. So now you've got your answer. But remember. It's all confidential."

"Boy, do I owe you one, Joe. My precious little kugel, you! A tummy tuck! Wow. Big time. OK. Well, sorry to abandon you to the herd, but now I have to catch up with

195

Carol Chen

our hostess, Ms. Chanson, and go fight crime. Would you please excuse me? Ciao, Baby!"

46
New Year's Eve Party
11:15 PM

As the party's earlier polite conversation began sloshing into the merry roar of a successful party, Konstantin commenced his search for Jane...down one passageway and into a glass cube; no sign of Jane; down another passageway and into the next cube; still no sign of Jane. He scanned the shapes and faces packed into the crowds around him...then, at the far end of the room, a glimpse of her...with her back to him. Yes!

Konstantin kept his orientation to her just so and followed her from a distance until the right moment presented itself. That right moment came when Chanson made a point of breaking away from some of her guests to approach Jane and tell her she should really take the time to head upstairs to the third floor for the view.

Jane made her way through the bunches of revelers and entered a side hallway. Konstantin followed discreetly behind as she left the gathering room. He could see the teasing arch of her back as she weaved along in a zig zag fashion. Her long, dark hair and cashmere stole floated up and down with each stride, revealing snatches of bare skin along the deep cut at the back of her gown. Konstantin paused as Jane slipped along the passageway, and then up a set of stairs. He heard the uneven clicking of her high heels as she ran up unsteadily. Once he was sure she had reached the head of the stairs, he looked around the corner to see which direction she had taken. He would give her enough time to get a bit ahead of him. Then he would bound up the stairs and close in on her. Down below, the jazzy music, the garbled conversations, the bustling of the party—they all swallowed up Konstantin's presence. When Jane reached the second floor, she remained oblivious of his pursuit.

....

Once they had parked their Massachusetts van in front of the Pratt estate, Ray Bun, Jay Bun, Man Bun, Van Bun, and Tiny Bun got out and surveyed the various lighted entryways in reference to the blueprints Ray had brought along. Diane Savoy had finally committed to hiring them to shame Chanson Pratt, and their plan began to unfold. Ray huddled with his team and did their final checklist:

"Jay Bun, you've got the mickey to douse the whore?" Check.

"Man Bun, you've got the blanket to wrap her up?" Check.

"Tiny Bun, you've got the all-important WHORE sign to put on her once she's out like a light?" Check.

"And just to be sure, does that sign refer to a woman of ill repute?"

"That's right, boss."

Their plan was for Diane Savoy to buttonhole the lady of the manor, or the "Whore" in Diane's book, aka Chanson Pratt, and tell her someone needed to speak with her in the side hallway next to the great room at 11:30 PM. Ray Bun and his team would grab the whore, knock her out with a little cocktail of this and that, and finally set her up on her throne of infamy under the tarp that was covering the 1,000 helium balloons set for release at midnight. Then the Buns would fly the hell out of there and get back to the mainland.

....

"Dimitri, do you see who I see?" Spartak asked him in Russian while they were doling out appetizers to Chanson's crowds. "Look at that Black man over there. Do you think he could be LL Cool J?"

"Don't be crazy, Spartak. How could that be? He looks like he might use chopsticks." But Dimitri looked closely and thought to himself the man actually did look an awfully lot like the rapper, or maybe even Michael Jordan.

"Maybe it's Michael Jordan," Spartak suggested. Dimitri laughed. Then both men looked at each other and got a little loopy. They began whispering while people were walking by and snatching snakebites off their trays. It wasn't that big a stretch that the famous rapper or maybe the famous basketball player would be here at the party. The Russian sailors looked at all the fancy people with their sparkling jewelry and big white teeth. This was not a bunch of serfs. These were American oligarchs, plus some crazy local peasants.

Why wouldn't LL Cool J or Michael Jordan want to party with these shiny people? Why else would they be here? It made all the sense in the world. And there was no way the Russians were not going to get an AUTOGRAPH! They set down their trays and started moving casually towards Ray Bun.

47
New Year's Eve Party
11:20 PM

It might not have been exactly 11:45 PM, but it was good enough for Jane Wayne from Maine. When she reached the second floor, she poked her head into each room while looking for a telephone. She found one in a study and shut the door behind her. By now, she and her three Aunt Robertas were entirely dedicated to the cause of keeping America safe. They must make contact with the Eagle, so the Eagle could land. Jane sat down at the phone and dialed in the Champus number at the FBI. .

"Mission code, please," an operator's voice requested.

"I'm sorry. I don't have a code. No one gave me a code," Jane said.

"Well, Ma'am, if that's the case, I'm required to send you to the regular switchboard at the FBI. They'll take down your message and it can go through the routine channels."

"But, wait!" Jane panicked. "I've got to report my intelligence to the SWAT team that's about to storm this New Year's Eve party on St. Frewin's Island."

"I'm sure you do, Ma'am. We're getting lots of those calls tonight...about our federal forces crashing New Year's Eve parties. If you don't mind my asking, Ma'am, have you perhaps had one too many this evening?"

"What? You mean my Aunt Robertas? I only had three...well, Ha ha!!, maybe four. They're helping Jane Wayne to keep America safe, if you really need to know.

DON'T TOUCH MY COCKTAIL!

Though I'm not supposed to talk about it. No yackety-yack-yack, that's what the Chimp said."

"Ma'am, there are no chimps at the FBI."

"Well, how about ICE or the CIA?"

"Not that I know of, Ma'am."

"What I don't understand, Operator, is that this mission I'm on is TOP SECRET and how am I supposed to keep it secret and pass on my TOPS if you and I keep yackety-yacking about it and you don't let me into the Homeland? I have to report my list of *unusual behaviors* to the Straddler. You me comprehendo?"

"Ma'am, I'll try one thing for you. Do you have the complete name of the party you're trying to contact?"

"I already told you, Party Pooper. It's Alex the CHIMP! But you say you no comprendo who is the Chimp! Well, I'll give you an idea and you can go stuff that up your switchboard. The Chimp is an ENFORCER. And he's going to grab you by your nuts. And chuck you to the ends of Shanghai if you don't put me through to him."

"OK, Ma'am. Stand by. I'll connect you to someone who can take your message. That should work."

A different voice came on the line. "Go ahead, Ma'am. I'm ready for your message."

"OK!" Jane took a deep breath. "This *unusual behavior* is all confidential, so keep it between you, me, and the Pentagon, all righty? Here goes:

"1. Potentially naughty waiters may be snorting the Big C in bathroom—leaving powdery residue on snakebites and armadillo eggs;

"2. Potential urban guerillas from forbidden fruit import/export entity may be up to no good concerning one Cigarette Man, but Jane Wayne unable to determine what kind of 'no good'—not too sure about identity of Cigarette Man either;

"3. Potential Russians racing around looking for Rhinestone Cowboy and Beyoncé; also snooping around roasted pigs;

"4. Unknown batch of Texans standing around not eating appetizers, like Texans know something about content of appetizers no one else knows;

"5. Potential urban operators hanging around in hallways with ropes, blankets, duct tape, blonde wig, and something that looks like a leopard hankie;

"6. Definite visa violator Gluella Trott is handing out tummy tucks to any Double Quarter Pounder who asks;

"7. Head bartender by name of Nathan Herinton, a St. Frewin's Island local from old money, but someone Jane Wayne has had long-standing doubts about as far as his real commitment to keeping America safe, is putting something hokey in the Aunt Robertas.

"Hooah!"

....

Zen-Ti circulated through the long ribbon of rooms as he looked for Chanson's husband. Salem Pratt was nowhere to be found. Maybe try to track down Chanson and get her to point the way. He started back towards the dining room, when a small hand reached for his arm and held him.

"Young man," Diane Savoy could not resist asking the handsome Black man, who, along with five or six others, seemed to have appeared from nowhere during the course of the evening. "Are you one of the Buns helping Ray Bun tonight?" Diane was sure she was asking the right person the right question. Why else would this man be here tonight if he wasn't with Ray Bun?

"And I have to ask you, does Ray really need nearly ten men to grab one woman, put her out for a while, and hang a whore sign around her neck? Is this going to cost me more? It's preposterous!"

Zen-Ti stopped in his tracks. He was a very sharp individual, and tonight on this freezing island off the coast of Maine at nearly midnight on New Year's Eve, he was sharper than ever. So, whoa, Baby. What did she just say? And what should he say? It was his time to be smooth, no hesitation, just play along.

"Actually, Ma'am, I am not a Bun. But I work with Ray Bun. How may I help you?" was Zen-Ti's measured response...agile, calculated.

"Well, you know, I wanted to be sure you're all going to take care of that Chanson whore of a woman, just like we planned," said Diane. Knots of tension suddenly leaped off her shoulders after saying aloud what she was dying to accomplish tonight.

"Yes, Ma'am. We're aiming to do our best to satisfy your plan. Now, Ray said we should wait for him to give us the sign. That's what you wish, correct?" Zen-Ti inquired with all the wiliness he could conjure up, without alerting Diane Savoy to the fact that Zen-Ti had no fucking idea what she was talking about.

"I think Ray wants me to send the whore into the hallway near the great room around 11:30 tonight, and you folks will take care of the rest, right?" Diane said with a slight question in her eyes.

"And we understand the great room is the cube with the grand piano?" Zen-Ti tossed out a clarifying guess.

"That's right. That's the one," said Diane, nodding at Zen-Ti and shaking the ice in her gin and tonic.

"Well, thank you Ma'am, for taking the time to check with me." And in that moment, Zen-Ti leaped to spread his wings and try a little rainmaking, because that's what the goal was all about in this business. The entrepreneur's seminar he had recently attended in Boston emphasized honing your brand, getting out the word, cultivating every potential client. So what if he happened to be a Lowell gang leader? Come on.

"By the way, Ma'am" he whispered to Diane Savoy, looking her straight in the eyes with his intense gaze and handing her his card, "if you ever need some small job done here or there, please feel free to get hold of me. I help Ray Bun with the big jobs, but on the side, he lets me take on more basic client needs."

Diane looked at Zen-Ti, stunned but flattered to be discussing unsavory business with this impressive "Mr. Zen-Ti Smith" of "LifeStyles, Ltd." She repeated her earlier question after eyeing Zen-Ti's business card. "Not to be pushy or anything, Mr. Smith, but Ray Bun is not hiking up his price by bringing you and all these extra men along for this event, is he?"

Zen-Ti took a deep breath and a plunge. "No, Ma'am, the extra staffing won't cost you more. In fact, Ray's decided to give you thirty percent off because it's been quite a perk, after all, for us to spend some time in this beautiful State of Maine. He'll be in touch with you about that shortly. It's the least he could do."

Zen-Ti roared inside himself over the idea of messing with Ray Bun's dome a little. Zen-Ti would shake up the man's cheddar flow. So what if Ray got a few less Presidents in the end?

DON'T TOUCH MY COCKTAIL!

"Well, that's very decent of Ray!" Diane said, obviously pleased by the special treatment.

Zen-Ti shook her hand. "So very nice to talk with you. I'll give Ray Bun your regards. Got to run now!" and Zen-Ti turned away quickly...to go on the hunt for Chanson...immediately...before any harm came to her. Midnight was nearly upon them. No way was his Cinderella going to end up in the wrong pumpkin.

48
New Year's Eve Party
11:30 PM

Jane gasped when she reached the third floor. The wall of glass at the head of the stairs reached out to infinity...a diamond-iced landscape and endless ocean surface, brilliantly lit, yet dark and unknowable under the full moon. A perfect backdrop for the weight of the old year disappearing beneath the new....

Before her next thought could jell, she sensed a movement of air from someone near and behind her. Before her shock could register into a yell, a hand came over her mouth and held her silent...not in an uncomfortable way, but strong enough to quash any sound she may have wanted to make. She could smell elegance; she could sense intensity. She had no idea what to do.

Her assailant slowly walked her towards a door ajar...and in they went...into a large storage closet...and absolute darkness. She heard the door close shut...and then the faint, barely audible word..."Flicka."

In the total darkness of the small space, Jane could feel herself being turned around to face her mysterious aggressor. His powerful arms drew the length of her into his chest and his terrain below. He was saying nothing, only holding her close and tight. Seconds before she knew she would be begging for air from these arms that bound her, the memories of their passionate nights and days and afternoons and mornings in Switzerland rocketed across

DON'T TOUCH MY COCKTAIL!

Jane's unseeing eyes. Could it be? Had he come for her? When the invisible face found Jane's cheek, her eager willingness to welcome his tongue into her mouth propelled her into him. Bristles crushed against her lips. Jane drew back shocked. Bristles?! She froze. Konstantin had no mustache.

....

ZK and ZM almost wept when they wandered into the euphoric fumes of citrusy, sweet, and salty pork...chops, ribs, and roasts. They hadn't eaten for hours. And since there was no Salem Pratt in silver and gold for all they could see while scouting in the glass castle, they decided to make a beeline for the pork. They hurried through the cube next to the kitchen and then snaked past the caterers' food frenzy to the outside patio. Lo and behold, if they didn't finally lay eyes on the good old silver and gold stripe suited Cigarette Man, surrounded by one monster-fuckin' pig roast.

The pressure was on to serve the masses, and Bernie had plunged into the slicing. Cora left him to gather platters in the kitchen, and he was now elbow-deep in succulent slabs of glistening pork. There wasn't much more on his mind than that when the two men in black fleece sidled up to him, ready for a friendly chat.

"Porker of the Year, Bro!" ZK crooned to Bernie. ZM came round Bernie's other side, full of praise as well. "Sweet Mama! Don't those ham hocks rock 'n roll!"

Bernie looked up and was beyond confusion. He had never set eyes on Black kung-fu men during his entire island life, and he was at an unusual loss for words.

"Sorry to interrupt," ZK began. "But Miss Chanson asked us to find you and bring you to her. She has a big emergency and needs your help right away."

Bernie knew this probably made no sense, but he was impressed that Chanson wanted his help and his ego got the better part of him. "Well, let's go see what's up," Bernie offered without a second thought. "There ain't many problems this man can't fix in a jiffy!" His see-sawing and glassy-eyes suggested otherwise to his companions.

The three men were walking towards the passageway outside the kitchen when Cora hurried past with platters. Before she could voice her curiosity, Bernie cut her off, his voice puffed up with officialdom. "I'll be right back, Cora. I gotta trouble-shoot somethin' for Chanson."

ZK and ZM walked with Bernie towards the large closet near the kitchen service entry. The two Lowell men were starving after smelling all that food in their midst. It occurred to both of them that it might be quite some time before Zen-Ti caught up with them. How could they keep up the small talk with Cigarette Man out here in the hallway in the meantime? And that's when they telegraphed to one another over Bernie's head. With no one in sight, ZK silenced Bernie's mouth with his hand and yanked him into the closet. "You're going to stay in here for one hour. We'll be back."

"That's fifty-nine minutes too long, Podnah!" Bernie ranted from under the palm smothering him. "What about Chanson? She needs me!" Bernie's muffled voice cried out.

"Sorry, old man. We've got to get something to eat before we starve. Then we'll get you over to Chanson," ZM assured Bernie.

DON'T TOUCH MY COCKTAIL!

"Well, shit! I ain't gonna sit here like I'm your pu-pu platter while you pile on the main course!" Bernie jabbered away under ZK's broad palm.

"Pu-pu platter? No way, man. You're too mousy!" And ZK let out a honk.

ZM swooped in and tied a gag around Bernie's mouth, and a second one around his eyes, followed by strips from a roll of duct tape he pulled from his fleece pocket. They bound him up further with rope they had hidden in the closet earlier. In that state, with all the party hoopla and music blasting throughout the residence, Bernie wasn't going anywhere and no one would hear him. The two men quickly stepped out of the closet and shut the door. Back to the kitchen and the mountains of food.

....

"Sir, don't you dare cut in front of me at the Armadillo Egg tray! I am trying to reach for some hors d'oeuvres, if you don't mind." Harriet Buxton shoved her arm closer to the tidbits and wedged in her hips to block the man's reach.

"Bitch," Van Man said under his breath, for no one but himself to hear. He made a quick grab around Harriet's bulk for an Armadillo Egg, but Harriet smacked his hand.

"Don't think I didn't hear that, you greedy delinquent," snapped Harriet. "Where is your respect for your elders?"

"OK, you rule, you old prune. Age before beauty any day." Van Man was no longer masking his daggers. He didn't need this shit. He walked away.

....

"There she is," Zen-Ti exhaled with relief when he spotted Chanson. She had just left a group of Texans, and Zen-Ti caught her eye and signaled with his head that they should move to the passageway.

"Zen-Ti!" Chanson exclaimed on catching up with him. "Is everything OK? Have you subdued Salem and tucked him away in your car? Are you ready to go?"

"We're getting there. But first I've got to warn you, Sugar Boo. I just found out there's another Massachusetts gang here tonight. And they're going to grab you and make you look bad. Some kind of humiliation thing...I have no idea what or why. So you've got to listen to me. Let's go in this closet over here and get you changed into some different duds I stashed away, just in case."

"Zen-Ti, are you crazy? This is absurd. I'm up to my neck in this huge party and you want me to put on some kind of a costume? A blonde wig and this tiny leopard scrunchy?" Chanson exclaimed as Zen-Ti reached into the closet and handed her the disguise. "What's come over you?"

"Honey Boo, I'm telling you the truth. It is absurd, but I wouldn't do anything on God's sweet earth to hurt you. I...you...oh, man. I think you need to just listen to me this once, OK?"

Chanson did believe him. She just couldn't believe *what* he was telling her. But she gave in to his gaze and his caring manner, and they ducked into the utility closet for whatever came next.

"Don't turn on the light, Sweet Tart. Let's just get you into this female gang gear and you'll be good to go." Zen-Ti helped Chanson disrobe in the dark. She couldn't believe it, but she knew she liked it.

DON'T TOUCH MY COCKTAIL!

"Promise me you're not looking, Zen-Ti," Chanson suggested, hoping for the opposite.

"Baby, I'm erasing anything I see or feel. You've got my word." His hands moved and paused over her breasts and then took their time down around her golden globes as he helped her pull on a stretchy top and the pencilest of skirts....

49
New Year's Eve Party
11:35 PM

"Hey, Mister...You are beeg, famous man, yes? We would lof to haf your autograph!" Spartak and Dimitri were trying to be respectful and enthusiastic in their approach to Michael Jordan. Or maybe it was LL Cool J. Either one would do.

Ray Bun looked at the white-jacketed men and thought about what they had just said. Every once in a while he got this treatment...this kind of request. He was big, he was Black and Cambodian, but he was neither Michael Jordan, nor LL Cool J. And no one ever wanted to hear that. People wanted their unexpected fantasy to be true, to think that they had run into one of the "greats." But hey. Tonight was New Year's Eve. Who would ever know? Why not sow a little thrill and happiness in his wake? "Gentlemen, how kind of you to ask. I'd be happy to sign your cocktail napkins."

"Fantastika!" The Russians broke out into genuine smiles. They'd bagged a beeg feesh...wait till they told their comrades back on the sheep!

Ray Bun took a pen out of his suit pocket, did his thing, and handed two napkins back to them with an indecipherable scrawl on each.

Spartak looked at his napkin. He couldn't tell which side was up. He wondered if he should ask. "So, you are Michael Jordan?"

DON'T TOUCH MY COCKTAIL!

Ray Bun tossed the choices in his mind and came down on center court. Ray could play a bit of basketball a hell of a lot better than he could rap out a song. "Right you are, my Man. Michael Jordan is correct. And now, if I may, I need to go see someone about an important matter. Very nice to meet you. Go Chicago Bulls!" He could see the men grinning wildly as he left them and headed towards a Black-Asian man he could see from a distance. A Black-Asian man with a ruby of a woman, whom he had not seen until now. An absolute ruby. Who were they?

"Yo, Black-A. What's happening, man?" Ray asked as he extended his hand to Zen-Ti. Zen-Ti knew this had to be it. The chance to save Chanson from whatever shit that crazy broad with the G&T had been yacking about earlier.

"Hey, Bro. We're just chilling. Friends of the owners up from Texas."

"I must say, you've got some beautiful hot spice on your arm, Amigo," Ray complimented Zen-Ti.

"She's my coochie mama for shizzle." Zen-Ti pulled in the blonde woman standing next to him in the cheek-tight leopard skirt and black leather bomber jacket. "Excuse me a moment while I assure this lady how much I love her." He dipped the blonde gang woman low and gave her a long, steamy kiss to send the point home. "Ownership" it said. "Off Limits" it implied. All without uttering a word.

....

After Ray Bun had wandered off, Zen-Ti led Chanson towards the closet in the passageway once again. "Babe, listen to me. Like I said, some banshee here tonight wants to do a Rambo on you and make you look real bad. And that banshee has hired Ray Bun to do the job. He's the

213

man we just saw. So I want you to stay in here until I come for you. I know hiding in the closet isn't the normal hostess shit, but you've got to trust me on this one. I'm not smoking you, OK?"

Chanson could see his fuzzy point. She had no idea who Ray Bun was or how he had happened to come to her party. So something must be afoot. And Zen-Ti was nobody's fool, so she knew to cooperate. She was also surprised but very, very pleased by the fervent kiss he had bestowed on her. She knew it was not the kind of kiss compelled by macho display. Definitely not raw hunger, or duty, or aggression. Love maybe? But how could it be love? Anyway, it was the kind of attention she'd been hungering for in recent years. And Salem Pratt and Wilton Savoy and a few forgotten types along the way had never kissed her quite like that. Never.

....

After all this time, Zen-Ti was hoping to catch up with ZK and ZM at the closet near the kitchen service entry. Surely they had found Cigarette Man by now. Time to fly the coop.

"All right, my boys! Where are we at?" Zen-Ti asked the two men.

"Take a look in the closet, Boss. We've got the goods all bundled up tight," ZK said.

Zen-Ti opened the door. The silver and gold tuxedo was buried in a layer of rope and knots. All set to go.

Zen-Ti, ZK, and ZM started hauling their bundle of Cigarette Man out into the hall. An intoxicated guest was teetering past them. Zen-Ti decided to make a bold but cautionary move.

DON'T TOUCH MY COCKTAIL!

"Excuse me, sir. We're moving Salem Pratt to get him some fresh air. His costume for tonight's party has gotten the better of him."

The guest wagged his head towards Salem and said, "Oh, is it a costume party? My goodness...Salem's not looking good at all, is he?"

"No, sir," Zen-Ti answered, feeling that he had received confirmation enough with that exchange. On their way out the door, Zen-Ti had a sudden thought. "ZK, ZM, I'm going to run back in and get some goodies we can give the man once he's tucked into the car. We don't want Chanson's hubby to go hungry. And we'll need food for tonight's ride. So go ahead and bring him out. I'll be there in a minute."

Zen-Ti ran into the kitchen and saw huge serving dishes brimming with black-eyed peas, white rice, collard greens, corn bread, and all manner of pork. Hallelujah! The radio news gabbling in the background was describing a significant snowfall on its way tonight. Ignoring the caterers' stares, Zen-Ti grabbed two large plastic containers from the counter and spooned in mounds of food. "This is for Ms. Chanson's clean-up crew!" he assured the startled waiters gawking at him.

Next he sprinted with his containers to the closet where he left Chanson. He opened the door to his wilting blossom. "Come on, Cupcake. For the time being, you come with me. I don't want any boogeyman doing you harm. And we've got a change of plans. Instead of driving you and your man all the way to Massachusetts to scare the bejesus out of him, we'll just go as far as HOJO's in Portland tonight. There's no use trying to leave the state with all this snow coming down. So let's go, OK?"

215

Chanson looked at Zen-Ti. She looked at herself. Life was short. Portland was not that far away. And she would be there in person to know Salem stayed safe. She stepped out of the closet and left with Zen-Ti.

50
New Year's Eve Party
11:40 PM

Ray Bun's crew was hanging around in the passageway outside the great room. The shit was about to nuzzle up to the fan.

"Ray, how long are we going to wait for this Chanson whore to show up? It's 11:40 and we're running out of time if we're going to pull this thing off." Man Bun felt more than antsy. Timing was everything.

"Yeah, Ray," Jay Bun chimed in. "What happened to that Diane Savoy woman anyway? We thought you said she was hot to get the skunk bitch out of here at 11:30 sharp. Now what?"

Ray Bun analyzed their plight aloud to his men. He had planned the logistics, they had traveled all this way, money was on the line, and he had his professional reputation to keep intact. An event was an event; the show must go on. They had to have something to report to the money man Tony Abanditono. OK. That was it. They would find a substitute. They would get the job done. It wouldn't be their fault if Diane Savoy screwed up and left them without a victim. They could say a certain so-and-so was in the passageway at the great room at a bit past 11:30 and they carried out the event. Case of mistaken identity? Not their problem. End of story. Receipt of payment. What did Jay, Van, Man, and Tiny think?

"Hey, no sweat, gang," Van Bun stepped up. "I think I have just the old shit waffle to wrap this up. You all come

217

with me. I'll point her out to you, and Ray can soft talk her into the great room near the tarps. Once she's there, we can do our magic and then break out of here."

....

"Ma'am, I'm so sorry to interrupt you," Ray Bun was speaking to the woman with the burgundy-colored hair. "Chanson Pratt is in the great room and asked me to bring you to see her. She has an important question for you."

"Well, that seems a bit strange. I only just met the woman tonight, and barely at that, Mr.? Pardon me, but what is your name?" the woman asked the tall Black man.

"Yes, Ma'am. I'm Michael Jordan. The Pratts employ me as their property manager. If you'll please step this way, Mrs. Pratt will only take a moment of your time."

....

Don't let on. Don't panic. Play along. Jane realized now was not the best time to coach herself about sexual assault in this absolutely dark closet with this libidinous, Unknown Asshole trying to pull one off. But still, there was no way in hell he was going to swamp Jane Roberts. She wouldn't freeze any longer; she wouldn't run. She would play into his lust. Lust...his Achilles heel. And the second she found her balance, she would smite him...with her evening attire...Hah!...Bring it! Then find the door and get the hell out of there.

She moved in synch with the human form flanking her own. What had been natural and impassioned seconds ago, was now a revolting exercise in concentration. Unknown Asshole moved to guide Jane further into his loins. God. Loins. That was the word, Jane thought, when she got there. Didn't D. H. Lawrence always mention "loins" in such moments? But, wait. What was this? A minor, little bundle? Her downstairs sensed...yes, her downstairs sensed a little mini...mini...g-h-e-r-k-i-n? Aha!...so that's what she was up against? "The Small Gherkin Complex"? Nubby, bumpy, tart, and crunchy!

But seriously, she had to focus...laser focus. And that's when she felt Unknown's hand moving down into her gown and twiddling with what came between Jane's breasts and the more generous bodice of Samantha's gown. *God damn it! He's pawing my bubble wrap! That's it. I've had ENOUGH!* Commanding her body to undulate in desire, Jane raised her right foot and swept it upward along Unknown's leg. Then, like a frenzied mustang kicking off a lunging cougar, she stomped down hard at his foot.

Fuck! Her heel hit the floor instead of Unknown's foot! Damn it! Her exploding adrenalin blew past this error with a second stomp, and this time the force of her furious heel sent shock waves through Unknown's shoe into all those slender bones and delicate tendons in the human upper foot. He yelled and leaped back.

Jane skidded towards where she remembered entering the room. Her hands started slapping at door knob level in an attempt to find the knob and turn it. Unknown was cursing under his breath, but she noticed he didn't raise his voice enough for her to hear how he talked, how he sounded. Which suggested to Jane he had done this before...and gotten away with it. The fucker.

She kept pounding along the wall and wondering if Unknown had turned her at some point, such that she was on the inner side of the closet, away from the door. In which case, she should continue to feel along the walls until she made her way back to the door. She renewed her

Carol Chen

search, but Unknown had the same thought of escape. Before Jane found the door, she heard and saw it open, and a dark figure rushed out and raced away.

For all her training, for all her innate pit bull, Jane's body refused to run after her assailant. Locked in place. Was it inebriation? Humiliation? She didn't care. She stood still, trying to remember what she had just seen. In the light from the hallway, was it someone tall, was it a dark suit...what about his hair, footwear? What about them? Could she recall? And on her gown, her leather gown...Ohhhhhh...that was it! Unknown's fingerprints! Drunken, sticky fingerprints. All over the leather surface...Jane was her own walking evidence...she had to proceed carefully. Maybe Chanson would lend her something to change into so Jane could wrap up her clothing for examination later. God, her mind was racing.

51
New Year's Eve Party
11:45 PM

Salem ended up on the phone far longer than he had anticipated. He had been informed that his major nightmare account with his overseas creditors was in some sort of limbo status at the moment and no one could give him an intelligent explanation.

Limbo might be good...suggesting the money bags were going to lighten up on Salem for a while. Or limbo could mean Salem might be tits up before the new year, with his creditors piling on to vacuum up his earthly assets. But he told himself he would have a heart attack if his mind went down that road.

He wasn't going to waste New Year's Eve imagining his note holders and mortgagees gobbling up his semiconductor fabrication plants. His hard-won "fabs"! All his industrial air showers; his scanners; his etching, cleaning, doping, and dicing machines; his integrated circuits; his transistors; his silicon chips; his Texas residence; his St. Frewin's Island residence; his vehicles; Chanson's jewelry; their artwork; their dog! Total breakdown. He couldn't go there.

And the curious thing was, against all odds, his forlorn corporation was slowly hauling itself back up on its sore feet, so that was good news. Right now his business could use all the forbearance it could get until it reestablished itself as the money machine it had been only three months earlier. Why the foreign creditors weren't throttling

Salem's neck was beyond him, but he was thankful for however long it would last.

So back to the party...oof...the God damn New Year's Eve party. And obnoxious people like Hitch McGill.... Time to return to the thick of it. Time to make the best of the long, shrill night, so tiring and expensive....

Salem started down the stairs and towards the passages that led to the ground floor. On the second floor, he suddenly heard people running behind him, and he turned to see what the commotion was. Far down the hallway and bearing down on him were two men in white jackets. He didn't recognize them but he was smart enough to know they must be trouble. He began running from them himself, maybe for his life? He couldn't stop to wonder. He tore down the set of stairs that he knew would lead towards the kitchen. He could race outside from there and hide in any number of places. But the white jackets were gaining on him. He had to change that. He rounded a corner, yanked open a closet door and, leaping inside, shut it.

He could hear footsteps pounding past and more yelling in some foreign language. The voices disappeared as the running footsteps receded.

Salem snuck out of the closet and saw no one. He darted into the kitchen and headed for the door. Outside he could see Samantha through the open door of her caterer's trailer. He flew to the trailer. He could hear the white jackets suddenly yelling in Russian back in the house. Russian. Maybe his foreign creditors were ready to break his neck after all.

"Samantha! You've got to help me! Hide me!" Salem was calling out as he raced up the trailer steps and practically crashed into her.

DON'T TOUCH MY COCKTAIL!

"Oh my God. Holy shit. OK. OK," Sam said, rising to the challenge and extricating herself from the tail ends of collard greens and cornbread. "Here! Take this trailer key," she blurted as she slipped it from its hook. "It's a deadlock!" They could see the Russians had once again caught sight of Salem from within the house.

Sam jumped out of the trailer and looked at Salem. "Race through the trailer and when the men follow you in, you run out the back end and lock the door behind you. I'll lock it from this side. HURRY!"

Less than a minute later, the white jackets stormed past Samantha to reach Salem inside the trailer. She rushed to lock the door behind them, just as she heard them shouting at Salem. In mere seconds, the trailer backdoor slammed shut, and Salem quickly reappeared at the front of the trailer, half hobbling and looking freaked. He was completely out of breath and panting for air, but he bent over laughing hard. "I can't believe we pulled that off, Sam! You genius, you!" Salem yelled as he plunged in to hug her.

Ever practical, Sam began thinking out loud. "There's more than enough food in there to keep them happy until Jane can figure out what to do with them. And I better turn off the gas tanks so the jerks don't blow up the trailer. Where is Jane anyway? We haven't seen her all night." Sam had a worried look on her face as she began walking towards the tanks.

She suddenly looked back at Salem with another thought. "You know what, Salem? You should hide somewhere in your house where you'll feel safe. There were two other Russians here tonight—all of them on some kind of hunt, I now realize—after the fact. And they may still be on the lookout for you. So you should hide, seriously!"

52

New Year's Eve Party
Near the Stroke of Midnight

"Thees peekin pie very good, Injun. Spartak fall in love with thees pie...jes' like mebbe Spartak fall in love weeth you, Injun, you teenk?"

India and Cora had dedicated far and enough of the night standing on their feet, serving people, baby-sitting pork, and searching for Jane Roberts. Now was their chance to lounge around and nibble on some food while the guests were licking their dessert plates and readying for the grand finale. The two women and their would-be Russian suitors were hanging out in a small sitting room far from the heart of the party. Their chocolate bourbon pecan pie was delicious—nutty and crunchy, with a kick of liquor and a generous lid of thick whipped cream.

Dimitri stuck his index finger into Cora's long brown hair and began absentmindedly curling it into a sausage. He sat there twirling away, hypnotized, not really talking, not eating much at all.

Spartak watched Dimitri's routine and nudged him while pushing his limits in English. "You are in fog, Dimitri, yes? You are here, but you are far away, with your finger in hairy wiener on your pretty friend's head. Why you do that?"

"You are too noosey, Spartak. How do they say in America...Mind your own beesnus."

"Jus' tell me what you theenkink, Dimitri? You theenkink too much sadness to leef America? You theenkink you want stay on this island?"

India looked from the one Russian to the other. "Are you serious? Stay here? Wouldn't you get into a lot of trouble with your bosses? And what happened to your other two comrades who were here tonight? I haven't seen them for quite a while. Last I knew they were handing out Snake Bites, and then they disappeared."

"We know noteenk, Injun," Spartak said. "No sign of comrades. Everyteenk tanked tonight, I teenk. Eef we go back to sheep now, we be in beeg sheet, you know what I mean?"

"No Meeshun Accumplisht tonight. Beeg sheet," said Dimitri.

"Oh God," Cora sounded worried as she looked inquiringly at India. She moved closer to her and whispered, "What do you think? Should we help these guys? I mean, this Dimitri...I am not really taken by him, but maybe this is a case of human rights or something like that? Isn't that what they call it in the news? It sounds like these guys will get creamed if they go back to their bosses. I have no idea what's going on, but it doesn't sound good."

"OK...let's try to think this through. Jane was hot to get more information about these guys and the Environmental Fields. So there's one question. And now it sounds like they're in trouble for some reason unknown to us...they didn't accomplish some assignment they had tonight. They were probably put here to be up to no good, but that aside, they really are two puppies, don't you think?"

"Yeah...hah...puppies. That need house training.... So what should we do?" Cora asked.

"Why don't we bring them to Grand Harbor Inn and the Russians can sleep on the sofas in the parlor. At least they'll have a place to crash for tonight, and we can worry about tomorrow tomorrow. I'm not even going to ask Maggie...I don't think she'll mind." India was satisfied, and that was good enough for Cora.

"Come on, you guys. You're going with us," India informed Spartak and Dimitri and stood up. "We've got to get our coats and then hit the road. We'll drive in my car."

"Where to?" they both asked.

India looked at them thoughtfully. "How does 'freedom' sound?"

53
New Year's Eve Party
Still Near the Stroke of Midnight

Van Bun was pleased they had no struggle with their female target. No biting or scratching or workout of any kind. Ray had convinced her to come to the hall outside the great room. Tiny Bun approached them from behind and deliberately bumped into the woman. Ray saved her drink from her hand as she pitched forward. He also slipped their little surprise into that drink and handed it back to the lady as she regained her balance. They chatted and sipped their cocktails for a few moments until the ingredients in the surprise took their effect on the woman. From there, it was only a matter of bundling her up in a large blanket they had stashed earlier.

While Ray and Jay Ban kept watch, and Man Bun was ready to create a diversion if necessary, Van Bun and Tiny Bun carried the woman's rolled-up form over to the tarps covering the balloons and put her down, as if she were just another prop for the evening's festivities.

All at once, the lighting went low—low enough for Van and Tiny to position a nearby chair beneath the balloon tarp. They dragged the body under the tarp, unwrapped her, and propped the slack form onto the chair as Ray had directed. Van positioned the infamous sign with its shrill, red lettering around her neck, and the job was done. Minutes away from ringing in the New Year, the DJ switched to Guy Lombardo for a little nostalgic jazz to sway the mood as people moved into the great room from the rest of the party.

All five Buns walked past the crush of merrymakers who were readying their confetti crackers and positioning their buzzers and blowouts. The Buns stopped near the door of the passageway to take in one final view of their long-awaited handiwork. Everyone started roaring with the countdown, and the tarp came off on cue...THREE, TWO, ONE!!!

Iridescent clouds, enormous rainbow clouds of balloons bubbled up and began floating over the guests and aloft towards the distant ceiling. People were yelling "Happy New Year!" all at once and tossing back gallons of champagne, their party favors crackling the air with squeals and quacks and garish clamor.

But then, a murmuring began, like some distant mechanical rumble, billowing into an unexpected wave of shocked whispering. Mild pandemonium rang through the crowd, competing with the cheering and the highs and the lows and the roads in "Auld Lang Syne."

Guests were turning and gazing at the figure enthroned in the center of the room. Who was she? What was happening?

Knocked out and disheveled, a forlorn woman sat slumped into her round body with a loud sign around her neck proclaiming in red, foot-high letters...WOMAN OF ILL REPUTE!!! The error caught Ray Bun utterly off guard.

He stared at the conceptual clusterfuck, his fingers clenching and unclenching in his taught palms. He had said one thing; his team had said another; and they both confirmed what they meant when it wasn't. Lord, what was the point? What was the point of trying to pound it all home, to keep communications clear...now that it was too late. He had had enough. It was time to call it a night. Time to drive home to Massachusetts.

Diane Savoy was cradling drinks in both hands and jabbering with several Texans when they became aware of the commotion near the middle of the room. Midnight had come and gone, and she didn't, for the life of her, know where Chanson the Whore had disappeared to. Diane had thrown up her hands as far as Ray Bun and his merry men carrying out her wishes to teach Chanson a lesson.

Diane took a swig of her fourth gin and tonic in the one hand, followed by a chug of champagne from the other. When she craned her neck to see what all the fuss was about, the embarrassing human centerpiece came into view, crumpled and wildly labeled.

Diane's mind could not translate. *I must be drunk. That's it. I'm way over the limit.* She blinked and swallowed. She tried remembering where her diaphragm was to take a deep breath. And it slowly dawned on Diane. She, Diane, was the epicenter here and now. The Diane Savoy Fault Line. All her fault. Her internal Richter scale blew inside out. She earthquaked, if that was possible. Her shattered pieces landed miles away from the woman she was, who still looked like Diane Savoy, and who was now screaming "HARRIET!"

54

New Year's Eve
Nearly the Stroke of Midnight

Zen-Ti and Chanson slipped out of the Pratt residence and ran to his car parked in the sea of guests' vehicles. ZK and ZM had been warming up their wheels for the getaway, with Cigarette Man bundled up in back. Zen-Ti warned Chanson to keep her blonde disguise on and not talk, with the faint hope that her kidnapped husband would not recognize her during the dark drive to Portland. ZK drove with Chanson in the front seat. Zen-Ti and ZM kept Cigarette Man company in the back.

Once they had driven the car onto the ferry, Cigarette Man started bouncing around in the back seat. Zen-Ti intended to offer him food, whether or not Chanson was present. No need to make the man suffer further. Zen-Ti removed the tape and gags from Salem's eyes and mouth and opened up enough knots to give him some breathing room for his arms.

"For fuck's sake, what's goin' on?!" Bernie exploded semi-hysterically at all the faces he could barely see. "Why do I feel like a string-tied salami? Ain't anyone gonna talk to me? I got rights you know!"

"Hey, man. Cool it. Calm down. I've got some roast pork and all the fixings for you right here in this Rubber Maid," Zen-Ti said to Cigarette Man. "You're going to be OK. We're just taking a little ride out of town. Go ahead. Have some pork."

"You got to be friggin' kiddin' me, Mister! I hope I don' see another piece of pork for the rest of my life! I've had it with pork! Pork's what got me into this pickled shit in the first place. And sure as hell, you're gonna be sorry you're messin' with Bernie Pushaw, you are!"

Zen-Ti could see Chanson jerk up in the front seat, but she kept quiet. He looked the partially cinched salami in the face and said, "You say your name is Bernie?"

"You're darn tootin', it is, man. And I still wanna know what I'm doin' in this jalopy with a bunch o' you outta town boys on New Year's Eve. What's Bernie Pushaw gone and done to get so clobbered and now you're stuffin' me with the God damn pork! Jesus all, give me a clue!"

"Well, for starters," Zen-Ti said, "why are you wearing that gold and silver tux?"

"Oh, this...I sure look like a fancy man, don' I?" Bernie actually let out a bit of a chuckle. "This pretty jacket belongs to Salem Pratt. You know Salem, right? I mean you was runnin' all over his house tonight like you fuckin' own it. You must know him. He lent it to me so I wouldn't look like such a mess. And now look at me. Shit. But what's Salem's monkey suit got to do with me gettin' hauled off my island? You ain't even stopped to think 'bout my ever-lovin' wife, have you? Like maybe Noreen's gonna miss me sooner or later and call the cops?"

"I am so sorry, Bernie," Zen-Ti decided it was best to let out some basic truths. "There's been a big mistake tonight, and you got balled up in it. But it wasn't your fault...none of it. So just relax and have some corn bread while we drive to Portland. We're going to sit out this snow storm at HOJO's tonight and get you back home bright and early tomorrow. How's that sound?"

DON'T TOUCH MY COCKTAIL!

"Sounds like you done wasted twenty-four hours of the rest of my life," Bernie groused. "That's what it sounds like! An' I'll tell you what. I am gonna get me a lawyer and sue the livin' daylights outta all o' you. And jus' wait till Jane Roberts hears what I gotta say about this. You're gonna be deep and sorry when she catches up with you. Take my word."

"Look, I don't blame you, bro, for wanting to belt us. We have to make it up to you somehow," Zen-Ti said. "It clearly isn't fair that you got hog-tied without your consent, muzzled, and dragged off your island just because you're wearing some kind of honky-shit silver and gold space blanket."

"That's right. You got it," Bernie was shaking his head and starting to nibble on some black-eyed peas. "And by the way, how come it's so fuckin' hot in this rig? I'm not sayin' I'm decomposin', but it's gotta be 130 degrees in here. Can't you turn off that damn radiator, whoever's drivin'?"

Zen-Ti leaned towards ZK and asked him to lower the car heat a bit. Settling back in next to Bernie, Zen-Ti had a suggestion. "So I'm going to tell you a secret and bestow something special on you, if you say it's OK. But you have to keep it a secret, OK, Man? This is the biggest secret of your life. OK?"

"Go on. Hit me. Can't get no worse than where I'm sittin'," Bernie said.

"Well, it's like this, Bernie. Some honcho wanted to shake Salem Pratt up a pinch you know? And don't ask me who or why, because I can't say. But this honcho hired me and my boys to do the gig, and here we are, mistakes and all. So to heal your wounds, we're going to make you a special honorary member of our Bay State gang. We call ourselves the Forbidden Fruits."

"Huh? *A fruit gang?! From Massachusetts?* How's any o' that gonna help me or be special if I'm kickin' around up here in Maine for the next fifty years? You gotta come up with somethin' better than me bein' the tail end of a bunch o' Bay State bananas. Bay State, my ass."

"Zen-Ti, I can't help it. I can't take this anymore," Chanson broke down and pulled off her wig. She turned her face around to look back at Bernie.

"Babe, wait," Zen-Ti tried to hold her off....

"Jesus Christ, Chanson! What's happened? You OK? They got you, too?" Bernie asked, trying to sit up more, entirely stunned.

"Oh Bernie, it's my fault. All my fault. I've been so foolish," Chanson felt she must confess. "But you can't say anything about any of this...not to anybody, Bernie. You've got to promise me."

Bernie never felt so discombobulated in his whole life. He had to shut up a minute and try to think this all through. No one else was talkin' either. Not a peep. He looked around him. What on God's earth was Chanson doin' with these fruit loops? And Chanson was sayin' it was all her fault. But that Bernie couldn't say a thing. Couldn't tell Noreen, or Jason Coombs, or Jane Roberts how he got kidnapped near the fuckin' stroke o' midnight 'cause he was dressed up like a gold an' tin foil freak.

"Yo, ZM, hand me a hunk of pork with some collard greens piled on top, will you?" ZK called from the front seat. They were finally on the open stretch of Route One heading down to Portland and he needed some more chow.

DON'T TOUCH MY COCKTAIL!

"Will you shut up, up front there, Taxi Driver? I'm still tryin' to get my head around all this, OK?" Bernie yelled. It occurred to him he wouldn't even be able to tell his mother-in-law. Ha ha!! That wouldn't hurt much.

But what about Chanson..."Mom" to Secret Agent Woman? And how about that screwball Secret Agent Woman? She told Bernie he couldn' talk about her or ask about her. Nevah again. Fuckin' A! He and his lips had crossed both their paths, Chanson AND Secret Agent Woman, and both of them were trying to seal his lips twice? Like mother, like daughter. God dang! How many times in one month did one grown man have to seal his lips?

"Look, Bernie," said Zen-Ti, still trying to be the diplomat who would solve their crisis. "How about, in addition to bestowing on you one handsome 'Forbidden Fruits' one hundred percent boiled wool jacket with the embroidered name, front and back, I also give you a super new, fresh-off-the-factory-floor Vipertek VTS-989 stun gun? Will that make you a happy camper?"

"Hey-o, now you're talkin', Captain Taser," Bernie piped up with a twinkle in his voice. "Finally some mano a mano. I jus' may be ready to cut a deal, so long as you're not shittin' me, Boss Man."

55
New Year's Day
Zero Zero Zero Zero Hour

The Federal tactical teams in their high-tech monster garb and gear were poised outside the Pratt residence, waiting for the imminent hand signals. Down went the arm from the commander's elbow, then the fisted arm pumped up and down, respectively signifying "Forward" and "Rush"...and the combined forces from ICE, the FBI, and the CIA raced through the main entry and into the New Year's Eve party. They immediately collided with the polite stampede of tipsy guests who were trying to escape what had turned into some sort of pooped-out Salem Witch Trial. Best to get away from that deflated, marked woman in the middle of the great room—whoever she was; whatever it meant: Woman of Ill Repute??? Too unnerving to stick around.

The commandos fanned out and scoured the departing crowd. Other team members asked for the caterers and then began questioning Samantha and Hamidi about Russian waiters who may have helped with the catering.

The team members followed Sam and Hamidi out to the catering trailer. Inside the trailer, the team members grabbed the two Russians who had chased Salem, and moved them out to the commando van.

"Where are the Pratts and Public Safety Officer Jane Roberts?" the commander asked Samantha. She led him to the closet where Salem was hiding, and she explained she had not seen Chanson for some hours. Officer

DON'T TOUCH MY COCKTAIL!

Roberts had been resting upstairs and was now changing. Samantha assured the commander Jane would be down shortly.

....

Nine hours difference between Maine and the Caspian Sea. It was now 1:00 AM early New Year's Day in Maine. Salem still had time to call his impatient creditors in Makhachkala...before they sat down to lunch. He needed to know why his whole universe was now safely in limbo. He would demand an explanation.

When the call went through, he got his answer, which was not what he had expected. It nearly put him on another planet, he was so astonished. Make that ecstatic. Wait until Chanson heard. Somehow, *somehow,* his Siberian-sized debt had been paid down sufficiently, such that he should have no more worries for now. Incomprehensible. It defied all logic.

Wait until Chanson heard, Salem thought. But Salem paled. Where was she? He had not seen her for several hours now. No one had...not even when ICE, the FBI, and the CIA had swept through the house on their unannounced raid. And who did he have left to talk to about all this chaos, after so many guests had fled the party feeling sullied by the turn of events they witnessed in the great room? Who was left, now that the residence was calm again, but one Harriet Buxton, a woman he may have blinked at once when she entered the party with Mr. and Mrs. Billings. And his daughter, Geneva, was at home. But he thought she had said she was going to bed before midnight.

Carol Chen

At the moment, on a settee in the Pratts' entry hallway, Harriet was lying there, terribly groggy and finally coming to. He supposed he could hustle her over to the Billings home before the night was through. But he also had another missing person bulletin to contend with.

"Salem, just what are we gonna do? What is Noreen gonna do if some New Year's Eve nutcakes have kidnapped Bernie for good?" Trudy Moody stared at Salem with a combination of alarm and annoyance. "My Noreen won't have her husband, her for-better-or-worse, no more. And look at you? Where's your wife, for God's sake? What's gone and happened to Chanson?"

"Trudy, we have to deal with these logistics one at a time. I'm going to deliver Harriet Buxton over to the Billings house before too long. In the meantime, let's find Jane to get her advice. She rushed past me a while ago hoping to change into some of Chanson's clothes. I told her it was OK. She said something about saving evidence. I don't know what's going on with her end of things." Salem put his head in his hands and rubbed his brow in exhaustion.

"You know what else, Salem," Trudy plunged in anew. "Someone told me they thought they saw a long, rolled-up somethin' or other—somethin' or other!—that looked like Bernie—gettin' carted out the door by two very strange actin' characters. And someone else told me they thought they saw Chanson jumpin' into a closet as herself and jumpin' right back out lookin' like, well, pardon my French, but lookin' like a toasty little slut. So I wanna know, WHO all did you invite to this wing ding of yours anyway?"

"I'm going to put aside what you just said about Chanson, OK, Trudy? By the way, where is Noreen with all of this?" Salem asked. "Does she have any idea what happened to Bernie?"

"Oh, she left the party early. She's got to get ready for a seminar she's givin' on NDEs up at Etna in a few days," Trudy replied.

"NDEs?"

"You know, 'Near Death Experiences.' You've heard of 'em haven't you?"

"Oh, yes. Right. People's testimonies when they've nearly died. Fascinating actually. I had no idea Noreen was knowledgeable about that area. And now that you mention NDEs, maybe Bernie is just out collecting raw material for Noreen's talk."

"Tell me you're not jokin' at my family's expense, Salem. As for Noreen, she's a bright one, my daughter. Got a lot of watts in her bulb, alright...'cept maybe when it comes to her husband. I will never know why she chose him. I will never know. And it's not like I can quiz her on it, either. Too late for that."

56
New Year's Day
Pre-Dawn

"Oh, Hi, Everyone. Sorry I took so long," Jane apologized to Salem and Trudy. Hamidi, Samantha, and Grace were finishing the last of the clean-up in the kitchen, and the residence was emptied of guests. "I just had to check in with the SWAT team...I think they're finally heading out."

"Jane, we have several issues to discuss with you," Salem began, with Trudy nodding vigorously at his side. "It seems both Chanson and Bernie Pushaw are missing. And Harriet Buxton, a friend of Mrs. Billings, was somehow overwhelmed tonight and probably drugged a bit, and left sitting on a chair in the middle of our balloon surprise at the stroke of midnight. There was a sign around her neck that read 'Woman of Ill Repute,' which I'm guessing was perhaps meant to read 'Whore'? Though what in hell it's all supposed to mean no one can figure out. So we're looking for your guidance on all of this."

"Good grief! I had no idea. All that happened to Harriet Buxton? How insane! I'm very sorry to hear all this news. A lot of the time tonight, I was...," Jane hesitated, "taking a tour of the house at Chanson's suggestion."

Jane sat a moment to digest Salem's news. She looked at the odd couple before her. "Well, concerning Harriet, you're saying Mrs. Billings brought Harriet to the party as her guest. So I think we should call the Billings family right now and tell them we're bringing Harriet to stay with them until she's ready to return home. When Harriet's more coherent, she needs to talk to the police about the assault on her person. I'll speak to Winnifred Billings and alert her about this step."

"I think I'll ask Samantha to take care of delivering Harriet Buxton to the Billings home," Salem suggested. "She'll be leaving soon and can drop Harriet off along the way."

"So, as far as Chanson and Bernie being missing persons," Jane said, "the first thing we should do is search this entire house to be sure neither of them is hidden or holed up somewhere in the house. If we don't find them, we should make sure Bernie isn't simply back at his home. And we can ask Noreen if there's anything that could help explain his disappearance. Tomorrow I'll talk to the State ferry people and the taxi shuttle service and see if they have any information. As you may know, missing people often surface in a day or so, so we shouldn't panic for now. But we'll open files on both Chanson and Bernie tomorrow and alert State law enforcement. We'll chase down everything and do our best to find them, OK?"

Salem stood up. "I'll ask Hamidi if he wouldn't mind looking through the house with me right now to confirm that neither Chanson nor Bernie are here. But first I'll help Harriet get settled in Samantha's car. I guess that means you can both head home," Salem said as he glanced from Jane Roberts to Trudy Moody.

57
New Year's Day
Not Yet Daylight

As Jane turned in towards her house, she immediately saw the black Mercedes SUV parked in her driveway. Now what, she thought irritably. The surprises just wouldn't quit. She turned off the key and stepped out of her truck into the snow...of course it was deeper than her boots, so of course the snow plopped down inside her boots and all over her cold feet. At least she had had the sense to remember to bring her boots to change into when she left the Pratts.

She held her bundled evening dress of evidence close to her chest and clomped through the snow and climbed the steps to her porch. What if Unknown Asshole had somehow figured out where Jane lived and had beaten her home? God forbid. No way. No second chance. She opened the front door and hesitantly called out. "Hello? Who's here? Anybody?" She slowly stuck her head inside.

"Jane! Finally! Where have you been?" Konstantin rose from his seat in the living room and walking briskly towards Jane. Before she could exclaim and leap on him, he held up his hand in a Stop sign.

She set the folded dress down on the hallway bench. Behind Konstantin on the living room couch were a couple in party attire. Jane assumed they must have come from the Pratts' party. She felt utterly exhausted, but totally mystified and jolted. What was Konstantin doing in Maine?! What was this couple doing in her home?

DON'T TOUCH MY COCKTAIL!

Konstantin quickly made the introductions. "Jane Roberts, let me introduce you to Texas Senator Hitch McGill and his wife, Shelby. They're old friends of our family. I ran into them tonight at Salem and Chanson's and invited them over. We're actually leaving now—I'll drive them to the Grand Harbor Inn and be right back. OK?"

Jane decided to be honest. "So sorry I can't ask you to stay longer, Senator and Mrs. McGill, but it's been quite a night. Hope you have a good visit in Maine. And hurry back, Konstantin! I can't believe you're here!"

The McGills and Konstantin gathered up their coats and started filing past Jane. They were all sharing polite, holiday phrases as they departed. She noticed the Senator was walking with a slight limp. As he passed her, she smiled in an automatic fashion while looking down at his limping. The foot section of his left boot appeared to have a discolored puncture mark. Jane looked up instantly. McGill had a mustache. *Don't,* Jane told herself. *Don't flinch. Lock it in. Get to it later, whatever it means.*

Once the front door was closed, Jane headed to her bedroom to prepare to collapse. Next to Konstantin!...and soon! But HOW did he know the McGills?

....

"Whatever happened to you tonight?" Konstantin called out from the hallway the minute he returned.

"Whatever are you doing in Maine?" Jane shot back.

"My compass is unconscious and unassailable," came his reply as he approached the bedroom.

"Well, my compass says nothing says lovin' like something from the oven...." His Pillsbury Dough Girl

243

was standing in the doorway with only her down quilt wrapped around her like a batch of inflatable buns. When Jane saw Konstantin, she turned into butter on a griddle. She buckled at the knees. She was relieved and hysterically happy and wild for hugging as they jumped into her bed, Konstantin yanking off his dinner jacket and unrolling Jane from her comforter.

A few minutes after their bouncing and tickling and smothering, Konstantin caught his breath. "No, wait! Wait! Before we get all crazy...tell me why I never found you at the party. Half the night I was looking for you, then I finally found you, and when I followed you, you vanished! What happened to Jane Roberts?"

What could she say? First, all those Aunt Robertas. Then Joe's revelation about Troy's tummy tuck. And her secret mission...Off Limits. And Konstantin knew the McGills! WHAT IF the Senator was Jane's Unknown Asshole? And how well did Konstantin know the McGills? Quite well—if they were old friends of his family. Quite well, if he had them over before Jane returned home. So should she tell Konstantin what she thought had happened? Should she tell anybody? Should she bother?

Nothing had actually transpired in the end. And what would she get out of telling people? She might get teased to death. And even if she could confirm Hitch McGill was Unknown Asshole, then what? He was a United States Senator for fuck's sake. What to do about that?

But his status, his public office, shouldn't be a shield at all. What Unknown Asshole did was so wrong. Jane couldn't remember the exact term, but it was on the books in Maine. Attempted sexual assault? Unlawful sexual contact? Some kind of Class C or D Crime...even if Unknown Asshole didn't get everything he wanted.

Maybe she was too tired to care tonight. Maybe she just wanted to be held warm and tight.

"Konstantin? Can we leave the details until tomorrow? I disappeared partly because of a work assignment, and partly due to a strange encounter. But right now, can we get under the covers and laugh, OK? Please? Can you make me laugh?"

"Come here, you crazy, crazy girl." And Konstantin wrapped Jane into him like a Brazil nut growing round its own flesh...two being one and nearly inseparable. "I've been holding off from showing you some of my more amazing skills."

"Haven't I seen them all?" Jane asked in wonder.

"Hardly, my dearest. Hang on...just let me chew this piece of gum for a moment. When I open my mouth, tell me what architectural wonder you see."

"Oh, come on...." Jane looked at him doubtfully and bumped him with her arm.

"Say another word, and I'll set you free."

"OK, OK...."

He worked on the gum, taking his time. "So, what is this?" he asked.

She looked at the stubby piece of gum on his tongue— a wrinkly piece of pink poked with a bunch of tiny teeth marks and nubs. "How should I know? You tell me."

"The Taj Mahal," he said. She stared at it. She looked into his eyes. Her whole face and throat exploded in laughter. And then they went crazy.

58
New Year's Day
Before Dawn

The Forbidden Fruits (including their newest member) and Chanson, plus one, rolled into HOJO's around 4:00 AM on New Year's Day. "Plus one" meant a scruffy, little stray puppy Zen-Ti had noticed through the falling snow near the dumpster at a gas station they had stopped at earlier on Route One. "We can't leave that little wankster shivering in the cold like that," Zen-Ti declared. "I'm going to grab him and then we can get going. And I'm not taking a group vote on this one."

The motley crew booked two rooms and split up...Zen-Ti, Chanson, and the little wankster in one room; ZK, ZM, and their new bro, Bernie, in the other. Bernie knew his lips were sealed.

....

"So how are we going to handle tonight, Zen-Ti?," Chanson asked, looking at the two queen-size beds and torn between wanting to go to Zen-Ti and wanting to do the right thing for the long haul.

"Chanson, I'm going to be totally straight with you now. You are my client above all else. I make it my motto never to mix pleasure and business, no matter if in your case, all I want to do is hold you all night long. And I'm serious about that. And not just tonight, but maybe forever. I don't know why I'm saying all this except you should know how I really feel, versus what I have to do to do the right thing by you...and your husband."

DON'T TOUCH MY COCKTAIL!

"I see," Chanson said, crestfallen that they would probably be behaving in this motel chain, but appreciating how Zen-Ti really felt.

"That doesn't mean we can't cuddle awhile with the little wankster and talk as much as you want. No one goes to jail for that, right?"

"So tell me about yourself, Zen-Ti...who you are. Tell me everything," Chanson said as they both lay down together on one bed with the puppy boomeranging between the two of them.

"Well, first off, Chanson, how was your Christmas?" Zen-Ti asked out of curiosity, wondering if Salem and Chanson had even spent the holiday together this year.

"Oh, Christmas. You know, it was kind of quiet. I was up in Maine. Salem was down in Texas. And our daughter was back and forth between her job in D.C. and our home in Maine. Nothing really to talk about."

"How about that," Zen-Ti said, actually surprised. "Kind of dull, huh?"

"Yes. Not a whole lot of Yuletide, caroling...or cookies...or wreaths. And the spirit of Christmas, all the magical or religious feelings, went out the door a long time ago. On top of that, I'm going to wake up in an ordinary HOJO's on New Year's Day. I am really batting 1000," Chanson said in dismay.

"Well, Honey, let me tell you how my granma used to tell us the Christmas story when we were just kids in Lowell, in Massachusetts." He leaned towards Chanson and tucked his head near her shoulder while the puppy bounced over and buried his face in between Chanson and Zen-Ti.

"My granma used to say Joseph and Mary didn't have a fancy hotel anywhere to check into on Christmas Eve...no one had space for them because they were Black-Asian people. They drove and drove till they saw a HOJO's on Route 93 near Lowell with a sign that said 'Pets Allowed.' And HOJO's was happy to give them a room, no matter if Joseph and Mary were Black-Asian. Plus HOJO's was the only motel that allowed animals for miles around...and that's how the cows and donkeys and sheep got to be there when Baby Jesus was born."

"You believed that story?" Chanson said as she wrapped both her arms around one of Zen-Ti's.

"Believe it? Hell, every year when we drove by HOJO's on Route 93 in December and January, us kids were always hanging out the car window looking and looking to see if we could see any donkeys or wise men trotting along on the highway. What did we know? When you're a kid, everything is true."

"Well, we've got a little Baby Jesus right here," Chanson said, snuggling the wankster up to her face. "What's going to happen to this little guy, Zen-Ti?"

"Why don't you keep him, Chanson? We can name him 'ZT Lowell,' so you have something to remember me by. ZT Lowell, the Little Wankster. Sounds kind of waspy, doesn't it? He'll fit right into your kind of life...no one will ever know he belongs to you and me. It'll be our furry secret. How's that?" Zen-Ti slowly stood up.

"And now I have got to go to sleep...in this other bed. Never mix love and work...," Zen-Ti repeated once again.

....

"Zen-Ti...Pssst! Zen-Ti, are you cold?" Chanson whispered into the darkness.

DON'T TOUCH MY COCKTAIL!

"...Huh?...What, Boo?" Zen-Ti was awake just enough to respond.

"Are you cold?"

"So cold, Babe."

"Is it us, or is it this room?"

"Both."

"Well, then...."

"You think so?"

"Yes..."

"Smart solution, Boo...."

"But, Zen-Ti. Your feet are freezing!"

"Only one way to take care of that, Babe."

"Oooooo! Hahahahaha!!"

PART THREE

59
Thursday, January 2, 2020

Helen Oberton thanked God for new mornings, and especially this one. She could feel all the High Cs of Christmas stress sliding away simply because the calendar read "January." It was always so easy. Took no effort. January and its perennial fresh start simply arrived. Such a welcomed relief to get out from under all those holiday frenzies and stale disappointments. Onward towards the bright white openness of a new year, with the gift of more light each day. Anything was possible.

She doublechecked her call list and was satisfied she had rung up everyone Jane needed to talk to or see today. Which meant Harriet Buxton, Salem Pratt, Chanson Pratt, and Bernie Pushaw.

Jane arrived sunny side up. "Good Morning, Helen. What a beautiful new day. The sky...the brilliant snowy countryside...the clean air. Life in Maine!"

"You certainly have a bounce in your step, Jane." Helen smiled at her. Not that it had anything to do with Konstantin being in town. Helen wasn't about to suggest that out loud. She arranged fresh coffee and tea and sour cream cinnamon nut cake on the PSO table so people could nibble while Jane cajoled them.

DON'T TOUCH MY COCKTAIL!

....

"Jane, Bernie's here for his interview. Don't say I didn't warn you." Helen bent down under her desk to whisper the second sentence into the phone.

Jane stepped out of her office. Missing Person Bernie Pushaw was no longer that. He stood there proudly, buried within a bulky black varsity jacket, which he spun around in to show off the colorful "Forbidden Fruits" logo on the back.

"Well look at who just walked in. Houdini, himself. How did you get your hands on that jacket, Bernie Pushaw?" Jane said.

"Hey, now, Jane. There you go again...all huffy on me." He began to weave his answer. "I jus' found this baby lyin' around at Chanson's party. I put 'er on while I was roastin' those God damn pigs because I was freezin' my butt off. Ain't every day your wife signs you up for pig duty, outside, when a blizzard's about to hit, right?"

"You found it, Bernie? And you took it? And then what happened? Did you just up and mysteriously disappear for twelve hours while the rest of us went mental trying to figure out who kidnapped you?" Jane was steaming.

"Well, I can't remember much o' what happened, Jane. Seems like a big blank. Wha' do they call it? Amneesher?"

"I'll tell you what they call it, Bernie. They call it the Stockholm Syndrome. That's what I think is going on here," Jane said, coming to the end of her patience.

"Come again?"

"The Stockholm Syndrome, you turnip," Jane said. "Where you're captured and you actually start to take a liking to your kidnapper. Instead of being angry, you bond

251

with that person—you don't want to blame that person for anything."

"Now that sure as hell ain't my style, Jane. Come on. You know me better 'n that. No way am I gonna fall for some guys from Massachusetts."

"Bernie! There you go again. What do you mean 'some guys from Massachusetts'? Are you saying people from Massachusetts grabbed you and spirited you away from Chanson's party? And those same someones dumped you right back here the next day? Why would anyone in his right mind do that?"

"Jane, I ain't got no idea what you're talkin' about. I don' know nothin' 'bout Stockham Syndrome or Massachusetts Syndrome. All I know about is MY syndrome. I got Post Traumatic Pork Syndrome. That's what's really goin' on here."

"What the hell is that?" Jane said, closing her eyes and shaking her head.

"Post Traumatic Pork Syndrome? I found out all about it on Google. At the ferry terminal cafe."

"So you played Dr. Google, did you?" Jane said.

"It's a syndrome, Jane! That's serious stuff where I come from. You can check it out on PorkBuddy.com."

"How the hell did you get this so-called Post Traumatic Pork Syndrome?" Jane was ready to choke Bernie.

"Well, now, that could be a long story, but it ain't. See, my one-and-only Noreen promised me to Chanson and Sam for the party pork prep. Just tryin' to keep me busy at doin' somethin' perductive on New Year's Eve, instead of drinkin' the whole night away...like I saw you hollerin' for your Aunt Robertas at the party, Jane."

"Bernie, I think that's enough. You can stop right there," Jane said, deciding to shut Bernie down. "I'll get back to you if I have any more questions. But to be clear...you are not interested in filing any police report or talking to us about any kidnapping. And no one has harmed you. Is that correct?"

"Sure as the day is long, Jane. An' if I ain't A-OK, then I'm B-OK." Bernie flashed her a toothy grin and grabbed a piece of sour cream cinnamon nut cake on his way out.

....

The office door opened and Chanson Pratt walked in wearing an oversized Forbidden Fruits varsity jacket. Jane eyed her from the PSO table. "Well, hello, Chanson. Come have a seat at the table. And don't tell me. Let me guess. You found that jacket lying around at your New Year's Eve party, right?"

"Hi, Jane! Happy New Year. Yes, the jacket was something someone must have forgotten...we have a pile of people's odds and ends up to my waist in our main entryway...left over from the party. Happens every time."

"Well, first of all, thank you for dropping in to talk, Chanson. We're all relieved that you're back at home and in one piece. But please tell me. What exactly happened to you and Bernie between the time you left your party and once you got back to the island? Is there anything you can divulge, Chanson?" Jane—eternal idiot optimist—was holding her breath that she'd get some kind of honest answer.

"Oh, Jane. New Year's Eve was insane! We'll never hear the end of it. And I especially have no idea what happened to Harriet Buxton. We're hoping she doesn't haul us into court." Chanson leaned over for a piece of sour cream cinnamon nut cake.

"Chanson, did you notice how you did not answer my question?"

"That's true. But what can I say? I probably drank more than I should have. You can appreciate that." Chanson rolled her eyes at Jane. "I really can't remember enough of the pieces to put them together. But one thing does stick in my mind. And it's profound...why can't we all live together in peace, no matter where we come from or what we look like?" She stood there looking perplexed and rather gang-like.

"What's any of that babbling got to do with my question about you going missing for a night and half a day, Chanson? First Bernie is incapable of remembering anything vital. And now you. Same incident; same problem. What am I dealing with here? Two brain-drained Houdinis?"

"I just don't know, Jane. I don't know what to say. I have no recollection of leaving the house, and I must have only woken up when I arrived back at my house. I can't remember any faces, or places, or people. It's all a blank...honestly. I'm so sorry! Mind if I have another piece of cake?"

"Oh, for God's sake. I am tired of this," Jane blurted out. "What am I supposed to do about you? I think you're also caught up in the Stockholm Syndrome, Chanson. You know what happened and you refuse to tell me."

"Well, my memory is not cooperating, Jane. But think about it. Does it really matter at this point? Bernie and I are both back home and we don't feel like anything happened to us to make a difference. So why don't we chalk it up to one bizarre night and leave it at that? Easy. Simple. No harm done."

DON'T TOUCH MY COCKTAIL!

"Chanson, you're driving me crazy. But I'll compromise with you. I'll close the books on your twelve-hour vanishing act. But if our investigation into those Russian fake waiters at your party points us back in your direction, things aren't going to be as easy and simple as you think."

"Oh, Jane. Sometimes you act like a she-bear in satin."

"Oh yah? Well, sometimes you're more slippery than a pocketful of pudding, Chanson."

"Why, Jane, I didn't know you know how to talk Texan. Well done!"

"Guess I still have some snap in my garters," Jane said, bouncing on her toes.

Chanson slapped her thigh and said, "If that ain't a fact, God's a possum!"

60
Thursday, January 2
Afternoon

"Thanks for coming in alone, Salem. I wanted to talk to you without Chanson present. Once you two split off to attend to your separate host duties at your New Year's Eve party, it seems like everything began to get kind of crazy."

Salem pulled out a chair and sat down at the PSO table. "I couldn't agree with you more, Jane," he said.

"Could you tell me what you think happened at your party that was out of the ordinary?"

"Yes, but before I forget, Jane, here's something I found buried inside our fridge this morning." Salem handed Jane a piece of paper smudged with grease and what looked like barbecue sauce. "It's some kind of love letter from Bernie Pushaw to you. I'm guessing he stuck it in the fridge while he was helping with the pigs. He goes on about walkie talkies and Russians. I'll leave it up to you to figure it out."

"Thanks, Salem. At this point, every detail may be helpful. So, getting back to your take on the party, tell me what you think," Jane said.

"I guess there's nothing that sticks in my mind until I came back downstairs after making a few business calls. Then all of a sudden, these two guys in white jackets were coming at me. I ran like hell. At some point, I think I heard them speaking Russian. I finally ran to the catering trailer, and Samantha, our chef, helped me lock the guys in the trailer." He helped himself to a piece of cake.

DON'T TOUCH MY COCKTAIL!

"Then at midnight, we had the frightful scene of Harriet Buxton with the supposed whore sign, and right after that some kind of federal posse piled into our house at the tail end of our party. And as you know, both Chanson and Bernie Pushaw went missing overnight, but they're back home now. So what do I think? Maybe I don't want to think, Jane. I can't recall a worse party. And here we are."

"Do you know if any of these strange incidents are connected?"

"No idea. Did Helen make this cake? It's fantastic."

"Thank you, Salem. Take all you want," said Helen.

"So why would Russians be running after you at your own party, Salem?" asked Jane.

"OK. This is in utter confidence, Jane. I'm only telling you because it might help explain the Russians. And it looks like I'm in the clear now, so this is just background information, OK? You see, due to some recent, unfortunate economic shifts, my semiconductor business was in deep trouble. It's all been resolved, but some of my major creditors are Russian, and they may have been getting impatient about my loans. Maybe they wanted to exert some pressure, shall we say?"

"But, Salem. That's awful! You could have been seriously hurt, if not worse, at your own party. And what do you mean, everything has been resolved? I take it you're talking about owing lots of money but now you're out from under that debt. Can you talk about how it got resolved?"

"I'd rather not go into the substance, Jane. If you need to dig further, my lawyers would probably suggest a subpoena. I'm not trying to give you hard time. But there are all these precautions about business security and so on."

"Well, let's leave it at that for now. For your own safety, though, as well as any law enforcement issues...if we need more information, I am going to have to get back to you."

"Sure."

"May I ask how well you know this Senator from Texas...I think his name is Hitch McGill?" Jane asked.

"Oh, Hitch and I are old buddies...Texans by birth. He was at the party," Salem added.

"Yes, I know," Jane said.

"It's funny you mention Hitch...and you'll have to tell me why. But he did have an odd question for me at one point. Wanted to know what the Environmental Fields was all about. He didn't bring it up again during the evening, so I don't know more than that."

"Really," said Jane, making a note of Salem's comment.

"In fact, you might want to talk to our daughter, Geneva. She's an assistant to Senator McGill in his Washington office."

"Well that's very helpful, Salem. I will plan on talking to Geneva. Is she still on the island through this weekend?"

"Yes. You can definitely get hold of her at the house until Monday morning. We're still cleaning up and putting things back in order. So what's your interest in Hitch?"

"Oh, nothing really. I met him and his wife briefly the night of your party...through Konstantin. So, ah, one last question, Salem. Do you know why the federal SWAT team invaded your home?"

"Jane, we were as stunned as anyone. No warning whatsoever. I have no idea what inspired them or motivated them to crash our party. A hell of a lot of mysteries all in one night...."

61
Thursday, January 2
Late Afternoon

"Helen, can you help me at the whiteboard?" Jane said after Salem Pratt departed the PSO. "I've got new intel to put into the columns."

"Sure, Jane. What should I do?" Helen asked.

"Let me add something to the white board and then we'll get started." Jane wrote a note about "Operation?" next to the note about "$?" in Troy's column, and a second note about Salem's debt to the Russians in the ICE column. She paused a moment and added Salem's debt to the CIA and FBI columns as well.

"OK. First off...here's Bernie's note to me. Why don't you read it out loud and then we'll decide how it's helpful."

Helen peered at Bernie's chicken scratch and began:

Jane—Bernie here. Gotta tell you bout them Ruskies! I just seen two of em at the pigs tonite. Every time the grease hits em, they yell out PIZ DETS. Now your probably wonderin why Im tellin you all this. Its cuz, Jane, and this is the God-awful truth...there come a night this December, maybe the second week in, when I was talkin to Jason Coombs on the walkie talkie. We had lots of static and then he started talkin funny, you know, like funny with an acent. So

DON'T TOUCH MY COCKTAIL!

Im goin along with him and every time he yells out PIZ DETS, Im thinkin hes bein silly and razzin me about a PIZZA DIET. I mean what would you do if you herd someone yelling PIZ DETS into your walkie talkie? So Im OK with his PIZZA DIET. I mean mans gotta eat, right? So Im asking him to get me some pizza too, like maybe with hamburger and pinapple or whatever black and gold thing he's talkin about. Anyway, we talk about our next barrel pickup an he tells me to go the boatyard, of all places in December, Jane! So I go to the boatyard and there ain't nothin there, Jane! Not a soul. Not a barrel. And the next day I sees my buddy Jason, he says I must be losin it, cause he don't know what the hell Im talkin about. He says he lost me on the walkie talkie that night. He says he never herd of PIZ DET, and he didn't say nothin to me about the boatyard. Now ain't that the stranjest thing, Jane? You need to know this, and Im tellin it to you. Cuz it says to me PIZ DETs got to be them Russians. And them Commie Russky guys must have walkie talkies and they are tryin to act like they are Jason, or they are tryin to order us around, or maybe it's jus one big fuckup, but you can figure it all out. OK, Jane? Over and out...your friend, Bernie Pushaw

"Wow, Helen. Let me see that letter," Jane said. She read it again, line by line, trying to decipher Bernie's meaning. Hoping to follow his train of thought about the pig roast, Russians yelling PIZ DETS, Bernie and Jason Combs on their walkie talkies in December, black and gold, and no barrels at the boatyard.

"So Bernie concludes the Russians have walkie talkies and it was a Russian who spoke to Bernie that night about the barrels at the boatyard. Pretty good analysis...and from Bernie, no less."

"Well, Jane," Helen spoke up. "You know how walkie talkies can accidentally pick up conversations intended for other parties. It sounds to me like that's what happened to Bernie that night. He and Jason were talking, and then a Russian joined the conversation by mistake."

Jane looked at Helen in surprise. "I think you've got it, Helen. And walkie talkies...they came up concerning Troy Overlock. His mother said he was on the walkie talkie quite a bit in November concerning winter storage. But Mr. Williams at the boatyard said there weren't a lot of boats delivered for winter storage in November. That's already on the white board. Where is it? OK. So what we can conclude is that Troy was on his walkie talkie more than usual in November, but it may not have been for work.

"Furthermore, does Bernie's account mean the Russians told him to pick up barrels at the boatyard? That's the point of it, don't you think."

"Why then would Bernie say he found no barrels at the boatyard?" Helen asked.

"Maybe there was so much confusion language-wise and meaning-wise, that nobody was making sense while the Russian was talking to Bernie," Jane said. "Or, maybe

Bernie's not telling the whole truth. There we go again. I'll add a question about 'Bernie's honesty re barrels at boatyard?'

"And what is this reference to black and gold? If the Russian didn't intend to talk to Bernie, who else would the Russian be trying to reach? Was that person Troy? And I've got to call Torrance Balankoff about PIZ DETS. She'll know what it means.

"And one more detail...Salem mentioned that Senator Hitch McGill was asking him about Environmental Fields at the party. Why would this Senator from Texas want to know about our septage recycling area?"

"I'm back!" Israel said when he walked into the office. "Sorry I'm about eight hours late. Vermont and New Hampshire are having a hell of a sleet storm...getting back to Maine was a slushy nightmare on the highways."

"You're just in time, Israel. Grab some coffee and join us," Jane said. "We're plowing through the columns on the whiteboard, and I think something's actually beginning to jell. Take a look at what we've got so far while I call Torrance Balankoff. I'll be right back."

....

"So what do you think, Israel?" Jane said when she returned. "And by the way, Torrance says PIZ DETS is a Russian swear phrase. She, too, overheard the Russians using that phrase the night of the Pratt party. She also says she saw Spartak and two or three of his mates masquerading as waiters that night."

"Well, here's another possible link. You've got Spartak, the Russian sailor, wandering around in Environmental Fields. Why is he there?" Israel pointed to the whiteboard.

"And you've also got Hitch McGill asking questions about Environmental Fields. Why would he want to know about our island septage recycling, as you say. So maybe there's a connection between Spartak and Hitch McGill."

"Good point, Israel," Jane cheered as she added a question to the Environmental Fields column and the CIA and FBI columns about a link between Spartak and Hitch McGill.

Jane jumped up and started swinging into jumping jacks. "The more we see how this all flows together," she said, throwing her arms in the air, "well, we may end up saving what's left of civilized life on this island! Ha ha!!"

"Did you happen to pick up anything helpful while you were at the Pratt party, Jane?" Helen said.

"Glad you ask. Look at Troy's column. Now, this is all confidential. Seriously. This cannot leave the building...Troy's safety may be at risk, OK? I've written down 'Operation' and '$?.' 'Operation' is my shorthand for the fact that Troy wants to get a tummy tuck. Can you believe it?"

The words "tummy tuck" ping-ponged between Helen's face and Israel's face and bounced around the office until landing back on the table.

"Jane, come on," said Israel. "How do you know that?"

"Oh dear. I can believe it," Helen said. "Troy has certainly gotten heavier in recent years. It's quite a shock, compared to when he was younger."

"Well, I may have been under the influence of spirits at the New Year's Eve party, but I swear to you one of Troy's colleagues revealed Troy's big secret to me at some point that night. I had asked him what Troy would do if he had a lot of money. And he said Troy had plans to get a tummy tuck."

DON'T TOUCH MY COCKTAIL!

"What money does Troy have?" Israel said.

"Right. That's the other detail I have to report. Troy's mother came to the office last Friday to admit something she and Mr. Overlock failed to tell us. Troy had five thousand in cash stashed at home, and the Overlocks don't know where it came from. That's what prompted me to ask Troy's friend what Troy would do with a lot of cash."

"Which friend is this, Jane?" Israel asked.

"I'd rather not say at this point...we need to keep this all under wraps for now. The friend asked for anonymity."

"But you believe this person?" said Israel.

"Well, think about it. Look at all these comments from Troy's associates in his column." Jane pointed to the items on the whiteboard.

"The central question is *did* Troy get involved in some deal so he could get money to pay for a tummy tuck? And did something go sour on this deal? What do you think?"

"What kind of deal? With whom?" said Israel.

"I don't know. Maybe with Senator McGill? Or the Russians? ...Which might make the most sense if they were trying to reach Troy and not Bernie the night of the walkie talkie mix-up."

"If we assume it's the Russians, then we want to know what was Troy doing with them?" Israel said.

"And whatever it was, did it have something to do with barrels? And barrels of what? Barrels that Bernie says the Russian told him to pick up on the walkie talkie, but which Bernie said he never found. So what went wrong? And how might it relate to Hitch McGill and/or Salem Pratt? And remember, the federal SWAT team didn't show up for nothing. They were looking for something criminal with an international angle. So like you said earlier, Israel, the appearance of the FBI and the CIA helps to pull the picture together, and tighter."

"Too bad Troy won't talk to us," said Israel. "Remember how he acted when we visited him? He's not ready to tell us anything."

"Exactly," Jane said. "OK. Let's give this a rest. I'll see if Storm can join us to think through the pieces."

62
Thursday, January 2
Late Afternoon

"Jane, Harriet Buxton's on the line for you."

"Oh, Sweet Jesus. This could be painful. She's going to gut me and hang me from our flag pole," Jane said.

"Jane Roberts! This is Harriet Buxton. We need to talk."

"Mrs. Buxton, I am so sorry to hear about the party. What happened?" Jane stuck her head outside her office and scrunched up her face at Helen.

"You mean, how did a felony land in my cocktail? Well, Jane, that's for you to find out," Harriet said. "In fact, you and I are going to work on this together. All hush, hush. Do you understand?"

"But, Mrs. Buxton, shouldn't you first talk to the police and have an official investigation?"

"Definitely not, Jane! If anyone thinks for a moment that Harriet Buxton is going to let this Pratt party incident go public or go through official channels, then that person is a supreme idiot. My name is not going to be smeared all over kingdom come with a whore sign like a choker round my neck."

"I can see your point." Jane flopped back into her chair. She caught Helen's eye a second time through the door and mimed a self-stabbing to the chest.

"So I'm taking you into utter confidence here, Jane. I am not going to sit around like a victim feeling sorry for herself. And I'm not leaving the digging to some schlepping detectives. But I can't figure out how I got roofied all by myself."

"Roofied?" said Jane.

"Well who knows what it was...Rohypnol, special K...something in my drink that didn't belong there!"

"So how do you want to proceed, Mrs. Buxton?" Jane said.

"You and I are going to solve this case together. Now I know you feel defiant towards authority, Jane. It shows in all the wacked out things you do in your job. And I can't say I've approved of your errant behavior, but I get it."

"What are you talking about, Mrs. Buxton?"

"Never mind. What's done is done. I just want you to realize that I understand your stance against officialdom and posturing. You young people can't always see it in your older colleagues. But some of us once marched on the wild side...until we came round to full-time careers in law enforcement and justice."

"The wild side, Mrs. Buxton?" Jane said.

"Very wild, Jane. I was the child of full-blown hippie parents. Drugs, sex, and rock and roll were only the beginning. Why do you think I have maroon-colored hair? It's henna! I've used it since my childhood in a commune out in Santa Cruz."

"Maybe you don't want to be telling me all of this, Mrs. Buxton," Jane said.

"But I do, Jane. And do you know why? I mean, yes, it's quite personal and I may be going overboard. But I'm trying to illuminate the common ground I share with you. We are not perched in such far opposite corners of the universe as you may think. I wasn't always a figure of authority. And now, well I feel electrified, Jane. This whole whore incident has energized me. I feel like I'm back in my 20s, ready to kick ass. And that's where you come in."

Oh lucky me, Jane thought. *Lackey to the wacky.*

"From the moment my head cleared, I began stewing over the assault," Mrs. Buxton said. "Winnie Billings and I sat at her kitchen table the next morning and dissected everything that went wrong at that damn party. We concluded this has got to be a revenge matter that screwed up mightily. There must be adultery involved, right? Woman of Ill Repute?—Whore would have been more succinct! So who would want something like that done? Who was the real target? Who actually carried out the deed? Winnifred and I talked and talked and POW! We realized, to our horror, that Diane Savoy has been grumbling about her husband, Wilton, playing around again."

"Wait a minute, Mrs. Buxton," Jane said. "Who is Diane Savoy? Who's Wilton? And can you walk me through everything that happened to you surrounding the whore event?"

"Diane Savoy is the wife of Wilton Savoy. He's the marketing chairman of J. T. Karl's Wild Open. And Wilton's infidelity is a stale tale, but he's at it again, and this time Diane is really pissed."

"But what's Diane got to do with the whore scene?" Jane said.

"Well she's the only one we've come up with who's angry about her husband's latest affair AND she was also a guest at the Pratts. No one in their right mind thinks I was meant to sit on that chair. I'm not a whore! But for some as yet to be explained reason, I got dragged into the whole thing. By mistake. Diane would never do that to a sorority sister. And besides, I would never sleep with Wilton Savoy. He isn't my type."

And he would never let your flesh near his flesh.... "And can you remember the details right before you were knocked out?" Jane said.

"It's gone right now, Jane. But it may all come back, and the minute it does, these perps are going to end up begging for mercy. Trust me."

"So what's next, Mrs. Buxton?" Jane asked.

"To start, I'm going to put in a work order under your name to get Diane Savoy's cell phone records."

"My name? You're kidding," Jane said.

"I am not kidding, Jane. If she's not the trigger, then we'll eliminate that possibility and move on to some other idea. But she's a good place to start. And you're going to read through those phone records to figure out what's going on...and find out who hung the whore sign on me. Then I'm going to plot my own revenge."

"Mrs. Buxton, this doesn't sound like the workings of the Director of Human Resources at the Maine State Police. I'm not so sure I should commit to this task. What if I don't?"

"You have no choice, Jane. You're in charge of public safety on this island, aren't you? And don't think I didn't hear about your exchange with Alex Champus. Don't think I didn't read that entire, half-witted report you called into the FBI on New Year's Eve. Such shabby, shoddy work, even if you do abhor authority! What were you thinking? What were you drinking? A four-year-old could have done better job."

"How did you know about Champus and his SWAT team?" Jane said, shocked to think that Mrs. Buxton had any idea.

"I referred you to the FBI."

"As in 'cheap and easy'?!" Jane said, gripping her hands around a would-be neck.

"Those were not my exact words. And I'll be the first to agree that Champus can be a rude bastard. But when the FBI calls, Jane, we jump."

"Mrs. Buxton, I'm sorry, but this whole situation makes no sense. Why didn't you and Lieutenant Adderley report to Champus about 'unusual behavior' at the party? Why pull me in?"

"My dear, we wanted to enjoy ourselves, without the burden of surveillance for the FBI. So we tapped you. Besides, it's good for your CV," Harriet said.

"Well, I'd like to know why a SWAT team barged into the party in the first place. Champus refused to tell me."

"I'll give you a little background, because I agree with you that it wasn't right to leave you in the dark. But don't go breathing a word about this to anyone anywhere outside your team. The FBI and the CIA have been monitoring some highflyers in Congress for several years—tracking corruption, receipt of foreign bribes, illegal importation of gold and Russian manufactured goods. It's a total nightmare."

"That's the level of crime here?" Jane said in awe.

"Yes," Mrs. Buxton said. "And when you called in your concerns to ICE about Lobster Brides! and illegal foreigners, it got sucked into an already complicated mess. By the way, I wish you'd lay off of Gluella Trott and all her hard work. She's such small fish compared to the scum the FBI and the CIA are chasing down. Anyway, I can't say more. But you owe it to your country to get to the bottom of my whore horror, Jane. That will help absolve you of some of your latest gaffs."

"Mrs. Buxton...something's just occurred to me. When you say highflyers in Congress, just how many highflyers were at the Pratts' party?" *Besides Hitch McGill,* Jane was wondering. *And illegal importation of gold?*

"How would I know the guest list, Jane? You can ask Chanson or Salem about that," said Harriet.

"OK. OK. I will talk to the Pratts. So where are you right now, Mrs. Buxton? And when were you planning to send me Diane Savoy's telephone records?"

"I'm still at Winnie Billings' home. I already had plans to stay a few days after the Pratt party. In fact, you could also help me with one little bit of back-up, Jane, just to be safe."

"Back-up? To be safe?" *Now what?*

"Yes. I have a little rendezvous planned for tonight at Curry in a Hurry. I'll explain everything at the restaurant. But I'd like you nearby, just in case."

"Just in case? What does that mean, Mrs. Buxton?" Jane said.

"Well, after the whore incident, I want to take precautions against anyone who might still be lurking on the island, ready to pounce on me."

Jane dropped her head onto her arms on her desk, almost losing the phone. "By nearby, do you mean I should be in the restaurant?"

"Definitely. Let's meet at 5:30 PM. And I'm happy to cover your meal, Jane, but no dessert."

No dessert. The nerve of this woman. "OK, Mrs. Buxton. I'll follow through per your plan. And fax me Diane Savoy's phone records when you can," Jane said.

63
Thursday, January 2
Evening

Jane stepped into Curry in a Hurry, none too eager to join Harriet Buxton. But there she was, waving Jane in from the booth at the back...looking a bit too happy possibly, uncharacteristically enthusiastic?

Jane walked past several booths and tables done up in pale wood. Rajiv Basrak had chosen Nordic simplicity for his new little cafe, and the colors of saris and Indian sweets called out from the napkins and plates...saffron, lime, magenta, persimmon, bright blue. Jane was relieved Rajiv hadn't succumbed to a tented, festooned interior of filmy curtains and elephants with jewels plastered in the middle of their foreheads.

She sat down with her back to the entrance. Harriet was beaming at her with unusual warmth. "Thank you for doing this, Jane. And make sure you order yourself some dinner. I just wanted you here tonight as my security blanket...not really for protection," she said. "More like emotional security."

"That's OK, Mrs. Buxton. Happy to calm your nerves."

"I should confess. And you'll probably laugh. But I've signed up with Lobster Brides!" Harriet leaned forward and Jane could smell the excess of perfume. "I'm about to meet up with my potential suitor."

Unbelievable. Who would believe this? "Wow. That's very brave of you, Mrs. Buxton," Jane said in faux support.

How on earth Harriet could qualify, Jane had no idea. Harriet did not live on the coast, and she wasn't a juicy, young chick. Jane could not imagine what Harriet had submitted for pictures and personal data. So much for Gluella Trott and her absurd algorithms.

"Yes, well, we're planning to meet in the first booth near the entrance at 6 PM, and it's nearly time. So I'll go anchor myself. The rest is in the hands of Gluella and Fate!" Harriet laughed bumpily as she maneuvered herself out of the booth and left Jane with only the menu for company.

....

Harriet sat with her back to the entrance. She was poised on her whoopee cushion of anticipation. Her skin felt like it was lathered in chili sauce. If she could only prolong this frisky suspense for the rest of the night. She even dared to ask the fateful question she had been shoving aside for weeks. *What* if she *clicked* with this man?

She could hear the door open, footsteps moving forward, then footsteps halting. Potentially Mr. Right was turning to sit down in the booth. She lifted her face to greet the promising specimen, but the sight of him ripped the syllables from her lips. Joseph Adderley hesitated in mid-air, looking like a baby gorilla with a big secret in his diaper. Not quite the knight of Harriet's dreams.

"Joseph! What is this? What are you doing here?"

"Is this the wrong booth?"

"What do you mean?"

Adderley leaned forward with a pained, self-conscious whisper. "Do the words 'Lobster Brides!' mean anything to you, Harriet? If not, please forgive me, and I'll be on my way. Though I don't mean to be abrupt."

DON'T TOUCH MY COCKTAIL!

"This is ludicrous, Lieutenant Adderley. You are exactly *not* the wealthy foreigner featured in your bio."

"What?" said Adderley, not instantly comprehending. "Oh...I see. But you? Mrs. Buxton?" Adderley's face flushed red. "You are hardly the foxy lady who loves jogging naked on the beach at midnight."

"Well, what did you expect, Joseph?"

"I expected the seductive nymph posted on the web."

"Oh, you did, did you?"

"I did indeed."

Harriet crossed her arms, holding in her pounding heart so recently flaming with internal hot sauce and passion. "It serves you right for trying to pull a fast one, Lieutenant. Trotting in here masquerading as a British don with a manor house in the Cotswolds."

"Now, Harriet. Hold on a minute," said Adderley.

"To think you sat across from me at the Billings breakfast table two mornings in a row, stuffing yourself silly with bacon and eggs and French toast and apricot jam, all the while plotting and hotting it up for your mystery date. Shame, shame on you for not bringing it up in polite conversation. If I'd had even a clue about your absurd intentions, I would have been forewarned."

"One might say the same to you, Harriet, if one weren't a gentleman."

"You forget, Lieutenant, that women are at a statistical disadvantage, come a certain age. Society *should* permit them judicious berth to manipulate how they will present themselves."

"All right, Harriet. This has got to stop. We're not going to get anywhere with this awkward blunder. I say it's time for a truce."

"And then what? What are we going to do?"

"Maybe apply for a refund from that ridiculous dating site?"

"Oh, shut up. Gluella is my niece. She was doing me a favor. I'm not going to drain her profits on account of your falsehoods."

"You know, I give up. Let's be civilized adults, shall we? Would you like a ride back to the Billings house?"

"Suit yourself. But I think we should get some take-out to bring back with us."

"That'll work. Let's order enough so we can sit down with Winnie and Kenmore. There's still time to catch the basketball game tonight."

"Basketball? You never mentioned basketball in your Lordship's bio."

"Blast it all, Harriet. Just ditch the website crap already. I'm sure you don't know the first thing about the Kama Sutra, unlike your dishy virtual self."

"Wouldn't you be surprised...."

"Then surprise me. Later tonight. I'm all in."

....

"I'll have some of that Indian fried rice, medium spicy, with some chicken tandoori, palak paneer, and an order of dal." Jane sighed over the menu one more time and smiled at the waitress. "Also an order of paratha, extra mango chutney, and a mango lassi. Thanks. And please give my bill to the woman with the dark red hair in the first booth, OK? She's treating me."

Jane took out her notepad and started scribbling down random ideas about Troy's troubles and her over-populated whiteboard. She wondered how to go about analyzing and pulling together all the points in her columns. As her mind strolled around, it occurred to her to string things together into coherent sense...like a necklace...maybe that was it. Each event was a bead to add to the necklace...one after another, wherever they fit the best. That's what she would suggest to Storm and Israel tomorrow....

"Ma'am, sorry to bother you, but there is no woman with red hair in the first booth to pay for your dinner."

"What? She was there when I arrived. You don't remember?" Jane leaned outside her booth to look back towards Harriet. *What the hell?* She was gone. "OK. Ah, do you remember seeing the woman with the red hair at all? ...You think she left with a man? OK. Never mind. I'll pay. No problem. Thanks."

Jane wasn't about to blubber into her tandoori, but she was ready to label Harriet a ditz. And she was not going to become Jane's responsibility. Not by a long shot. Harriet could take care of herself. Especially since she had run off without paying Jane's tab.

After a few minutes, Jane got up and walked towards the kitchen cut-out window to say Hi to Rajiv who was busy cooking. He stepped away from the stove, and she handed him a package. "Here's what I promised you. Make me happy, OK?" They both laughed and Jane returned to her seat.

64
Thursday, January 2
Later in the Evening

Jane was washing down a mouthful of fried rice with mango lassi when she became aware of loud male voices approaching the booth seating area. There was something familiar in those voices, and the people attached to them seated themselves in the booth behind Jane.

She could discern only two men talking once they were settled. The waitress came over and took their drinks order.

Wait a minute. Is that Champus speaking?! Jane listened closely. *Did he say 'Hitch...as in Hitch McGill?* Scrunching down in her seat, Jane tried to think what she would do if they saw her. She grabbed her trapper hat out of her hobo bag, pulled it down low, and tucked her hair up inside. After she fished around in her bag again, she found what she was looking for and put it on the table. Then she hugged the booth with her ear to listen further.

"So, here's to skirting disaster, hey, Hitch?"

"You bet, Alex. Shelby and I definitely appreciate that heads up you gave us. Who'd of thought the Feds would come pissing on the Pratts' party. Seems like it's getting harder and harder to stay ahead of these goon squads."

Hitch McGill AND Champus. Traitors to their country? ...My country. Jane wanted to disappear or kill. She couldn't decide which.

DON'T TOUCH MY COCKTAIL!

"But that damn Environmental Fields, Alex. What the hell is going on there? Did you find anything?" McGill said.

"Nah...I scoped it out late last night, tried cracking through in a few spots. It's a fucking glacier out there. Don't think you're ever going to find your goods. At least not until spring."

Goods buried in Environmental Fields? That belong to Hitch? That's it! But what is IT? Jane held her breath.

"How did this happen, Champ? How did my stuff end up in those fields? One fucking surprise after another. This whole island makes a hornet look cuddly. No internet, cold as a banker's heart, and too many tater heads runnin' around," said McGill.

"No kidding. I swear the Public Safety Officer out here was loaded when I sent her to the party on assignment. I had to pretend we needed some law enforcement bozo to give our team local support. What a joke."

You asshole! Such a jerk. Jane stuffed a piece of paratha into her mouth.

"What intelligence she did provide was all garbled...and she may have even brought along her Aunt Roberta. Totally unprofessional," said Champus.

Idiot!

"The Public Safety Officer, you say? What's her name again?"

"Jane Roberts," said Champus.

"She the tall flicka with the full dark mane? Prancing around in some kind of black opera glove for a dress?" said McGill.

Flicka! I knew it. It's got to be him.

Carol Chen

"Might have. I'm not sure. When she caught up with my team at the end, all I saw was casual clothes. After I specifically told her to wear a gown. Pathetic public servant," said Champus.

"Hmm, I may have crossed her path at the party. But not to worry. Just as well she doesn't have a clue about what we're up to."

Jane pondered what she should do. Arrest both of them? Without handcuffs, or a proper jail? Without back-up? Threaten to smear them with hot mango chutney if they misbehaved?

OK. She should just wait. Think about it. They weren't running away—they didn't know that Jane knew they were in cahoots. Even when they left the island, it wasn't like they would flee the country. Jane decided to simply wait. To figure it out. And in the meantime, after the duo left the restaurant, she would head to the ferry cafe and review what intelligence she had gained in the last half hour.

65
Friday, January 3
Morning

"Jane, Harriet Buxton's on the phone. She says a lightbulb went off in her head and she needs to talk."

"Oh God help me, Helen..." Jane said, hesitating over the phone like it was a hand grenade.

"Jane! Harriet here. I've got it. It came to me while we were watching basketball last night."

"What's that?"

"The night of the party. When I got knocked out. It was Michael Jordan, Jane."

"Mrs. Buxton...you're saying the basketball player Michael Jordan was at Chanson's party?" Jane said.

"Well, someone named Michael Jordan grabbed me in the hallway. I couldn't say if he was the basketball player. And then the next thing I knew, I came to on a sofa in the Pratts' hallway. So, yes, it was *A* Michael Jordan. Though not necessarily *THE* Michael Jordan."

"OK. I'm taking notes and I'll plug this new information into the big picture. Anything else you can think of, Mrs. Buxton?"

"That's about it, Jane. But aren't you going to ask me how my date went last night?"

"Oh, sorry. How did it go?"

"Exceedingly well, Jane. But more I cannot say."

"Well, congratulations thus far, Mrs. Buxton. Well done!"

"Yes, thus far...I'm hoping for the best!"

Before Jane could raise the topic of her meal reimbursement, Harriet Buxton hung up.

66
Friday, January 3
Late Morning

Storm and Israel walked into the PSO office together.

"There you are, Storm," Jane said. "Happy New Year! Thanks for coming over."

"You're looking good, Jane. I trust being PSO continues to suit you?" Storm swooped in to give her a big hug. Looking at Israel, Storm demurred. "You don't get one."

"Hah! I don't want one," Israel said, coming out of his ducking feint.

Jane walked over to the white board. "OK. All set to get started?"

Storm's eyes ran up and down the columns and back to Jane. "God Almighty. You've got the FBI, CIA, a manure pile, a tummy tuck, Russians. What is all this? Camp Runamuck?"

"I warned you," Jane said.

Storm read through the whiteboard for several minutes. "Well, let's see how we do with all your columns and details...try to string events together like a necklace, as you suggested, in a way that makes sense. Harriet Buxton, on the other hand...she's got to be in a league all her own. That sign around her neck, the absurdity of it, suggests there's no connection to anything else up on your board. I'm betting Harriet's incident is unrelated. Bizarre, yes. But unrelated."

"We also think the disappearance of Bernie Pushaw and Chanson Pratt is an isolated incident. No connection with the federal stuff," said Israel.

"OK," Jane said, "before we take the plunge, I need to write down several new points. Harriet finally revealed to me that the federal SWAT team was at the Pratt party to track down corruption among Congressional types, related to illegal Russian goods—both gold and manufactured stuff."

"I heard some buzz about that back at the office," said Storm. "But sounds like nothing came of it."

"Hold on to that point, Storm. I also spoke with Geneva Pratt, who is Chanson and Salem Pratt's daughter. Geneva works with Texas Senator Hitch McGill in his D.C. office. She confirmed he was the only government official at the Pratt party. So McGill must be the SWAT target, right?"

"That's logical," said Israel.

"Unfortunately, Geneva Pratt had very little to offer about McGill's interest in Environmental Fields. She kind of glided over everything and said he may be looking into field recycling as an alternative to Texas hog waste pits. I say that's pure bull shit."

"What makes you so sure, Jane?" Storm asked.

"Because...and this is the juicy part...I overheard Senator McGill and Alex Champus, my FBI contact, at Curry in a Hurry last night. Or rather, I eavesdropped on their conversation. Those guys are a team! Champus *warned* McGill about the SWAT raid ahead of time. Which gave McGill enough time to slip away from the Pratts' party close to midnight...to my house, of all places. It so happens the McGills know the Balankoffs—all old family friends—Konstantin invited them over for a night cap. I even met them when I finally got home."

"That's wild, Jane," said Storm.

"Anyway, McGill asked Champus at the restaurant about Environmental Fields. McGill sounded irritated. Champus said he was afraid McGill might never see his goods. Something about the ground being frozen, and it seemed hopeless they'd dig anything up until maybe spring. So what are McGill's goods? And are those goods tied to the federal corruption investigation? Those goods have to be crucial to our necklace of events."

"So let's start at the beginning of this necklace" Storm said. "Or maybe it would work better if we started at the end of the known timeline." He moved back and forth again to continue studying the columns.

Israel scanned the whiteboard. "You're saying we start with the Pratt party, where Senator Hitch McGill avoided getting nabbed by the FBI/CIA/ICE team. Because the FBI guy, Alex Champus, tipped off the Senator."

"And before that, McGill expected to get some goods delivered to St. Frewin's Island, but they apparently got lost in Environmental Fields," said Jane.

"So," Storm said, "we're wondering *why* those goods ended up at Environmental Fields. And *how* did those goods become lost in the first place."

Jane picked up the theoretical necklace. "Another mysterious angle is those barrels that Bernie Pushaw heard about on the walkie talkie in December. The Russians intended to have those barrels picked up. But some Russian guy spoke to Bernie Pushaw by mistake that night...and not to someone else who also had a walkie talkie."

"And we think the other person with a walkie talkie was Troy Overlock," Israel said.

"Then there's Bernie Pushaw's letter left in the Pratts' refrigerator at the party. Your notes on his letter conclude that the Russians intended to speak to Troy in December about picking up the barrels...and *not* Bernie Pushaw," said Storm.

"That's right. I think that makes sense," said Jane. "You agree?"

"Well, the story line is holding up at this point. But what about Bernie Pushaw not finding the barrels at the boatyard. What then?" asked Storm.

"That's where I think we run into some truth decay, as they say in politics. Bernie is all over the map when he goes on about what did or didn't happen."

"And remember, Jane," said Israel. "Stan Helmstadt said Bernie watched Stan's cows the weekend those holes mysteriously appeared in Stan's manure pile. And you also have a note here that Bernie joked about Stan's manure pile. Why would he even mention the manure pile out of the blue? That's a Freudian slip, don't you think?"

"If Bernie caused those holes in Stan's manure pile, and we're wondering what happened to some barrels, are we trying to connect the missing barrels with the holes in Stan's manure pile?" said Jane.

"I'm losing both of you here. What are you saying?" asked Storm.

"We're considering a side event in early December, Storm," said Jane. She summarized the matter of the holes in the manure pile belonging to local dairy farmer, Stan Helmstadt.

Storm arched his back and stood there trying to limber up his stocky frame. "OK. If we have barrels of the

DON'T TOUCH MY COCKTAIL!

Senator's mystery goods, and then suddenly we're looking at smaller holes in Stan's manure pile, what's our guess? That someone, maybe Bernie Pushaw, found out what was in those barrels, and it wasn't septic waste. So that someone repackaged those goods and moved them around somehow, including burying them in Stan's manure pile...but only for a short time. What do you think?"

"Hold on. Harriet said the SWAT team's concern was corruption surrounding gold and manufactured goods...see, there in my notes. So could the Senator's goods be gold? Gold is heavy enough...I could see someone dividing up a barrel full of gold into small parcels. That would make sense," Jane said.

"So now where are we?" Storm asked. "Let's keep tracing backwards to figure out *how* the gold, assuming it's gold, got to St. Frewin's Island."

"But, wait," Jane said. "Who moved the gold? What about Bernie? And what happened to that gold, if McGill didn't get his hands on it?"

"That's one of our mysteries, isn't it, Jane?" Storm agreed. "What happened to the gold?"

"Anyway, gold aside for the moment, we were making the connection between Troy's walkie talkie and the Russians trying to reach someone at night. Via walkie talkie for a barrel pick-up. Can we assume Troy was the contact person for the Russians?" said Israel.

"Good. That's good. That fits in with the report that Troy wanted money to pay for a tummy tuck," said Jane.

"So the Russians would pay Troy for his help," said Israel.

"Right."

"On this tummy tuck," Storm interrupted. "You're serious, Jane?"

"Yes. The night of the party, one of Troy's colleagues informed me that Troy wants a tummy tuck," said Jane. "He's extremely overweight and thinks it's ruining his life...something like that."

"OK. OK. Continue," said Storm.

They discussed further Troy's role, the apparent mistake where the barrels went off to the Environmental Fields when they were likely meant for the Senator, and the lack of the internet on St. Frewin's Island, making it the perfect niche for illegal activity.

"I'd say my head's starting to spin, though this does seem to fit together. But how can McGill know so much about St. Frewin's?" Israel said.

"Well, he's friendly with the Pratts, right? He was at their party. And they're all Texans." Storm said.

"I wonder if the Pratts are involved? Salem did say some of his big creditors are Russians," Jane said.

"If Salem Pratt is to be believed," said Storm, "your notes over here show that he didn't know anything about the SWAT team coming to his party. And he had no idea why Senator McGill was so interested in Environmental Fields."

"So back to Environmental Fields," Jane continued. "That sailor Spartak was nosing around there soon after the attack on Troy Overlock. Which suggests the Russians found out where their barrels had landed, if Storm's right about the Russians delivering the barrels to St. Frewin's Island. And eventually Hitch McGill also found out where his barrels ended up. So there's another link between the Russians and the Senator, right?"

DON'T TOUCH MY COCKTAIL!

Israel took up their thoughts. "And the link between the Russians and the Senator was the reason the SWAT team raided the party. The federal government must have collected enough intelligence about the Senator's dealings with the Russians to try and scoop up McGill on New Year's Eve. But, as Jane pointed out, that failed because Champus warned McGill."

"About the attack on Troy Overlock, Jane. You think that was tied to the fuck-up with the barrels?" said Storm.

"Yes, I do. Timing-wise it fits. Let me check my notes on Bernie's letter to me. OK...he says in December, about the second week, the walkie talkie incident happened. And I had to come home from Switzerland early for the TV interview on December 12. That's when Troy stumbled into view and then crashed on the beach. So the Russians could have gone looking for Troy to beat him up, after they realized there was a mix-up on the walkie talkies."

"And they would want to beat him up to try and find out what happened to the barrels?" asked Israel.

"Right. Except that under our hypothesis, Troy apparently had no idea," Jane said. "By the way, his mother called to let us know he's back home now. On the mend, she reported, but the medical bills are making them faint."

"Well, let's type up our analytical timeline and get it to Adderley for his review. But we have to be honest with ourselves," Storm said. "Today's effort is really nothing more than a necklace. It's not hard-core proof. There's no direct evidence, only bits and pieces of circumstantial evidence, and too much hearsay. We've created a logical concept of what happened, but we can't prove any of it."

"You're such a downer, Storm," Jane said.

"Hard realist, my dear."

"There's got to be a solution we can coax out of all of this," Jane insisted. "Something to put things right...at least for Troy. He's my main concern right now."

She looked at the overloaded whiteboard and cursed. "You know what? Some other cog in the wheel can take care of the Feds' botched raid and the Russians and the gold gone missing."

And then it clicked. *The gold had not gone missing.* Jane blinked twice and her confusion evaporated. She now understood the motives and the outcome—they had been in front of her all along—human nature, desire, greed, and the unanticipated joker...Human Error. *The gold had not gone missing.* The gold had flowed to St. Frewin's Island on a harebrained scheme, ill-begotten treasure meant for the coffers of a Senator. But the wealth of that gold would remain on St. Frewin's Island. And Jane was content to let the gilt settle in right here at home, to let all other guilt disappear. "THINK LOCAL." She knew Bernie Pushaw had decided the same.

"Jane, are you forgetting about Harriet's misadventure?" said Storm.

"Are you about to miss your ferry, Mr. Nosmot?"

67
Wednesday, January 8
Somewhere in the Caribbean

Noreen Pushaw reached over her husband Bernie's less-than-remarkable body to borrow his Mai Tai for a quick sip. The refreshing lime kick tickled her throat as the drink slid downward. She gazed past the cruise ship railing towards the turquoise blue ocean.

Those travel brochures always talked about the electric blue bays, the emerald coves, the azure sea, and now damn if she wasn't floating in it and looking at it right outside her suite. Suite! Not just a cabin. She patted Bernie's remarkable stomach. Nothing he said or did from here on would ever irritate her again, or make her feel like bashing him over the head with a frying pan.

Noreen's mother, Trudy Moody, turned in her own lounge chair and whispered to her daughter, "I always knew Bernie had a glimmer of MENSA in him."

"Really, Mom?"

"Well, granted it took a while for his genius to catch up with him, but it did, didn't it?" Trudy stretched her very satisfied smile wider across her lips. She offered her hand to husband Wilbur to hold. There wasn't another mother-in-law on St. Frewin's who could boast an upcoming home renovation to be paid for by a beloved son-in-law. Who was also paying for this very snazzy cruise to the Bahamas. Noreen had had freakin' good sense to marry so well, and Trudy knew just where that sense came from.

....

When their cruise ship anchored in Nassau in the Bahamas, Noreen, Wilbur, and Trudy were eager to rent scooters and bounce around town, but Bernie put his foot down.

"Everyone on this candy-coated island thinks they is James Bond, my ass. Ain't no way I'm gonna pay to git on one of them jet-skis on wheels. And you're gonna suck in all that crappy air comin' out of those trucks whizzin' by at a hunred miles an hour? Foe-get-it."

The rest of the Mainers took their brain trust's opinion to heart and boarded a bus instead. Bernie opted for a stroll over to the Atlantis Resort to use his free day-pass. He had overheard fellow passengers talkin' about some Cinderella towers or somethin' like that. He'd go see for himself and have somethin' special to tell Wilbur and the gals when they got back.

Once he entered the hotel fairyland, Bernie saw what folks meant about the towers. But the closer he got and the more he could see, it all made him think of Las Vegas and a Walmart Gahden Center smooshed together on a golf course with some puddles thrown in. Way too much of too much.

When he finally found the hotel beach, Bernie was glad to be around more air and less people. Fun to walk on the sand barefoot. In the warm sunshine. With palm trees leanin' over him. No snow. No windshield to scrape. Nothin' like Maine in wintah.

But for cryin' out loud. He did a double take. Was it happenin' again? Another vision? Just like Mt. Manure back home? What the fuck? The Virgin Mary sunbathin' in a bikini? On a lounge chair with an unlit cigarette in her hand right there in front of him. But Bernie Pushaw knew better this time. And he had his matches on him. He pushed his toes along in the warm sand until he stood before his apparition. "Hey there, Secret Agent Woman. Need a light?"

68
Saturday, January 11

"All I ask is that you give our recipient some gentle prodding," Jane said on the three-way conference call. "A little peer pressure from both of you ought to do it."

"And you think this will mean no need for subpoenas or legal counsel?" Salem said.

"That's what I'm hoping."

"Jane," Konstantin said, "you're certain about the final amount? You're not going to come back with a revised figure or additional requests?"

"That's right. The information I'm sending you sums it all up, including a private digital document only the recipient can access. It explains why the recipient will want to cooperate with us. Sorry I can't say more. It's work sensitive...can't be divulged."

"Well, I'm happy to give it a shot. He's certainly good for it, as far as I know," Salem said.

"Konstantin, are you on board?" Jane said.

"Awkward as this task seems, I believe you when you say it's for a good and just cause, Jane."

"OK then. That's all I need. And apologies if I sound all business and brusque here. I'm in a time crunch. Thank you both—tons!" Jane closed out the call.

She flipped through her paper copy of the digital document meant only for the recipient, who was Jane's Unknown Asshole, who was none other than Senator Hitch McGill. She wanted to race around outside and jump up and down and yell her head off, but it was too early to celebrate. How delicious, though, to see Rajiv's forensic conclusions about sticky finger prints on leather and to recall what her Spy Guy recorder had picked up that night at Curry in a Hurry. And there, on the last page...Jane laughed...at her own signature on the document. Flicka.

69
Late March

People on St. Frewin's Island often found the barometer dragging them backwards in early spring as they concentrated on just "making it up the March hill," as the saying went. No longer cold enough to complain about winter's blast; not warm enough yet to do a darn thing outside.

Chanson Pratt was feeling the effects of the March hill. She was staying at her summer home off-season when she should have known better. But being away from Texas was a good idea. She could reflect, and her body was letting her know. Things had changed. She leaned over and stroked puppy ZT Lowell on his neck.

During her phone call with Wilton Savoy, the shivering thrill no longer ran through Chanson. He had reached her just now, trying to move forward with whatever they had left between them, under the guise of their J. T. Karl's Wild Open corporate roles.

"It would do us all good if you would stay on the Board through our summer catalog printing, Chanson. I could really use your creative spunk and enthusiasm," said Wilton.

"Thanks, Wilton. I appreciate your asking, but I feel like I've got too much on my plate right now. Too many commitments, socially, personally, and back in Texas."

"But you'll miss out on all the launch fun...the parties, the interviews. You were the one who got us rolling on this prison chic concept. Don't you want to be at the center of it all?"

DON'T TOUCH MY COCKTAIL!

"Oh, before I forget, Wilton, and before I hang up, because I really do need to hang up, Wilton. I have a name—a label—to suggest, in case you expand the prison chic look into a whole line of prison-inspired clothing. How about 'U Hauled Away'? Get it? Grabs you, doesn't it?" She could hear Wilton begin chuckling out loud.

"That's very catchy, Chanson. We'll have to check the obvious trademark conflict issues and so forth. But I'll run it by the rest of the Board and the marketing team. You may have a winner yet again."

"Of course I have another winner, Wilton. Don't worry about obvious trademark conflicts. You can cultivate this opportunity full throttle. Get U-Haul to underwrite the prison chic project. Trust me—it'll boost their rentals sky high.

"And one last question, Wilton. An awkward question. How is Diane doing?" After the uproar at the end of the New Year's Eve party, Chanson felt something tingling between guilt and curiosity.

"Well...." She heard his pause string itself out on the phone line.

"Yes?" she asked.

"You know, even small resentments can have a long shelf life," Wilton said. "And I now realize Diane has been nursing a monster of resentment over you and me. I think we both know who that whore sign was meant for, don't we, Chanson?"

He heard her "Hmm."

"Anyway, I've been busy tearing down the stone-cold Berlin wall at home since your party. And if you and I are taking some time out, it's probably for the better. I'll concentrate on helping Diane tame her furies. She's been in such a foul mood, especially since she came clean with Harriet Buxton about the whore business."

Chanson put down the phone when they were done and headed for the bathroom.

70
Early April

Jane and Helen were closing up shop late at the Public Safety Office. It wasn't quite 7 PM, but it was Thursday and getting dark out and their dinners were calling to them.

"What did you say you were going to make tonight, Helen?"

"Probably fried haddock and a hot potato salad."

The office door opened and Bernie Pushaw plowed in.

"Now what, Bernie?" Jane tried not to snap at him. "Your fifteen minutes of fame ran out a while back, you know. And we're about to lock up."

"Bet you haven't heard the latest, Jane." Bernie looked around him, ready to burst.

"OK. Tell us and get it over with," Jane said.

"Well, it looks like Chanson Pratt may have been playin' hide the pickle. And now she's got a pea in the pod. How about that?" Bernie seemed so proud of himself, master of the metaphors.

"Do we need to hear this? And did you have anything to do with it?" Jane looked at him suspiciously.

"Me? Hell, no! I'm wonderin' myself if it's a case of immaculate conception."

"You don't really believe that, do you?" Helen asked.

"All I'm sayin' is there's always room for one more Baby Jesus," Bernie said.

"Oh, God. This has got to stop," Jane said. "Go home, Bernie. Noreen needs you."

Bernie held his ground.

Carol Chen

The office door opened yet again. Joe Miller stuck his head in. "Anybody home?" he called out, looking directly at Jane and Helen and Bernie.

"We should be so lucky. What's up, Joe?" Jane waved her hand at Bernie to signal he could go. He didn't budge.

"Just thought you would love to know that Troy Overlock is heading home from Portland tomorrow. His tummy tuck was a breeze, and he says he feels like a million bucks."

"That's wonderful, Joe," Helen said.

"No kidding," Jane said.

"And get a load of this," Joe said. "Some anonymous donor paid for Troy's stomach surgery *and* all his medical bills from his attack. Troy and his parents are stunned."

Bernie was already out the door. Rushing to spread more good news.

So, Nature finally shook hands with the Universe. Jane had been in suspense for months, but now it had all come together like cake batter in a hot oven...Rajiv's findings on the dress Jane had borrowed from Samantha for the New Year's Eve party, and Salem and Konstantin teaming up to sway Senator McGill to do the right thing. Jane could finally relax. She stepped off the imaginary tightrope inside her head, and looked over at Joe Miller and Helen.

"What do you say, you two? Time to celebrate?"

DON'T TOUCH MY COCKTAIL! is the second Jane Roberts Mystery. Carol Chen lives in Camden, Maine.

Jane Roberts Mysteries in order:
LOBSTERS WITHOUT BORDERS
DON'T TOUCH MY COCKTAIL!